The moment the door intensified.

As if the room had exhaled the world's worst bad breath on us. I stopped breathing through my nose entirely, but that helped only a little. My lunch churned around inside my stomach.

The room was absolutely black. My flashlight beam speared the darkness and came to rest on a twin-size bed. A long shape lay beneath a blanket. At the foot of the bed sat a wheelchair. Uncle Howard's, no doubt. Someone would have to check that bundle. The thought of twitching the blanket aside to expose what lay beneath made my skin crawl. I looked over my shoulder at Slava and Ms. Hawk. Slava gave me a wide-eyed look and backed away.

"Not my job," she said. "You get paid for looking, not me."

"If you don't want to, Terry," Ms. Hawk said gently, "I'll go take a look."

That gentle tone of voice did it for me. What was I, a little kid? As if I'd never looked at a dead body before! I marched into the room, banged my shin on a pile of newspapers and fell against the bed. My hand sank into the bundle beneath the blanket and came away wet. I set my mouth and whisked the blankets aside.

A pair of cloudy eyes behind Coke-bottle glasses stared up at me from a blackened, decaying face.

"It's Uncle Howard," I said, and threw up.

PENNY DRAKE

is a retired nurse in Michigan. She's taking advantage of her spare time to travel. So far she's been to Italy, England, Ukraine, the Caribbean and a number of places within the United States. Penny writes with the encouragement of her son, novelist Steven Harper, and is hard at work on her next book.

PENNY DRAKE

TRASH COURSE

CARINA PRESS™

To Sarah Zettel, with gratitude.

CARINA
PRESS™

Recycling programs
for this product may
not exist in your area.

ISBN-13: 978-0-373-06256-0

TRASH COURSE

TRASH COURSE

ONE

THE CHILDREN SHUFFLED across the warehouse floor in shackles and chains. There were a dozen of them—nine girls and three boys. They ranged in age from five to twelve and wore ragged, filthy clothes. I watched them through the mesh floor of a catwalk, feeling like a mother bear separated from her cubs, even though the kids weren't mine.

One of the thugs riding herd on the little group gave a girl a shove to make her move faster. She stumbled and nearly fell. I started to growl, then shut myself up. No way I could take on six guys unless I had serious surprise on my side, and most crooks get over their surprise real fast when they hear snarling noises from the shadows above them.

A sixth man was with the kids and the guards: Stanislav Yerin, the *Pakhan* himself. Yerin reminded me of a pile of alphabet blocks—sturdy, square and cornered. A knife scar split his right eyebrow which, like his hair, was the medium brown of a wooden horse. I'd learned a lot about the Russian Mafia in the last few days, and knew the *Pakhan*—bosses—don't usually get involved in day-to-day doings on the street. Yerin's presence meant something special was going down.

The corner of my eye twitched. *Special* always meant complicated, and *complicated* always meant *injury* or *pain*—probably mine. Blood tanged my mouth with copper, and I realized I was biting the inside of my cheek. I wondered if Batgirl ever felt this way.

My catwalk was a full story above the main floor. The guards were herding the kids toward a set of loading doors. Some of the kids shuffled along in a stupor, but most looked terrified. Their chains made them *clink* like baby ghosts. I felt sick to my stomach, and angry. I wanted to break those damned chains with my bare hands and rip the hearts out of those gorillas with my bare teeth. Mama Bear tried to growl again and I had to clamp my lips hard to keep her quiet.

One of the boys had straw-blond hair, brown eyes and a little Matt Damon nose that would get the girls' blood racing when he got older. *If* he got older. He was chained in the exact center of the line, and while the others stared straight ahead, he darted frightened glances around the warehouse. I recognized him from the picture his mother had given Ms. Hawk. His name was Andy Maine. The Maines had been visiting Russia on vacation and were shopping in a street market when Andy had disappeared. The St. Petersburg police hadn't had any luck in finding him, which was how Ms. Hawk and I got involved.

Four days with almost no sleep and a hell of a lot of footwork had produced a trail that led us to this warehouse. We eventually decided Andy had been taken by mistake—most of the children kidnapped into underground slavery are orphans and street kids. But, hey, once you've got the kid, you may as well finish the job and sell him, right? He'd be worth the same to a pimp, no matter what language he spoke.

Mama Bear bared her teeth, and I fingered the stun gun holstered at my waist. I wished hard for my Glock, but smuggling a pistol from Michigan to Mother Russia wouldn't be worth the risk. I don't relish a strip-search unless it's done by a cabana boy named Rico. Handguns are illegal in Russia anyway, though someone might want to tell that to the Mafia—the thugs below me were armed to the teeth. I kept a wary eye on them as I set my little MP3 player on the catwalk and clipped the remote to my belt. The player's tiny green light said everything was a go.

The thugs had the kids almost to the door. Outside was a launch that would take them to a tramp steamer bound for who-knew-where. France. The Netherlands. Maybe even the

United States. Hell, the child traffic industry has tentacles everywhere. Once those children got outside, we'd lose them forever.

My earpiece crackled softly. *"We have to move, Terry,"* came Ms. Hawk's voice. *"The police won't get here in time."*

"Right," I whispered into the button mike clipped to my collar. "I'm moving closer."

I eased across the catwalk and down a set of metal stairs to the main floor, my crepe-soled shoes making a whisper of sound. I wore a black jumpsuit that made me feel like Catwoman and made it easier to slip from shadow to shadow. Stacks of wooden crates created convenient places to hide, though the same crates also blocked easy viewing of the thugs. The place smelled of salt water, and the air was damp and cold as a used washcloth. Male voices ahead of me spoke in Russian, which is Greek to me.

I crept around a crate, my heart thundering in my ears. The thugs and kids were only about ten feet ahead, and their backs were to me.

Yerin said something to one of the thugs, and they all laughed. A little girl flinched at the sound, and I wondered what had happened to make her fear adult laughter. I quickly scanned the area but didn't see Ms. Hawk. Most of the warehouse lay in shadow—the traffickers were only planning to stop here for a couple hours before moving the kids again, and they hadn't bothered to turn on all the lights. Thank God for that.

"I'm in position," I whispered. Tension threatened to tighten my muscles like bungee cord, and I forced myself to relax. Adrenaline pulsed through my veins. Part of it was fear and part of it was anticipation. My fingers itched.

"On my mark," Ms. Hawk replied. *"Three...."*

I drew my stun gun, a flat, plastic box with two electrodes poking out of one end like a pair of cat ears. Foreign-made stun guns are illegal in Russia, too, but you can buy all the locally made ones you like. Unfortunately, Russian stun guns are about as shocking as a Disney movie. Ms. Hawk and I had gotten around this by dismantling our American models and spreading the innards around our checked luggage, which we hoped would fool a casual inspection. A small risk, but necessary. It had also worked. Our luggage had sailed through security without a hitch, and we'd reassembled the weapons in our hotel room with no one the wiser. Too bad this little trick wouldn't work with a pistol.

I powered up my little kitty-cat, and a spark snapped softly between the electrodes. I smelled ozone.

"Two..."

I tensed again, then took another relaxing breath and tried to make my muscles fluid as water. It was hard—Mama Bear was snarling again.

"One..."

A coppery taste flooded my mouth, as always happens when I get excited. Anger boiled a pot of bile inside me. These men were going to pay for their scaring and their scarring.

"Mark!"

I moved.

Common wisdom says that women don't like to fight. We're supposed to shy away from physical conflict, use words and careful prodding to get what we want. That's bullshit. We're just *told* to shy away from physical conflict. I did just that for most of my life. I was quiet and retiring for years until I got into my first real fight, and you know what? I liked it. Hell, I *loved* it. And not only that, I realized I was damned good at it. Yeah, there are plenty of guys out there who are stronger than I am. So what? You fight smart, and the bigger guys don't even get a chance to use those muscles they put so much stock in.

A *frisson* of adrenaline thrilled through me as I rushed the closest guard. Time slowed and stretched like a spandex jumpsuit. I love it when that happens. Not only does it give my own little combat computer time to figure out what I'm doing, it lets me enjoy what's going on. I jabbed my stun gun into the small of the thug's back and heard the sweet *zzzzzap* of muffled electricity. The thug stiffened, then dropped to the floor in slow motion, gasping and twitching like a landed salmon. No more chained children for him. Before he had finished collapsing, I was swinging at a second thug—the stun gun needed time to recharge, time I didn't have.

My mark had good reflexes, I'll give him that. He was already turning, arms at the defensive, his face an animal snarl. I dropped to the floor and lashed out with a sweep kick that would have knocked him off his feet if he hadn't jumped over it. He tried to land on my shin, but I yanked myself out of the way and flashed to my feet. *Missed me, you bastard,* I thought.

Then the thug's left fist flicked at me, quick as a snake, and clipped the side of my head. A flashbulb popped behind my eyes, but I felt no pain—not yet. Without pausing, I grabbed his outstretched wrist and used his own momentum to flip him over my thigh. He landed flat on his back with a satisfying crash.

I was vaguely aware of Ms. Hawk. She flickered out of the shadows to my right, swift and silent as black silk, and rammed her own stun gun into the kidneys of thug number three. He dropped, and she delivered a midriff kick to thug number four before he could react. Thug four folded neatly in half, but managed to grab her knee and take her down with him. She grunted when she hit the cement floor.

My hand dipped down to my belt and came up with a small black canister. I aimed it at my own thug and flicked the spray button. He screamed and clawed at his eyes. People always do that, even though it's the last thing you should do when you're hit with pepper spray—rubbing drives chili oil even deeper into your mucous membranes and makes it worse. I spun to help Ms. Hawk, but she had already snap-kicked her guy in the face. He went, "Oof!" and lay still. I guess some expressions are universal to all languages.

All this left Stanislav Yerin and one last thug standing. And me. Ms. Hawk was still on the ground, eight or ten feet away from Yerin. The last thug grabbed one of the kids—a little girl maybe six years old with brown eyes as big as peanut-butter cups—and aimed a gun at her head. She whimpered like a puppy, and the thug barked something in Russian. I didn't get the words, but his meaning was clear enough. I think he must have figured we had guns somewhere on us, or he would have shot us right off. Or maybe he just panicked and grabbed a hostage without thinking. Good old Stan Yerin backed up a couple of steps with a look of shock on his face. The scar that split his eyebrow looked like a startled stroke of lightning. It had probably freaked the hell out of him when two women popped out of the shadows to take down four of his men in five seconds. The children stared with wide, un-comprehending eyes.

The thug barked in Russian again—same command, I think—and dug the barrel of his pistol harder into the girl's temple. Tears trickled down her face, and Mama Bear roared inside me. An angry red haze tinged the edges of my vision. Yerin retreated a couple more steps, then stopped to watch, clearly undecided about the situation. I scanned the ground, hoping one of the thugs had dropped a pistol within snatch-ing range. Two guns lay on the floor, but neither was close enough to do me any good.

"How's that in English?" I said, and tapped my belt with a subtle motion. "My Russian's a little rusty."

"You to leave, or she die," he said in a thick accent. I men-tally rolled my eyes at his rotten usage. On the other hand, his English was better than my Russian and he had a gun, so I wasn't exactly in a position to complain. "Put up hands!"

I slowly complied. Ms. Hawk didn't move. Thug five wag-gled the gun again, and she slowly raised her hands. Even in the dim light, her face stood out sharp and beautiful, as if it had been caught in a stone frieze. Ms. Hawk has night-black hair, sky-blue eyes, and the classically beautiful profile of a Greek statue. I think she looks kind of like Artemis, if Arte-mis ever wore a black jumpsuit and put her hair in a French twist.

"Let the girl go," Ms. Hawk barked in a voice that reminded me of Kathleen Turner. "If that child is harmed, you will die. Hawk Enterprises will see to that."

I noticed with admiration that Ms. Hawk was aiming a pistol at the thug. She must have snatched it up from one of the guys she'd taken down. Stanislav Yerin's gaze flicked from Ms. Hawk to his thug to me. A fair number of *Pakhan* don't carry guns of their own, disdaining them as something for the hired help. He was probably regretting that decision just now. My boss got to her feet, though her aim never wavered.

The thug hesitated, uncertain about what to do. And then Russian police sirens wailed in the distance.

"Wow," I said as the sirens grew louder. "Frying pan, fire, you. I hear your cell mate's name is Ivan and he keeps a big jar of olive oil under his pillow. Hope you like that hot monkey love."

I don't know how much the thug actually understood, but a panicked look crossed his face, and he snapped his pistol around to aim at me. In that moment, Ms. Hawk lunged. She tackled the girl, wrenching her out of the guy's grip. He fired, but Ms. Hawk had thrown him off balance, and the shot caromed into the darkness. Me, I was already moving. I dove for the floor, stomach-surfed the four or five feet that separated me from my target like Pete Rose sliding into second, and jammed my now-recharged stun gun into the thug's thigh. A choking sound emerged from his throat, and he crumpled like a used Kleenex.

I scrambled to my feet and scanned the visible area. Stan Yerin was gone. I started to swear, then automatically checked myself when I remembered the kids. They were staring at me and Ms. Hawk like frightened kittens.

"You speak English," Andy Maine piped up in a voice that was both relieved and scared. "Are you cops? Are you going to take me home?"

"We're not cops, Andy," I said. "But Ms. Hawk and I are here to help."

"How do you know my name?" he asked.

I ignored the question. The sirens grew louder still, and I tapped the remote clipped to my belt. Above me, the MP3 player fell silent and the sirens stopped. I looked around. Five child stealers—three of them stunned, two of them moaning in pain and clawing at their eyes. These guys would never touch another child, all because of Ms. Hawk. And me. I felt like I'd just gotten off the world's wildest roller coaster—a little shaky and wanting to go again. Inside me, Mama Bear felt pleased, like someone had given her cub back and a big comb of honey to boot.

Then the pain caught up with me. It drove a chisel into my temple, and my midriff felt tenderized from that little belly-flop on the concrete floor. I knew from experience that I needed to keep moving or I'd stiffen up. The exultation faded a little.

"Are the cops coming?" Andy asked.

"Eventually," Ms. Hawk said in her rich voice. "Terry, let's see what we can do about those chains."

I found a set of keys in a stunned thug's pocket. The other kids shied away from me when I tried to unlock them, so I unchained Andy first. Once they saw that I didn't hurt him, they let me free them as well. I can't describe the mixture of ecstasy and loathing I felt as those horrible chains dropped with clatters and clanks to the ground. How many other kids around the world were having their chains unlocked by someone whose motives were completely different from mine? At least these kids would go free. They clustered around me, and I gave some of them hugs. Three hung back, still not quite trusting us.

I had just unchained the last child—a little girl with dark skin and hair that said "Gypsy" to me—when police sirens, real ones, howled outside.

"I think," Ms. Hawk said, "that we should step outside for some fresh air about now. We'll bring Andy with us."

I didn't want to leave. The girl with the peanut-butter-cup

eyes grabbed my hand and chattered at me in Russian, probably begging me to be her new mommy or maybe just show her
where the bathroom was. Her hand felt fragile as a little bird,
and I ached to hold on, let her know that everything would be
fine as long as she stayed with me. But Ms. Hawk was right.
It would create a difficult and ultimately unnecessary incident if two American citizens were discovered interfering in
a Russian police matter, especially when said women were
carrying illegal stun guns.

We quickly cuffed the groaning thugs with the kids' chains,
then grabbed Andy and towed him to the little side door we'd
first used to enter. The other kids tried to follow us, and Ms.
Hawk used emphatic gestures to tell them they had to stay.
They didn't want to. Three of the girls and one of the boys
burst into tears. I wanted to scoop them into my arms and re-
assure them, but I didn't know the words and anyway, I didn't
have time. I told myself that they'd get the help they needed
from the police more quickly than from us, but I didn't feel
much better. The sharp chisel in my temple dug a little deeper.

Police burst through the main door just as the three of us
slipped out the side. Luckily, the cops hadn't taken the time to
establish a perimeter, or we would have been sunk. We hus-
tled Andy away into a damp and chilly night illuminated by
spinning red-and-blue police lights. I wondered what the cops
would think when they found a flock of thugs trussed up like
roasting chickens, and a gaggle of children with a wild story.
The thought brought a little glow of satisfaction to my bruised
and aching stomach as we jogged away with Andy in tow.

TWO

FOUR DAYS LATER, I was behind my desk, engaged in brave battle with my keyboard. Outside, the August sun shone hot and harsh, but in the air-conditioned lobby of Hawk Enterprises the air was cool and soothing. Blue carpet and green plants hushed the muted hum of the air system, though my mood was much more restless. The cursor flicked across the screen, and I replaced "teh" with "the" for the third time on the same page. I sighed and looked up from my typing for a moment. Big mistake. The reception area has a big bay window with a built-in seat, and I have a primo view of the back yard. Soft green grass, fragrant flowers, singing birds. My fingers drummed the keyboard, sending random letters skittering across the screen. Maybe just a quick stroll outside for some sunshine. I could—

A lawnmower roared to life outside, and Melissa, our landlady, pushed the machine into view. She'll turn forty soon—about ten years older than me—brown hair, stick thin, deeply tanned. Her face glistened with perspiration. Only ten seconds outside, and she was sweating enough to drip. I grimaced. Suddenly the idea of going outdoors was about as tempting as a blind date with Rush Limbaugh. I went back to my keyboard, content to stay inside with the lovely, refreshing air-conditioning.

The office building itself is an enormous twenties-style Victorian that was split into apartments sometime in the sixties. The residents—mostly University of Michigan students—had been pretty rough on the place, and Melissa had bought it for a song and a joke. Some serious renovation turned it into a series of offices for small businesses.

Two doors open off my area. One leads to a conference room complete with a tiny fridge and an industrial-sized coffee maker. The other door leads to Ms. Hawk's office, and it's usually closed to preserve Ms. Hawk's privacy. That's fine with me. I don't have to wonder if the boss is peering at me through the doorway or listening in on phone conversations. Not that it would bother me. I love working for Diana Hawk, and wouldn't quit if I won ten million in tomorrow's lottery.

Computer keys chattered like chilly teeth under my fingers and I was humming "Bad Romance" as I typed, putting the final touches on the Maine report. Andy made it safely back to his parents, and the U.S. consulate has no record of our involvement—Andy didn't know our names, and Mrs. Maine was glad to keep her mouth shut. Someone in charge probably knew *something* was up, but as long as none of it led to Hawk Enterprises, Ms. Hawk would be happy. There was no way for me to find out what happened to the other kids, but I liked to think they were fine, especially the girl with the peanut-butter-cup eyes who had grabbed my hand.

The mail came, and I set the computer to printing three copies of the report while I sorted through it. Two bills, some junk mail, a business catalog, and three personal letters for Ms. Hawk. I automatically checked the postmarks. One from Seattle, Washington. One from London, England. And one from someplace I couldn't puzzle out. I didn't even recognize the alphabet. I was dying of curiosity, but they were personal letters, and I wasn't going to ask.

The printer finished up the report. I attached the final statement for what Mrs. Maine owed us, grabbed the mail, and was just about to bring everything to Ms. Hawk when the front door opened. A fifty-ish woman bustled in, slammed the door shut, and leaned against it like she was afraid Godzilla would try to break it down. She was breathing funny.

I blinked. "Can I help you?" I asked, setting down the papers.

But the woman was already rooting around in a capacious handbag. She produced an inhaler, shoved the business end into her mouth, and sucked like a crystal-meth addict. Her breathing immediately eased, and she closed her eyes in obvious relief.

"Are you all right?" Maybe I should dial 911.

The woman nodded and took a deep breath. "I will be. Humidity and fresh-cut grass always make my asthma worse." She crossed the room with short, tripping steps and held out her hand. "My name is Belinda Harris. I'm looking for Hawk Enterprises."

"Terry Faye," I said, shaking it. Her grip was light and dry. "And you've found us."

"Oh, good. I wasn't sure. There's no sign outside the building." Belinda had a Southern accent. She was a little on the plump side, and her face was just starting to show signs of grandma jowls, her short, curly hair colored a careful brown. She wore a yellow sun dress with big buttons down the front and large, clunky shoes.

"What can we help you with?" I said, putting on my Soothing Receptionist voice. "Would you like a seat? Some coffee or water?"

Belinda Harris politely declined coffee and water, and I came around my desk to offer her a spot in the window seat. I sat opposite her with a legal pad on my lap. Ms. Hawk doesn't like consulting with clients over a desk—she says men do that to establish authority, and she'll have none of it in her office.

Once Belinda was settled, her handbag within easy reach beside her like a favored cat, she said, "I have a problem. I haven't heard from my uncles in almost three months, and I'm worried about them."

"All right," I said in a voice that asked her to continue.

"I get a letter from Uncle Lawrence once every other week, like clockwork, and I always write back within a day or two.

These are paper letters, you understand—not e-mail. The last one arrived back in May. I've written seven times since, but haven't heard a word. He and Uncle Howard are elderly, you understand, and I'm worried something has happened to them. They don't own a telephone, so I couldn't call."

"Where do your uncles live?" I asked.

"Right here in Ann Arbor. I flew up from Missouri—" she pronounced it *Missoura* "—to find them."

"You've been out to their house, then?"

"I rented a car and went straight there from the airport," she said. "But I couldn't get into the house."

"The doors were locked?"

"They were blocked," she corrected.

"Blocked," I repeated.

"With junk."

"I don't understand," I said, confused.

Belinda gave a heavy sigh. "This is… Well, it's a little embarrassing."

It always surprises me what some people call embarrassing. Women get robbed or raped and call it embarrassing. They get abused or molested by their fathers and call it embarrassing. They get hit over the head by a carjacker and call it embarrassing. That's bullshit. The dog pooping on the rug in front of company is embarrassing. Getting caught snooping in the host's medicine cabinet at a party is embarrassing. Finding spinach stuck in your teeth after a job interview is embarrassing. Getting raped, ripped off, or molested is more in the range of horrifying, outrageous, or appalling. But I would never say this to a client.

"All our consultations are kept in strict confidence," I said. "Ms. Hawk and I will not discuss your case with an outsider unless we have your express permission. We could also go into the conference room, if you'd like more privacy."

She waved a hand. "It's nothing the neighbors don't already know, I'm sure. My uncles are…eccentric, you understand." She cleared her throat. "They hoard."

I was still confused. "Hoard?"

"They've lived in the same house for over fifty years, and I don't think they've thrown anything out in all that time." Belinda gave a little cough. "The doors and windows are completely blocked by junk. I found two unlocked doors, but I couldn't get either one to open more than an inch or two. I looked in the windows, and couldn't see anything but piles of boxes and stacks of books. By then, my asthma was acting up, and I had to go back to the car."

"When was this?" I asked.

"Yesterday. I called the police and they sent over a pair of officers, but they couldn't get in, either, and not for lack of trying. Then they checked the mailbox, and there wasn't a thing in it. Someone was moving around well enough to pick up the mail, the officers said. Right after that, they got called away to investigate a robbery and left. I did learn that social services has tried to investigate my uncles'…habits a few times because the neighbors have complained about the messy yard, but social services can't do anything unless my uncles specifically ask them to."

I gave another sympathetic nod and mentally filled in a few blanks. Budget cuts all over the state had made things difficult for both cops and social workers, and very few resources were devoted to looking after adults with a mental illness. Crime took precedence over checking on two reclusive old men.

"Did you try the fire department?" I asked. "They're good at getting into difficult places."

"I did," Belinda said. "They said I should call the police or social services."

"Don't you have any relatives who could come up and help?"

Belinda shook her head. "I thought of that, of course. But my husband and my brother can't get away from work to come up, and my daughter lives in California. I didn't know what to do, so I came to see you."

"How did you hear of us?"

"The motel where I'm staying gave me a bunch of promotional flyers. A card for Hawk Enterprises was in them. It said you solve problems, so here I am."

I blinked at this. Ms. Hawk and I both have cards, but we don't hand them out as promotional material. Maybe it got in there by accident? Our clients frequently stay in hotels and one of them could have dropped the card. I supposed it was a minor point.

"So it's been three months since you last heard from your uncles?" I said.

"Yes."

I suppressed a grimace, dreading what I had to say next. "Ms. Harris, you know that it's possible your uncles are…"

"Dead?" she said. "Yes, I'm aware of that. It's the most logical explanation—except that someone's getting the mail. Maybe someone's stealing it, hoping for a Social Security check. No matter what, I need to find out. If they *are* dead, I certainly can't leave them in that house."

"Did you notice… I'm sorry, but I have to ask…any kind of odor?"

"Like a corpse?" Belinda said. "No. Nothing. That's another reason the police weren't thrilled about trying to break in."

I gave Belinda Harris a casual once-over without seeming to stare, trying to assess her position. For someone who had flown all the way up from *Missoura* to check on two missing uncles, she seemed awfully willing to toss around words like *dead* and *corpse*. On the other hand, if her only contact with them was through letters, how concerned could she get?

"Is there any other family?" I asked. "Someone who might want to be involved besides your husband and brother?"

Belinda shook her head. "There are some distant relatives—cousins, great-nieces and nephews, you understand. They're out in Chicago, last I knew. But I don't know how to contact any of them." She sighed. "I think I'm the only family member my uncles talked to, if you could call it talking."

I was furiously scribbling notes in my own improvised shorthand. "How long have you been writing to your uncles? It doesn't sound like something you've been doing since you were a kid."

"Oh, no. I knew about them, of course, but I never laid eyes on them until my mother died about five years ago. Mom was their younger sister, you understand. I was at her viewing when I noticed these two old men hovering around the back, shy as wild turkeys. One of them was in a wheelchair and wore thick, heavy glasses. Both of them had dressed in these rumpled brown suits that probably hadn't seen the light of day in twenty years. When I saw them, I knew right off who they were, so I went over and introduced myself. Uncle Howard—he was the one in the wheelchair—never did say more than hello, but Uncle Lawrence and I hit it off surprisingly well, considering where we were."

"How old are they?" I asked, careful to keep my question in the present tense.

"Well, let me see. Mom was a week short of seventy when she went, so that would put both uncles in their mid-eighties."

"Did you have more conversations after the funeral?"

"No, we never spoke again. Uncle Lawrence did give me his address, and after Mom died I felt a need to connect with her family, you understand. So I wrote a letter. I didn't think I'd hear back, but a few weeks later I got a letter back. It was such a nice surprise, so I wrote again. He wrote me again, I wrote him, and it became a little tradition with us. I told him about my husband and my daughter and what we were up to, and he wrote me about the Peale family history—where we came from, old family stories, that sort of thing. We came from Philadelphia, you understand, and before that, southern England. He didn't write much about himself. I guess people can be shy even in a letter."

Belinda sighed heavily, suddenly looking old and worn, like an overused shoe. "I would like to know what's going on at that house. It's a family duty, you understand, but I'm also worried about those two. Uncle Lawrence was so nice in his letters, and I always looked forward to the next one. The idea that he and Uncle Howard could be dead... Well, I can't stand the idea that their bodies might be locked up in that awful house, all alone. And if they *aren't* dead, why did Uncle Lawrence stop writing to me? It just doesn't make sense."

I made a couple more notes, growing more intrigued as I wrote. You always hear about these kinds of people, collectors gone haywire. I wondered what kind of stuff might be in that house, and after spending most of a week in Russia chasing down child traffickers, the chance to go poking around inside an old house filled with who-knew-what sounded like a fun change of pace. I'd also spent the last two days typing up notes and reports, and I was getting antsy. My butt felt numb from sitting in my desk chair, and this would be the perfect excuse to shut down my computer and move around.

Provided Ms. Hawk took the case.

"Let me discuss this with Ms. Hawk," I said. "This case sounds just like the sort of thing we handle, but I have to run it past her."

Belinda nodded. I rapped briskly on Ms. Hawk's door and entered, feeling my heart beat a little faster. Even after three years of working for her, I got a little thrill at introducing her to a potential new case.

Diana Hawk's office is done in Early American Potted Plant, and the place smells like a greenhouse in the spring. I don't know the names of half the greenery, but plants sit, hang, and spread over every surface except her polished mahogany desk. The windowsill looks like a jungle. Ms. Hawk herself was on the phone, and she waved me in. She wore watered-blue silk today, and her black hair hung down to her shoulders. A wide-brimmed blue hat graced her head. Ms. Hawk usually wears some kind of hat, even indoors, and I envy her ability to pull off that look. At her throat glittered a silver pendant. It's shaped like a hawk flaring its wings, about to strike its prey. I've never seen her without it.

"...of course, darling," she was saying in her low, rich voice. "We can talk more then. How far ahead is the time in Kyiv? Fine. I'll call you later."

I closed the door as she hung up. "Kyiv? Anything to do with the Maine case?"

"Hardly. That was my brother," she said, smiling.

"I didn't know you had a brother," I said. Come to that, I didn't know anything about Ms. Hawk's family. "Does he live in Kyiv?"

"Sometimes," she said briskly. "Who's out front?"

"Potential new client," I said, and sketched out Belinda's situation.

"Sounds fascinating," she said. "Draw up a contract for her. Five hundred, with two."

I nodded and went back to the outer office. Belinda was reading a paperback book which she stowed in her purse when I emerged. "Ms. Hawk has asked me to draw up a contract for you," I said. "Let me tell you the terms, and you can decide if you're interested."

"All right."

"We charge a daily rate of five hundred dollars, plus expenses," I told her. "Any expense over a hundred dollars, we'll clear with you first. In addition to the monetary fee, you'll owe Hawk Enterprises two favors."

Belinda looked blank, the usual client response. "Favors?"

"At some point in the future, Ms. Hawk or I will contact you for some kind of favor," I explained. "And you'll need to do it. It will never be something that will risk your safety or reputation, but we *will* ask."

"What sort things do you ask for?" she asked warily.

"It depends on you, actually," I said. "Some of our high-society clients have provided us with invitations to particular events and introductions to particular people. A computer-programmer client might help us get an important password. A cleaning lady can get us the contents of an office wastebasket. That sort of thing."

"I see."

"Most of our clients find it a little exciting," I said with a smile. "Getting involved in a case, and all that. As I said, there's never a risk to you. Unless you want to take one."

Belinda cocked her head. "Do many women take risks for Hawk Enterprises?"

"A few."

"A few like you?"

Silence, and a little wave of memory washed over me. My husband, gray and dead in a drawer. Three men pouncing on me in my kitchen. Ms. Hawk blurring into action. Then I recovered myself and laughed. "You've got me," I said. "Yes, I was originally one of Ms. Hawk's clients. Now I work for her, though that wasn't the favor she called in."

"What favor did she call in?"

"She hasn't yet," I said. "I still owe her."

"What did she do for you?"

I raised a finger in mock admonishment. "Now that would be breaking confidentiality. Would you like me to draw up a contract?"

"Please," she said with a small smile.

I called up a contract boilerplate on the computer and entered Belinda's information. She wrote Hawk Enterprises a retainer check for two thousand bucks and didn't bat an eye when she did it. Ms. Hawk has done some cases for a pittance and at least two for the favors alone, but Belinda obviously wasn't worried much about the money.

We were just finishing up when Ms. Hawk emerged from her office. She had changed into khaki slacks, a long-sleeved khaki shirt, and steel-toed boots. Her hair was twisted into a knot at the back of her head. Even in explorer gear she looked cool and elegant.

"You might want to change clothes, too, Terry," she said. "If the house is everything Ms. Harris says it is, we might get grubby."

"Yes, Ms. Hawk." I keep a couple changes of clothes in

the conference-room closet for exactly this reason. Once I had changed into an outfit similar to Ms. Hawk's, the three of us headed outside. The August heat hit like a liquid-gold hammer, and I was sweating before we made it off the front porch. Belinda took a hit from her inhaler.

Our office building was on Catherine Street near downtown Ann Arbor. The city is home to the University of Michigan, and a few years ago one of the swankier business magazines listed our fair town as *the* hot place for yuppies looking to relocate. We got flooded with newcomers. They pushed up housing prices, created tentacles of urban sprawl, and sucked up the few remaining parking spaces. Even the economic implosion didn't have an impact—Ann Arbor has the lowest unemployment rate in the state, thanks to the University. Today, every inch of curb space on the street was occupied. Hawk Enterprises is allotted a single parking space in the office's tiny lot, and that goes to Ms. Hawk's mid-sized green Plymouth. I have to walk from a parking structure. Belinda told us her car was about three blocks away, and she had tried to take the walk too fast, triggering an asthma attack.

"We'll all go in my car," Ms. Hawk said, leading the way. Then she halted. On the public sidewalk ahead of us stood a tall, sturdy woman in a wine-red dress and black pantyhose. She wore three-inch heels that made her taller than most men, which, I happened to know, was the way she liked it. Her hair lay in a dark, curly tail down her back, and her lipstick was just a little too red for mid-day. An insulated lunch bag dangled from one hand. The bag was mine, and the woman was my best friend, Slava Cherenko.

"You! Theresa!" she bellowed, as if I were leaning out an upstairs window instead of standing right in front of her. "You forget your lunch this morning. I bring it for you."

I blushed a little and shot a glance at Ms. Hawk to see if she'd noticed. She made no indication she had. It was well past two o'clock and I was well aware that I'd forgotten my lunch. I'd grabbed a ham sandwich, corn chips and pop from the party store up the street, savored every mayonnaise-drenched, cholesterol-laden mouthful, and felt virtuous because the soda had been diet.

"Thanks, Slava." I took the bag from her, figuring I could use it tomorrow. "But you didn't have to come all the way down here just to bring me my lunch."

Slava shrugged and gave Ms. Hawk a brief nod. "I cancel office hours today, so I have time. Besides, my mother always say, 'If you don't eat lunch, you get very hungry.'"

I smiled. Slava is a professor of Eastern European studies at the University. Her family fled the Chernobyl disaster when she was nine, spent several years wandering Europe as refugees, and finally ended up in the United States. Slava's written English is flawless, and she can speak the language perfectly well—when she wants to. She usually doesn't bother. Instead, she prefers to bulldoze her way through grammar and pronunciation like a developer plowing through virgin woodland.

"I also come to say I e-mail translation of Romanian documents to you, Ms. Hawk," Slava continued. "Everything is finished."

"Excellent, Dr. Cherenko," Ms. Hawk said. "I look forward to reading them."

"Who is this?" she demanded, gesturing at Belinda.

"A client," I said. "We're on our way out."

"Where are you from?" Belinda asked politely.

"Ukraine," she said. "Where are *you* from?"

"Missoura."

"Ah. You are foreigner like me."

Belinda laughed. "It sure feels that way sometimes."

The sun was getting hotter by the second. Ms. Hawk was already moving toward her car. I edged that way myself, hoping Slava would take the hint. She didn't.

"You have problem for Theresa and Ms. Hawk to fix?" she said. "It is good you come to them. They always know what to do."

"I hope so," Belinda said.

"Perhaps I come with you, give more help, yes?"

"No," I said firmly.

"Why not?" Slava shot back. "I make good investigator. I grow up under KGB, you know."

"No," I said again. Although Ms. Hawk hires Slava on a regular basis whenever we need help with anything Eastern European, she's been reluctant to use Slava for field work. Hawk Enterprises requires a certain…subtlety. Slava is about as subtle as a Molotov cocktail.

Slava sniffed and turned back to Belinda. "What problem do you bring? I look at you and think it must be huge, yes?"

"Slava," I warned. "Ms. Harris doesn't want to—"

"It's all right," Belinda said. "The more I think about it, the more I realize it's silly to be embarrassed. We're going to check on my uncles." And to my astonishment, she gave Slava a thumbnail sketch of the problem.

Slava nodded sagely and drew a pack of cigarettes from her shoulder bag. "I know this house. My students sometimes talk of it, and I wonder how these old men survive alone. It is good to have family check up on you. You are very nice to come all this way to help them, and I commend you."

"Why, thank you," Belinda said, looking both surprised and gratified.

"Now you go," Slava said, lighting her cigarette. "You have uncles to save and I have boring papers to grade."

Ms. Hawk, meanwhile, was backing her car down the narrow driveway, and we climbed in with a final wave to Slava. Belinda took shotgun, and I took the back, feeling a little like a kid out with Mom and Grandma. Although her car isn't flashy or particularly new—anonymous-looking wheels are an asset in our line of work—Ms. Hawk has it detailed regularly, and the interior keeps that new-car smell. Mine always smells like Fritos.

Ms. Hawk pulled smoothly out of the lot and Belinda gave directions. We headed through downtown and turned west on Liberty, driving until the business buildings faded into a residential district. Western Ann Arbor is peppered with aging bungalows and Victorian mansions left over from the lumber-baron days. Most of them have been broken up into student apartments, but a few hang on as single-family dwellings. Ms. Hawk followed Belinda's directions down a series of side streets until she came to the end of a cul-de-sac, where a three-story mansion struggled to stay above knee-deep grass like a mammoth caught in quicksand. Huge maple trees dominated the lawn, and unkempt bushes clung to the sides of the house in suffocating swaths of green. A rickety split-rail fence ran around the boundary, marking off a triple-sized lot. Two neighboring houses tried to keep their distance, and a thick stripe of woodland formed a backdrop around them all. Ms. Hawk pulled into the gravel driveway with caution.

The house itself was done in the blocky Greek Revival style popular in Ann Arbor during the eighteen-hundreds. Two-story front porch, tall columns, square corners, flat walls. And absolutely enormous. It looked like it would be more comfortable somewhere in the deep South. Several of the windows had been boarded up, as if the house had shut its eyes. A mailbox stood on post like a sentry at the front of the driveway, and Belinda got out to check it. Empty.

"See?" she said, scooting back into the car. A wave of heat and humidity came in with her, overpowering the AC for a moment.

"Someone's picking up the mail," Belinda continued. "The police said this was more evidence that my uncles had simply stopped writing me and there was no reason for them to break into the house."

"Hmm," Ms. Hawk said, and I would have given a lot to know what she was thinking. The hawk pendant at her throat flashed in a bit of sunlight. Gravel poked and pinged against the underside of the car like popcorn in a covered pan. Once we were alongside the house, I could see the driveway continued around back, though Ms. Hawk braked to a halt out front.

"Let's see what we can do," she said, and all three of us climbed out of the car.

THREE

THE HEAT WASN'T so bad near the house, where maple trees provided leafy shade. Something rustled in the tall grass, and two rabbits sprinted away. A cracked and broken sidewalk wandered up to the front door, so the three of us followed it. My clunky tool belt dragged at my hips, and I resisted the urge to hitch it up—that never helped. Ms. Hawk wore one like it, though on her it look stylish. Both of us were equipped with flashlight, extra batteries, water bottle, camera, pepper spray, and cell phone. The trunk held more equipment—advanced first-aid kit, flares, night-vision goggles, and more stuff I hoped we wouldn't need.

A short flight of steps led up to a pillared front porch. Boards shifted and creaked beneath my feet. Ms. Hawk pressed the doorbell and rapped sharply on the wood. No response. She tried the knob. Locked.

"Worth a try," she muttered. "Terry, you go that way—" she gestured to the right "—while Ms. Harris and I go this way. Check for other ways in."

"If you don't mind," Belinda put in, "I'd rather stay near the car. I'm not sure how long I can last out here, even in the shade. Bad asthma day, you understand."

"Of course," Ms. Hawk said, and handed Belinda the keys. "I should have realized. Don't hesitate to start it up if you need the air conditioning."

I, meanwhile, followed the house wall past two boarded-up windows to the end of the porch at the corner. There was no wall or rail, so I simply stepped down into the long grass, then paused to look up at the tall, flat expanse of wall above me. Vigorous vines and bushes were climbing for the roof. The second-and third-story windows were gray with grime, and bare wood showed through peeling paint. I wondered what kind of people could let such a grand house fall into ruin.

The shrubbery made a tall, scratchy barrier between me and the outer wall of the house. I walked slowly around the house, pushing into the bushes every so often to look for a window or an overgrown door. My chest felt a little tight with nervousness. Working solo always makes me uneasy— no backup. But it was either that or admit to my boss that I couldn't handle this alone. I comforted myself with the fact that Ms. Hawk was within easy shouting distance and kept going.

Half a block later, I found a window that wasn't boarded up and stood on tiptoe to peep inside. I only saw a few vague shapes and no movement. What the hell was in there? I made a mental note of the spot—we could break the glass to get in, if necessary—and kept going. A few minutes later, I found a side door behind some bushes. Leaves and twigs prickled against my sides and face as I tried the knob, expecting resistance. It turned easily in my hand. The door moved about an inch, then stopped dead. I leaned hard against it, but it refused to budge. Of course. Belinda had mentioned this. I pressed my eye to the crack and tried to peer inside. Pitch blackness. A breath of damp air wafted past my face and I smelled mold, dust, and something…rotten. Garbage? Human flesh? I couldn't tell. I pressed my mouth to the crack and hallooed into the interior. No response.

By now my vision had adjusted a little, and I could make out boxy shapes packed around the door. Someone had deliberately blocked it up. Ooookay. I shoved the door one more time just for the hell of it, but whatever was on the other side weighed more than a stack of anvils. I pulled it shut again and continued on my way. August humidity moved in for the kill, and I felt my hair head for the frizzy zone. A few brown tendrils escaped from my scrunchie, and I could almost hear them go *boing*.

I looked in another window, but couldn't see anything. This whole thing was getting weirder and weirder.

I rounded the corner into the back yard. Fewer trees stood guard back here, and large patches of sunlight did their best to fry the tall grass. It smelled like drying hay. The neighboring houses weren't visible, though I could hear traffic noises beyond the thick tree line that stretched across the rear boundary of the property. Sweat trickled between my breasts and soaked my sports bra. Great. When I got home, I'd have to peel it off. Why had I wanted to come out here again?

I shoved through more prickly bushes to check another window—no luck—then caught sight of Ms. Hawk coming around the other corner. I waved to her, started to step around the shrubbery—

—and fell. The world blurred into green leaves and hard stone. My right elbow cracked against something and I lost all feeling in that arm. Yelping and cursing, I crashed down a lumpy, slanted surface until I fetched up flat on my back. I lay there, and for a second I was married to Noel again, my head aching from one of his ringing slaps.

"Shit!" I said, then said it again just to make sure I'd gotten it right. My arm throbbed. Gingerly I reached up to feel my head. No lumps or tender spots. Well, Mom had always said I had a head like granite.

Ms. Hawk's head poked through the leafy canopy above me. "Are you all right?"

I felt like an idiot, lying at her feet. "Still assessing the damage," I said, then sat up and looked around. I was sitting at the bottom of a short flight of flagstone steps sunk into the ground. Bushes had grown around the top of the stairs, hiding them from view. Behind me was a wooden door that probably led into the cellar of the house. "What happened?"

"You took a step and disappeared. It looked like the bushes swallowed you up." The greenery parted, and Ms. Hawk descended the stairs gracefully as a queen. I was glad to see her. She offered me a hand and hauled me upright with easy strength.

"Fun," I said, brushing myself down. A few scrapes and bruises—no major damage. "But I don't think Disney World will offer it as a ride."

Ms. Hawk gave a thin smile, then pulled out her flashlight. It was gloomy down here, and cooler. She shined the light at the door, then at the area just in front of it. "No debris," she said. "And that door appears to be in better repair than the others. This must be how the uncles have been getting in and out."

I examined it with my own flashlight. The doorknob wasn't more than a few years old. Fresh scratches marked the area around the lock. "Oopsie. Looks like someone lost his key."

"Did the intruder manage to open it?" Ms. Hawk asked.

I tried the door, and it opened easily on silent hinges. The basement beyond exhaled damp, musty air that smelled of old stone. I pointed my flashlight inside. The area just inside the door was clear, but beyond that was a wall of… Well, a wall of junk. A whole bunch of shoeboxes jumbled up with a rusty rake, three shovels, and an ancient rototiller. A stack of old-style oil cans were piled near a mass of broken lawn chairs that looked like shattered skeletons in the bad light. Flowerpots, half bags of peat moss, more chairs. Stuff that any normal person would have tossed on the trash heap years ago, and all of it piled to the ceiling beams.

"This is something else," I said, stepping inside. "Maybe we should—"

And then everything happened very, very fast. Something caught my ankle at the exact moment Ms. Hawk grabbed the back of my shirt and yanked me backward. My flashlight went flying. I heard an explosive crash, and a cloud of dust billowed up. I landed hard against Ms. Hawk, and we both went down. The ground vibrated, then everything went still. Dust clogged my mouth and nose. I lay there, a little dazed, until I realized I was still on top of Ms. Hawk. I rolled free, coughing, and helped her up.

"What the hell—?" I said.

Ms. Hawk, also coughing, pointed at the door. The dust cloud cleared a bit, and beneath the haze, I could see a shin-high pile of cinder blocks occupying the space I had been standing in a moment before. I swallowed and my legs went shaky.

"We almost had the ingredients to a Terry Faye pancake," I said, and my voice would have done credit to Minnie Mouse.

Ms. Hawk nodded. "Ms. Harris did say something about booby traps. I saw the wire half a second before you tripped it."

I looked at the bricky pile. The handle of my flashlight stuck out from under one of the blocks, and I tried to tug it free without success. One more piece of junk for the basement.

"I suppose," Ms. Hawk continued, "we should tell Ms. Harris we've found a way in."

Back at the car, Belinda expressed cautious optimism about our news. We led her around back and down the steps. By now, the dust had settled, but Belinda reached the doorway and stopped dead.

"Oh, dear," she muttered.

"What's wrong?" I asked.

"Mold. Dust. Mildew. I can smell it from here. If I go into that house, I'll land in the hospital." Her mouth twisted. "I've been like this my whole life, you understand. My brother used to call me 'limp lungs' until Dad took a strap to him. Couldn't play outside for half the year, and the other half I had to keep an inhaler handy. It's like being in prison, except there's no parole."

Her words were flat and her face was hard. I wondered what it would be like to live with that and took an unobtrusive deep breath of my own. Air flowed freely, easy to take for granted.

"We'll go in and let you know what we find," Ms. Hawk said.

Belinda nodded and headed back to the car. I followed her, retrieved a spare flashlight from the trunk, and went back to the basement. Ms. Hawk was just inside—I could see her light beam dancing around.

The basement had a low ceiling, with thick wooden beams that could crush a Volkswagen if they fell. The only light came from our flashlights and the tiny bit of sun that snuck in through the bushes outside the door. My hands were sweating, though the cellar itself was cool and damp. I couldn't see the walls—they were blocked by stacks of junk. An old bookshelf filled with mildewy stuffed animals. A weird cast-iron machine. Anonymous boxes covered in mold. A piano with missing keys that gaped like broken dentures. Stacks and stacks of newspapers, neatly bundled and tied with twine. One stack was only shoulder high, and I shined my light at the top paper. *Detroit Free Press,* October 18, 1968. President Johnson might order a cessation of bombing in Viet Nam. Yoko Ono and John Lennon had been arrested for drug possession. Geez.

A narrow pathway wound through the piles, and we had to turn sideways to squeeze through. Boxes and crates pressed in on all sides, and I couldn't see over the tops. Dust clogged my nose, and I kept pausing to sneeze. Ms. Hawk seemed unbothered.

The path led us through a low doorway into another room. The darkness and damp air pressed in around us, and cobwebs hung over everything like sleeping ghosts. They dragged through my hair and left dusty trails across my face. I shivered. Ms. Hawk kept her flashlight beam on the floor, scanning for more little wires. It slowed our pace to a crawl. Tiny noises scritched in the darkness beyond the light beams. Mice?

My foot came down on something that crunched. I jumped back, my heart beating at the back of my throat. Then I saw the little dark smear. Hundreds of tiny shadows scurried for cover.

"Cockroaches," Ms. Hawk said. "The floor is covered with them here." She made a small sound of disgust. "It's like living in Madagascar all over again."

Madagascar? Wasn't that near Africa? Ms. Hawk didn't have an accent, so I doubted she grew up there. Another strange piece of the puzzle that made up Diana Hawk. As for me, I reached down and tucked my pant legs into the top of my socks. Ms. Hawk noticed.

"Good idea," she said, and stooped to do the same. I felt oddly pleased. This was the way I liked it—me and Ms. Hawk, working as a team. Sometimes I still couldn't believe she had hired me, or that I'd had the guts to ask her for a job. Desperation had played a big role. My husband was dead, my parents weren't speaking to me, and I had no degree, skills, or income. I thought long and hard about what I wanted to do with my life, and a week later, I forced myself to stride into Ms. Hawk's plant-filled office.

"You want to hire me as your assistant," I said.

Ms. Hawk raised a graceful eyebrow, and I rushed on to sell myself. I had no ties to hold me down, I was organized, I learned fast, and I was willing to work long hours. In the end, Ms. Hawk agreed to take me on—as a file clerk. I drove home to Toledo, breathless with joy, and started packing. For the first time in my life, I felt like I had a purpose, even if that purpose was shuffling pieces of paper around a filing cabinet. Once I was settled in town, I enrolled in martial-arts training and learned to shoot. I discovered a talent and a taste for combat. My body and mind hardened, and Ms. Hawk began taking me along on some of her cases. Now, four years later, I had my PI license and an advanced red belt in karate, and I was involved in almost all investigations at Hawk Enterprises. I still don't know why Ms. Hawk had invested so much in me, but gratitude for her decision drenched my every waking moment. I would walk across hot coals for her. Cockroaches? Bring 'em on!

We continued across the crispy floor. It felt like we were walking on Cheetos. The two of us crunched through another room, this one filled with just boxes. The ones on the floor were being squashed by the weight of those above. Another had burst open, revealing a tangle of wire coat hangers and a single light bulb. Saved so the uncles could see to count the hangers?

The path ended at a set of stone stairs tucked against one wall. The steps were predictably piled with more junk—old dishes, bundles of cooking magazines, a microwave oven with a missing door. It had a dead potted plant inside.

"You think any of this stuff might be valuable?" I asked as we picked our way upward.

Ms. Hawk skirted a milk crate filled with flattened cans. "I doubt it. Hoarders are usually unable to tell the difference between what's valuable and what's worthless. They simply can't bear to throw anything away."

We reached the first-floor landing, opened a creaky door, and found ourselves in another room. Open boxes of paper spilled their contents onto the floor. I grabbed a handful and checked it by flashlight. Uncle Lawrence was a million-dollar finalist. And he could refinance his mortgage for low, low rates. He could even get a pre-approved home equity loan for ten thousand bucks. Gosh. No wonder he never wanted to leave the house.

Ms. Hawk, meanwhile, shined her light around. Dust-covered junk from floor to ceiling. The closest window was boarded up from the inside, and ragged curtains covered the others. Ms. Hawk blinked.

"I think we're in the kitchen," she said at last.

"We are?" I shined my own light over the area. After a moment, I could see that what I had taken for stacks of loose papers and food boxes was actually a stove. The refrigerator was obscured by a mountain of foam take-out trays. No one had used this kitchen for cooking in years. My foot crushed another cockroach, and I decided that maybe this was a good thing.

"Hello?" Ms. Hawk shouted, and I jumped. Even though we had Belinda's permission to be here, it felt like we were trespassing. "Can anyone hear me?"

We listened. Nothing.

"So the big question is," Ms. Hawk said, "do we split up or stay together?"

I thought about facing more cockroaches by myself. "Let's stick together. I'm willing to bet Uncle Lawrence has a few more booby traps up his sleeve, and four eyes are better than two for spotting them."

"True," Ms. Hawk said. "Let's go, then."

A narrow trail through the piles led out of the kitchen into what we figured was a grand dining room. Or it would have been if not for the junk. Mounds of papers, stacks of milk crates, leaning towers of books. In one corner sat a pile of bags of instant cement. They had gotten damp, and the cement had set, creating a stack of paper-wrapped bricks. Perched on top of them was an old bird cage with a dusty plush parrot in it. A table long enough to seat thirty guests ran the length of the room. I saw no chairs. What looked like a hundred years' worth of mail mounded every square inch of table space. Ms. Hawk found some windows that weren't too badly blocked and flung the curtains open like a movie star from the forties. Sunlight, possibly the first bunch of natural photons to venture in since the sixties, flooded the room, and I flinched until my eyes adjusted. The mail on the dining-room table differed from the junk flyers in the kitchen. These seemed to be old bills, bank statements, and other financial mailings. None of the ones I glanced at were less than ten years old. I checked the floor. It was uncarpeted hardwood, and the thin strip of bare floor that wound around the table was clear of dust. Someone was still walking around in here recently. I pointed this out to Ms. Hawk, who nodded.

"I noticed that, too," she said. "Next room."

We checked the threshold for tripwires before crossing it and found ourselves in a long, dim hallway faced with closed doors. Dusty gold-colored magazines were stacked against the walls all the way to the ceiling. *National Geographic*. Thousands of them. The air was hot and stuffy and tinged with something rotten again. I wrinkled my nose. How could anyone keep all this stuff? What was—

Something creaked. Ms. Hawk and I both froze. I shot her a glance, and she put a finger to her lips. We listened some more, and I heard it again—a faint creaking. It might have been footsteps, or it might have been the house scttling. I felt reluctant to shout and announce our presence. Apparently Ms. Hawk felt the same way, because she eased up the hallway without a word. I followed.

The creaking stopped. I was nervous now, and a little excited. At the end of the hall, we found a staircase. It was piled with shoes. Men's loafers, women's pumps, slippers, baby booties, even a pair of snowshoes. A narrow path twisted up the left side like a mountain-goat track. The steps were dusty, more or less. Something about them bugged me, but I couldn't put my finger on it. Ms. Hawk checked for tripwires, then moved to head upward. At the last moment, it clicked. I lunged forward and grabbed Ms. Hawk's arm.

"Wait!" I hissed. "Look!"

With my flashlight I pointed out the staircase. Every other step was clean.

"Someone skips certain steps," I said. I knelt down and wiped the board with my sleeve. A perpendicular line appeared in the exposed part of the riser. I set my palm on it and leaned down, gently at first, then with more force. The wood snapped, plunging my arm into the staircase up to the shoulder. Half a dozen shoes tumbled into the hole and vanished.

"Precut staircase," I said. "I think we need to skip every other stair."

"Good eye, Terry," Ms. Hawk said approvingly, and I felt a rush of pride. "Let's go up."

"House is in terrible condition," Slava said. "You should find new housekeeper."

Both of us jerked around. My friend was standing behind us looking at the stairs with interest. She had replaced the high heels with tennis shoes but was wearing the same red dress I had seen her in earlier.

"Slava!" I gasped. "What the hell are you—"

"Is all right," she interrupted. "I already told you I know of this house. I decide is too nice a day to waste grading freshman essays, so I come here for look inside. Belinda was in car, and she say everything fine I come in. So I come in to find experience as field agent. Three heads better than two, yes?"

"No," I said. "You're not even dressed for this sort of thing."

"So my dress get dirty," she said. "I am rich American now—I have many."

"Dr. Cherenko," Ms. Hawk said, "it might be best if you waited outside. It isn't safe in here."

"Probably true," Slava agreed. "But on day of big disaster, Chernobyl give me huge dose of radiation. My parents both die of cancer before I turn thirty. I will probably die same way. So I decide, what the hell? Either radiation kill me or big pile of cinder blocks smash me flat. At least with cinder blocks, I get to explore interesting house first. Besides—" she flicked a speck of dust from her sleeve "—Belinda give me permission. I have perfect right to be here."

Ms. Hawk sighed. "Just stay out of the way."

I glared at Slava, who pretended not to notice. "All right," she said. "I follow you. Just be sure to cut tripwire at top of stairs."

Ms. Hawk, who was halfway up the staircase, stopped. "You see a tripwire?"

"You don't?"

We both shined our lights upward. A thin wire stretched across the top of the staircase maybe two inches above floor level. It was perfectly straight, held rigid with ominous tension. I was suddenly less eager to explore the second floor.

Avoiding every other step, Ms. Hawk crept cautiously up to the top. Her flashlight beam followed the wire to a two-by-four wedged against the wall. The wire was wrapped around the two-by-four. The other end disappeared into a hole drilled

through the door jamb. Ms. Hawk checked the floor beyond
the trap, satisfied herself it was safe, and lithely stepped over
the wire. She gave the all-clear, and I made my way after her,
being careful to step only on the good steps, too. An entryway
opened up beyond the stairwell. It was crammed with—well,
you know by now. Brown light leaked in around a boarded-
up window. Above the door was a heavy shelf piled high with
books that made the *Oxford English Dictionary* look like a
small-town phonebook. One end of the shelf was held up by
a support nailed deep into the wall joists. The other end was
held up by the two-by-four. Anyone who hit the wire would
yank the two-by-four out from under the shelf and bring down
four or five hundred pounds of serious knowledge.

Slava came up the steps with surprising grace. She has a
lush figure that reminds me of Marilyn Monroe or Mae West,
and Slava carries herself with the same assurance. Must be
nice.

"Crude, but serviceable," she said, eyeing the trap. "This
Uncle Lawrence—he would have had fun in old KGB."

I sniffed the dusty air. Definite sweet-yet-nasty smell of
rot. "You guys catch that delightful scent?"

"We almost certainly have bad news for Belinda," Ms.
Hawk mused, still studying the trap. "Though right now I'm
more concerned about possible bad news for us."

"Should we leave this trap or disarm it?" I said.

"I don't want to leave it here in case one of us forgets about
it," Ms. Hawk replied.

"No big deal," Slava said, bending down and grasping the
wire. "Stand back."

"Slava!" I shouted. "No!"

But it was too late. Slava yanked the tripwire and scam-
pered backward. The two-by-four popped out from under the
shelf, and the entire thing came down with a thunderous crash.
A hurricane of dust exploded into the air. Coughing and spit-
ting, I retreated from the landing and backed down the hallway. My eyes streamed with tears, and dust coated the inside

of my mouth, my nose, my ears. I'd also be washing the stuff out of some other more personal places.

When at last I could see, I made out Slava and Ms. Hawk standing next to me. Ms. Hawk gave me a chilly stare. I looked away, feeling my cheeks flush. Slava was my friend, and her screwups were my fault. I turned to face her. Her wine-red dress had gone completely gray. So had her hair and face. She looked like a witch out of a fairy tale.

"Slava," I croaked, then spat dust and tried again. "Slava, that wasn't very smart. That tripwire could have been linked to more than one thing. You might have set off a cascade of traps and killed all three of us."

Slava shrugged. "But I didn't. We should keep looking. Follow our noses to old men."

Ms. Hawk produced a water bottle from her belt and took a swig. I did the same, sighing with relief as the lukewarm liquid washed the dust from my throat. I dashed a bit into my face to clear the dust from my eyes and nose. When I was finished, Slava held out her hand, eyebrows raised. Peevishly, I considered refusing her unspoken request, then shrugged and raised the bottle.

"You have to promise not to touch anything else," I said.

"But how can I help if I can't touch?" she said.

I waggled the bottle. "Nice, refreshing water. But only if you promise."

A burst of Ukrainian swearwords followed my attempt at blackmail, but then Slava said, "Very well. I promise."

I handed over the bottle. While Slava drank, Ms. Hawk and I checked the hallway. Old furniture, mostly broken lamps and tattered shades, lined the walls. Every so often a gap opened, indicating the presence of a door. The corridor ended in some sort of open space. I swung my light around.

"This place is more organized than it looks," I said. "Gardening tools and miscellaneous outdoor stuff in the back basement, newspapers toward the front, kitchen things on the stairs. Junk mail in the kitchen, regular mail in the dining room. Shoes on the steps. Lamps and accessories in the hall here. It's not perfect—cement in the dining room, for example—but there's definitely a pattern."

"Interesting," Ms. Hawk said. "I don't see any more wires, but step carefully."

We eased down the hall in silence, and the rotten meat smell grew noticeably stronger. I checked the first door. Unlocked. I stiff-armed it open and jumped back. Darkness beyond. I shined my flashlight inside. Monstrous shapes loomed in the shadows. My beam picked out a piano in slightly better condition than the one in the basement, a pedal harp with most of the strings missing, a small forest of bent and twisted trombones, two more pianos, and a stack of violin cases among the many, many boxes.

"It's a conservatory," I said. "Weird. How many pianos do you need, anyway?"

Slava peered over my shoulder at the violin cases. "Is too much to hope for a hidden Stradivarius, yes?"

"How on earth did they get all that up the stairs?" I wondered aloud.

"There must be another staircase," Ms. Hawk said. "A wider one. Let's keep moving."

As I shut the door, I heard more creaking above me. This was more rhythmic, like footsteps. My heart jerked, and I shined my flashlight upward, as if I'd be able to see through the ceiling. Slava and Ms. Hawk had heard it, too.

"Someone else still in house," Slava whispered. "Or else is really big cockroach."

"Whoever it is had to have heard that book trap fall," I whispered back. "They must know we're here. If it's one of the uncles, wouldn't he say something?"

"Not if he's scared of us," Ms. Hawk murmured. "And *someone* scratched up the basement-door lock. That person may still be here."

We wove our way through the junk piles in the hallway. I wondered who could be in the house, and if the person might be dangerous. Maybe there'd be a fight. A familiar mixture of fear and anticipation thrilled through me. I'm good at fighting. Earned my advanced red belt in karate last year, and I'm inches away from earning a black. I *like* fights—once I'm in one. Beforehand, I worry about pain and injury, but once the fists start flying, I'm *there*. Punch, block, dodge, kick, throw. It's like a dance I make up as I go.

The creaking upstairs continued. It was apparently moving down the hallway above us, getting farther away. Ms. Hawk had said the person was probably afraid of us, and that made me feel braver. The three of us moved as quickly as we dared down the corridor, past several more doors and still more junk. An open box of eight-track tapes caught my eye, and I wondered if they were still playable.

The hall ended in a grand staircase that curved down into shadow. A narrower set of stairs led upward, around an elbow of a landing, and then to the third floor. A half wall topped by a banister partitioned off the upper stairs. Only a narrow trail of space allowed passage up or down either staircase. The grand stairs were almost completely blocked with bundles of more magazines. *Life, TV Guide, People, Time, Newsweek.* Some looked pristine, others were crumpled or water stained. The staircase to the third floor was buried beneath mounds and mounds of pans. Sauce pans. Frying pans. Soup pans. Griddles. Dutch ovens. All of them dusty, rusty, or both. Some were cracked. Lids perched precariously on lips and rims like lily pads on a steel pond.

"Dishwasher is broken," Slava commented.

I checked the stairs with my flashlight. No tripwires or weakened risers. "I'll go up first," I said, and slipped upward without waiting for a response. I was kind of hoping Ms. Hawk would be impressed with my bravery, though she didn't say anything. The creaking footsteps had stopped, and the rotten smell gained serious strength. I was about a third of the way to the landing when I saw a human-shaped shadow flicker up near the landing.

"Terry!" Ms. Hawk shouted. "Look out!"

A metallic crash boomed above me, and an avalanche of pots and pans cascaded down the steps. I didn't even think. I leaped over the half wall into empty space, catching the banister as I went over. With an ear-shattering howl, the cast-iron avalanche swept past me down the stairs. I hung by one hand, my feet dangling a good ten feet above the ground. Ms. Hawk and Slava had already jumped aside. Pots, pans, and lids hit the wooden floor at the bottom of the stairs with the sound of a thousand knights in armor slamming into the enemy. My hand started to slip. By a miracle, my other hand still held the flashlight. I checked the area below me. Boxes. No telling what was in them or how fun it would be to land on them. They could be filled with skewers and knives, for all I knew. I tossed the flashlight over the rail onto the stairs, then flung my free hand up so I could get a double-grip on the banister. My shoulders were screaming at me that this kind of activity wasn't in their contract. I gritted my teeth. My feet scrabbled at the smooth plaster of the half wall and found no toe-holds.

My sweaty hands started to slip. I heard desperate clanking as Slava and Ms. Hawk shoved pots and pans around in an effort to clear the stairs so they could get to me, but in a few more seconds I was going to plunge down into those boxes, and something told me they weren't for storing pillows. I drew back one leg and kicked the aging plaster as hard as I could. I heard a *crack*. I kicked again. My left hand slipped off the banister. I flung my arm back up and regained a tentative hold.

"We're coming!" Ms. Hawk shouted. "Hold on, Terry!"

I gritted my teeth and focused like *Kyosa* Parkinson had taught me. My world narrowed. No sound but my breathing. No sensation but my heart beating. No problem but the plaster at the end of my boot. I thought of all my strength drawing into a single point in my foot. I drew back my leg and *kicked*.

My steel-tipped toe smashed through the wall and I was standing, however precariously, on the edge of the hole I'd created. Holding on was much easier now. A moment later,

Ms. Hawk and Slava pulled me over the half wall and onto the stairs. A mound of cookware lay at the bottom, though plenty of pans were left on the steps. I sat down on shaky legs and took a swig from my water bottle. It was almost empty.

"Very exciting," Slava said. "Much better than grading stupid essays."

"That wasn't an accident," Ms. Hawk said.

"I know," I said, retrieving my flashlight. "I saw a shadow at the top of the stairs."

"Uncle Lawrence!" Slava boomed. "We're friends! Belinda send us to check on you! Is all right you come out!"

My first instinct was to shush her. Then I grimaced. Our presence here was definitely not a secret. Why not shout?

No one answered. The stairs were much clearer now, and we got to the third floor without any more trouble. The air was even stuffier up there, and the smell was enough to curl my nose hairs. Ms. Hawk fished a crisp, white handkerchief out of her pocket and tied it around her face. No one carries handkerchiefs in this day and age—except Ms. Hawk.

The third floor was another long corridor, though I saw what looked like side niches and hidden nooks. You were supposed to fill them with comfy chairs so you could steal a few moments with a book or hold a private conversation. These nooks were crammed with still more stuff. Wine bottles made a glass jumble in one, old stereo speakers were stacked in another. At the end of the hallway, I saw a shadowy, uneven mountain. I couldn't make out what it was—we were back to near blackness except for the flashlights. The stench was awful.

Slava went straight to the first door. "I think smell is coming from here." She twisted the handle before I could say anything, then made a disgusted noise. "Locked."

I checked. Slava was right—the smell was stronger over here. I took shallow breaths and tried to breathe through my mouth, though the ambient dust made that difficult.

The door was solid, but I thought I felt it give a little when

I pushed. I glanced at Ms. Hawk, who shrugged. I motioned Slava away from the door.

"What you do?" she asked.

"I'm going to break it down," I said.

"Huh," Slava snorted.

"What?"

"That door is laughing at you. You hit it, you bounce off like tennis ball."

"I know what I'm doing," I said. "It's all a matter of focus."

"I see you focus," Slava said. "I see you focus on cherry cheesecake after supper. I see you focus on movies with Orlando Florida. I never see you focus on smashing down door."

"It's Orlando *Bloom*," I said. "And don't you diss my brown-eyed boy toy, radiation girl. Just stand back and watch."

"Huh," Slava snorted again.

I stood in front of the door and focused, as I'd done on the stairs. No sound but my breathing. No sensation but my heart beating. No problem but the door before me. I thought of all my strength drawing into a single point in my foot. I cocked a leg, drew back, and *kicked*.

The shock jolted me from skull to coccyx. I stood there for a moment, one foot on the ground, one planted against the door. Then I made a small, squeaky noise and fell backward. Ms. Hawk caught me. I swore I heard wooden laughter.

"Don't say it," I groaned to Slava.

"I would not," Slava replied airily. "I am very *good* friend."

Ms. Hawk set me upright. Once she was sure I was all right, she stood in front of the door and gave it a long look. The dark oak had a dusty boot print on it, but looked otherwise completely unfazed. My head and spine throbbed. Maybe we could find a sledgehammer among the tools in the basement. Or maybe we could—

Ms. Hawk's scream raised the hair on my neck. Her foot lashed out and crashed into the door. Wood shattered, and the door burst inward with a bang. I stared at Ms. Hawk, mouth agape. The white handkerchief tied around her lower face made her look like a karate bandit.

"You loosened it for me, Terry," she said charitably.

"I am *good* friend," Slava muttered. "Very, very good friend. I don't say nasty things to my friends."

"Thank you," I drawled.

The moment the door opened, the smell intensified, as if the room had exhaled the world's worst bad breath on us. I stopped breathing through my nose entirely, dust or no dust, but that only helped a little. My lunch churned around inside my stomach.

The room was absolutely black. My flashlight beam speared the darkness and came to rest on a twin-sized bed. A long shape lay beneath a blanket. At the foot of the bed sat a wheelchair. Uncle Howard's, no doubt. Someone would have to check that bundle. The thought of twitching the blanket aside to expose what lay beneath made my skin crawl like it was covered with cold worms. I looked over my shoulder at Slava and Ms. Hawk. Slava gave me a wide-eyed look and backed away.

"Not my job," she said. "You get paid for looking, not me."

"If you don't want to, Terry," Ms. Hawk said gently, "I'll go take a look."

That gentle tone of voice did it for me. What was I, a little kid? As if I'd never looked at a dead body before! I'd seen my ex-husband dead in coroner's drawer with a ligature mark on his neck, for God's sake. I'd watched *Saving Private Ryan*. Twice! I marched into the room, banged my shin on a pile of newspapers, and fell against the bed. My hand sank into the bundle beneath the blanket and came away wet. I set my mouth and whisked the blankets aside.

A pair of cloudy eyes behind coke-bottle glasses stared up at me from a blackened, decaying face.

"It's Uncle Howard," I said, and threw up.

THE NEXT THING I knew, I was sitting in the hallway with my head between my knees and a water bottle in my hand. Slava was kneeling next to me, her hand on my shoulder.

"Just breathe," she was saying. "My mother always say, 'If you don't breathe, you die.'"

"I feel stupid," I said, trying not to sob. "It's just a...a dead body."

"Is disgusting, rotten body," Slava said. "If you see nasty body like this and have no reaction, *then* you are stupid."

"She's right about that," Ms. Hawk said. She had shut the bedroom door and was leaning against it. "I feel a bit queasy myself."

"There, you see? The great Diana Hawk says is okay. You feel better now."

I did feel better. I swished a little water through my mouth and spat it onto the floor, then used some to rinse my hand. After a moment, Slava hauled me to my feet. Sweat and dust sludged into an itchy paste on my skin, and my stomach quivered. I wanted nothing more than a cool, relaxing shower, an Orlando Bloom DVD and a drink that would burn all the way down. And some cherry cheesecake.

"We should go out and tell Belinda," I said. "And call the police."

"Yes," said Ms. Hawk. "But I want to know the why of a few things. Like why Uncle Lawrence didn't call the police himself when his brother died in there—it's clear he passed away some time ago. I also want to know who started that avalanche and just where Uncle Lawrence *is*." She pulled her handkerchief down and gingerly sniffed the air. "I also want to know why the smell gets worse farther down this hallway."

Me, I *didn't* want to know, but gave no sign of that to Ms. Hawk. "Let's get this over with," I said instead, and headed carefully down the hall. We passed more junk and more closed doors, all of which we ignored. Our footsteps creaked on the bare wood floor, but we didn't speak. I found myself mulling over the points Ms. Hawk had brought up. Why *hadn't*

Uncle Lawrence called the cops after Uncle Howard's death?
A number of explanations went through my head, but most of
them brought up more questions. Probably Uncle Lawrence
was dead, too, and we were smelling his corpse right now.

The huge shadow I had seen at the end of the hallway began
to resolve itself. It was a mountain of magazines, some bundled, some loose. They were piled to the ceiling in an uneven
pyramid, completely blocking the rest of the hallway beyond.
I shined my light over it. It looked…out of place. All the other
piles of reading material had been almost tidy, if dusty and
neglected. This was random chaos.

"What is that?" Slava said, pointing down to my feet. I
pointed my flashlight beam downward. Sticking out from the
bottom of the pile was a human hand.

FOUR

A SHUTTER CLICKED and a light flashed. All three of us spun around. A male figure with a camera in front of its face stood behind us. Before I could react, another flash blasted straight into my retina, filling my eyesight with a red haze. As a result, I only heard what came next: a crack, a yelp of pain, a meaty thud and a strange crunch.

When my vision cleared, I saw Ms. Hawk standing over a prone man. She held a digital camera in one hand and was grinding her heel against the floor with a gritty, sandy sound.

"Hey!" the man protested from the floor. "My memory stick!"

Ms. Hawk dropped the camera onto his chest without comment. He grunted, but caught the object before it slid away.

"Get out," Ms. Hawk told the man in a voice that would have chilled a polar bear.

"Look, I just want—"

"Get out," Ms. Hawk repeated. "Or I'll have Terry here do something even worse. Her imagination is more colorful than mine."

Even though I knew Ms. Hawk was just saying that to scare the guy, I felt my chest puff up a little. "I think I saw a box of rusty skewers in the kitchen," I lied.

The guy sat up. "All right, all right. Violence isn't the answer here."

"You expect me to burst into song?" I asked. "That might be even worse than the skewers."

"God forbid." He tried to inspect the camera for damage, then gave up in the dim light. "Can you help me up, at least?

Jesus, I'm going to have bruises in places even my doctor doesn't check."

"I can check, if you like," Slava said.

I sighed and reached down to give the guy a hand. A hand. Just like the one sticking out from the monstrous pile of magazines. My stomach turned and I swallowed. Funny as Slava might find it, I didn't want to heave all over the guy. He grabbed my hand in a firm dry grip and came upright, straight into Ms. Hawk's flashlight beam.

Oh, my.

Okay, let's get one thing straight. I *like* men. I like the way they look, I like the way they move, I like the way they smell. I like to watch a well-dressed masculine figure in a candlelit restaurant. I like to see a tousled, scratchy face on the pillow come morning. And every day I thank God and the FDA for reliable birth control.

The moment I realized this guy was a photographer sneaking around taking pictures of squidgy corpses and mangled hands, I imagined a piggy-eyed, weasel-faced guy with receding greasy hair and acne on his nose. Instead I got gold hair, sea-green eyes and a long jaw that screamed for a finger to stroke it. He had the lean, lithe build you earn through honest physical activity instead of in a gym, and he looked to be somewhere in his early thirties. His red polo shirt and brown khakis were streaked with dust. A belt similar to mine was hung with photography equipment. And just below the belt...

I yanked my eyes back upward. Had he caught me checking? I doubted it—Ms. Hawk's flashlight was still shining in his face. He was probably half-blind. I flushed anyway, and my face grew hot.

"Thanks," he said, and I realized we were still holding hands. I dropped his.

"Yeah," I said. "Who the hell are you?"

He stuck his hand back out. "Zack Archer. I'm a photographer."

"What the hell are you doing here?" I said, ignoring the gesture. Gorgeous or not, a photographer wasn't someone Hawk Enterprises wanted to mess around with. Ms. Hawk kept a low profile for herself and the agency, and I suspect she cashed in a lot of favors to keep us out of the news.

Zack flashed a white smile that turned his face into pure sunshine. I became acutely aware of the grime encrusting my skin and the sweat plastering my hair to my head. Sexy I wasn't, but Zack looked thoroughly edible, even covered in dust. The dirt just made me want to give him a nice long bath. I told my hormones to take a hike, but all they did was jump up and down and complain that it had been way too long since they'd gotten any decent exercise.

"I'm here to take photos," he said, holding up the cameras. "Pho-tos. I can spell it for you, if you want."

"We aren't stupid," Slava said. "Answer question before I go KGB on your ass."

"Who do you work for?" Ms. Hawk interjected.

"I work freelance," Zack said. "I do a lot for Reuters, and my stuff's been in *Time* and *Newsweek.* Right now I'm hoping for the *Detroit Free Press.*"

"Why not the *National Inquirer?*" I asked nastily, just to prove that I had no interest in jumping him then and there.

Zack curled his lip. "I've got better things to do than dangle from a helicopter hoping to catch Taylor Swift bonking someone in her back yard. Look, this house is an unofficial Ann Arbor landmark. I figured there might be a story in it, so I came out to check around."

I narrowed my eyes. "You just *happened* to come out today. When we were here finding dead bodies. Amazing luck you have."

"Yeah," Zack said easily. Then, "Hey! What are you implying?"

"Please leave, Mr. Archer," Ms. Hawk said in a deadly even voice. Her crackling presence filled every corner of the dusty hallway, making everything else seem small and insignificant. I would have fled. Zack, however, turned to face her.

"You gonna call the cops?"

His tone held a hint of sneer, and I got pissed. My hands balled into fists and I started forward again. Ms. Hawk made a small gesture. I pulled myself up short. Slava gave me a hard look, but I kept my eyes on my boss.

"The cops can't do anything," Zack continued, completely unaware that death—or least great pain—was breathing down his collar.

"They could arrest you for trespassing," Ms. Hawk said. "Or on suspicion of murder."

"Doubtful," Zack said. There was that near-sneer again. "Trespassing charges are hard to make stick when the owners aren't…available to press charges. And judging from the smell, these guys have been unavailable for a long time. Besides, I was in Alaska until three days ago. No way I could have killed them."

"I didn't mean you might have killed *them*," Ms. Hawk said. "I meant you tried to kill Terry with that pan avalanche."

"Yeah!" I said, surprised this hadn't occurred to me.

"You're reaching," Zack said. "The hall in front of you is completely blocked by…by stuff. I came up behind you, on the pan staircase. I couldn't have pushed the pans, then snuck down past you to come up the stairs a second time. You would have seen me."

You could see the implications of this statement steal over everyone's faces, one by one. Ms. Hawk got it first. Slava got it a second before Zack and I did.

"Okay, who wants to say it?" I said.

"Only other stairway down is blocked by mountain of magazines," Slava said. "That mean person who started pan avalanche still upstairs. With us."

The door across from Uncle Howard's bedroom exploded open and a figure fled down the stairs. Ms. Hawk and I instantly charged after him, but Zack was between us and the stairway, so he got a head start. Leaving a startled Slava behind, the three of us bolted down the hall. This turned into a dance when we hit the stairs and had to dodge pots and pans. The figure reached the bottom of the stairs and turned to flee down the cluttered hallway.

"Freeze!" I shouted, but the figure kept going.

Ms. Hawk hit a pot lid and stumbled. She caught the rail just before she fell. My heart lurched, and I slowed to help her.

"Keep going!" she snapped. "I'm fine."

Zack, meanwhile, had reached the landing and was already sprinting away. I took a calculated risk and jumped, landing with a thud a few steps behind him. The figure had avoided the main staircase and was fleeing down the hall toward the shoe stairs instead with Zack in hot pursuit. I followed, all my senses set on high. My flashlight beam bobbled and jumped. I caught a glimpse of a baseball cap and some iron-gray hair.

"Hold it!" Zack shouted. "I just want to talk. I'm not going to hurt you."

The figure pulled a stack of boxes down to block the hall behind him. They burst open, revealing mounds of old clothes. Zack dove over them and tried to roll to his feet, but the open space in the hallway was too narrow and he ended up wrestling with a pair of farmer jeans. Dust rose in a choking cloud, and I heard the *thump* and *thud* of uncertain footsteps clambering over a pile of books—the booby trap Slava had set off. I shoved some boxes aside and clambered over others as Zack leaped back up and charged ahead. Footsteps clattered down the back steps in an uneven rhythm. Zack reached the top of the stairwell and started down.

"Zack!" I screamed. "Wait!"

Too late. Wood cracked and Zack screamed. I vaulted over the pile of books and found Zack clinging to the hand rail at the top of the stairs. He was knee-deep in shoes, and his face was drawn with pain. The figure had vanished.

"What the hell happened?" he gasped.

I shoved shoes aside and sent them spilling down the steps. They were surprisingly heavy and difficult to move. Once the top step was clear, I could see Zack's right foot had broken through one of the weakened risers. If he hadn't grabbed the rail, he would have broken his leg, or maybe fallen forward and broken his neck.

"Every other step is trapped," I said. "Didn't you see the broken one at the bottom when you came up?"

"I didn't know they were *all* like that," Zack hissed through clenched teeth.

I examined his leg with my flashlight. The broken wood had trapped his ankle and blood seeped through the khakis on his lower calf. I ducked under his free arm and put my own arm around his waist. His body was warm and solid and it felt…nice. He smelled of clean, masculine sweat. I remembered his earlier condescension and was forced to admit feeling a little conflicted right then.

"We'll go straight up on three," I said briskly. "Ready? One…two…three!" I lifted. Zack hissed again and I felt his muscles tighten. His foot came free of the stair, and a few more shoes tumbled down into darkness. With my help, he took a couple hops backward and we both plunked down onto the pile of dusty books.

"Let me look at that," I said, sliding up Zack's trouser cuff and shining my flashlight on his calf without waiting for an answer. His leg was covered with fine, red-gold hairs. A nasty set of abrasions oozed scarlet, but they looked more painful than serious.

"Will I be able to play the bagpipes, doc?" he asked, though his tone was forced.

"God, I hope not," I said. "You'll need to wash this. We have a first-aid kit in the car. Can you flex your ankle and wiggle your toes?"

"Yeah," he grunted, flexing. "It's twisted, but I think I can walk on it. Hurts like a mother, though."

"How come you didn't break through on the way up?" I asked.

"I always skip steps when I go up," he said. "The first one was broken anyway, so it was a natural thing to do."

Slava and Ms. Hawk caught up with us then. We all agreed
it was high time to exit the house and call the police. I noticed
with some satisfaction that although Zack limped, Ms. Hawk
walked just fine.

Another trip through crunchy cockroach county in the
basement, and we were outside, breathing summer air that
smelled delightfully of brown grass and sunshine instead of
dust and dead bodies. Ms. Hawk trotted over to the car to
update Belinda while I called the cops to tell them what my
boss and I had found. The dispatcher told me to wait, no surprise. I relayed this information to Zack and Slava, and we all
took up seats on the ground beneath one of the oak trees not
far from Ms. Hawk's car. Belinda got out of the car, and Ms.
Hawk talked earnestly to her for several minutes. A squirrel
cheebled at us and I threw an acorn at him. He fled in a huff.

Ms. Hawk returned bearing several unopened bottles of
water and a first-aid kit. Belinda followed, her clunky shoes
forcing her to walk carefully on the unkempt lawn. Her face
wore the neutral expression of someone trying to keep her
emotions under control. Ms. Hawk handed the water bottles
around, and even Zack got one. I drank thirstily, dashed some
into my face, and poured more over my head. Zack copied
me. The water soaked his shirt and made it cling to his body,
showing off lines I had only imagined before. Then he pushed
up his pant leg and set about cleaning the scrapes on his calf
with the first-aid kit. I resisted the urge to poke at the wounds
and make him yelp.

"I suppose I was expecting this," Belinda was saying. "But
it's still a shock to get the news, you understand. Poor Uncle
Howard. After the magazines crushed Uncle Lawrence, he
must have died of dehydration, stuck in bed like that. God. I
feel like I should go in there, but..." She trailed off.

"There's no need," Ms. Hawk said firmly. "Your uncles'
remains aren't in any condition for viewing, even if the house
were safe for you. You're doing absolutely the right thing by
staying out here until the police arrive."

"And who is this?" Belinda asked with a nod to Zack, who set aside the first-aid kit and got to his feet.

"Zack Archer, ma'am," he said, flashing a wide, sunshine grin. "You must be Mr. Peale's niece Belinda."

A startled silence dropped over us. I turned to face Zack. "I hope you're smart enough to figure out what I'm going to ask next."

"'How do you know Lawrence Peale, Zack?'" he said in an irritatingly high-pitched voice. I wanted to smack him.

"Let's hear the answer," Ms. Hawk said.

"I met him when I was doing a photo shoot on the homeless," Zack said. "I found him going through a Dumpster. I thought he was homeless. He almost ran away from me, but I called after him to stay, and he actually did. It was cold out, so I bought him a cup of coffee and we talked for a while. This was six or seven months ago."

"My uncle *talked* to you?" Belinda said. "That's...unusual, from what I know of him. He was painfully shy, you understand."

"Yeah, I got that sense," Zack told her. "But I think the old guy was also lonely. He told me that he had some pretty amazing collections and that I might want to shoot some of them, though he was pretty adamant that I never shoot *him*. I thought, what the hell. Mr. Peale took me home—here—in this old, rattle-trap truck. Like I said earlier, I knew the house and I was dying to know what was inside. Mr. Peale wouldn't let me see much of it, though. He brought me in through the basement and showed me a whole bunch of leaves ironed in wax paper, like you do in second grade. Big whoop."

"He brought you in through the basement?" Ms. Hawk said. "What about the cement blocks?"

"He told me where to step, but he didn't say why." Zack shuddered. "Now I understand. Anyway, after he showed me his leaves, he told me *I* had to leave—ha ha—but I could write to him if I wanted."

"And you did," Belinda said. She looked a bit put out. I

guess the idea that Uncle Lawrence corresponded with some-one besides her made Belinda a little jealous.

"Yeah," Zack said. "Peale was kind of strange, but kind of interesting, too. A few weeks ago, he wrote to say he had something important to show me, something big. But I was flying to Alaska the next day and couldn't come over. I wrote him to say I'd drop by when I got back, but he didn't respond. I got worried and decided to check on him. I saw your car, but it looked empty."

"I lay down for a nap," Belinda said. "You probably couldn't see me."

Zack nodded. "So I went in through the basement. A little later, I heard the Great Pan Avalanche, and you know the rest."

I fixed him with a hard glare. "Why didn't you tell us this before?"

He glared back at me. "I didn't know who the hell you were. Mr. Peale is—was—my friend, and you were trespass-ing in his house."

I started to snarl at this, then paused. He had a point, much as I hated to admit it. "I'll give you that," I said.

"Gee, thanks."

"Where is your car?" Slava asked. "I don't see it in drive-way."

"Rode my bike," Zack said, "and put it in the back yard so no one would wander off with it."

"You rode a bike?" Slava looked surprised. "You could boil eggs on sidewalk today."

"The ride keeps me in shape," Zack said with a shrug, and I thought I saw vague embarrassment in the gesture. Slava gave him a hard look, and he rolled his eyes. "Okay, so I like keeping green, too. Nothing weird in that."

"Not in this town," Slava agreed.

"What about the guy who started the avalanche?" I said. "Ms. Harris, did you see anyone leave?"

Belinda shook her head. "I read for a while, then dozed off.

I didn't see anyone leave the house, but that doesn't mean no one did." She paused. "Though I wonder…"

"Wonder what?" I asked.

"Maybe the person was looking for something," Belinda said. "Something specific."

"In that place?" Zack said. "Good luck."

"Something like what?" Ms. Hawk said.

"Well, there's the important thing Uncle Lawrence wanted to show Zack," I said.

"That, and possibly my uncles' wills," Belinda said. "I know they each had one, and they didn't file them with a lawyer, you understand. They didn't trust anyone that far."

"You think your uncles mentioned you in their wills?" I asked.

"It's possible," Belinda said. "As far as I know, I'm the only relative they had any contact with. They might have left me the house and property. Uncle Lawrence hinted he might, you understand, but he never came out and said so."

"That place is a total loss," Zack said. "I'm no engineer, but most houses aren't built to hold that much junk. You can tell by walking on them that the floors are warped."

"House may be loss," Slava said, "but this much property on west side of Ann Arbor is worth nice piece of change."

"You mentioned other family members in Chicago," I said. "Do you think one of them may be involved? That they may have killed your uncles to get their hands on the house?"

"I have no idea." Belinda's face remained stony. She took another hit on her inhaler, then said, "Listen, you've done what I hired you to do, but would you be willing to continue on this contract for a while yet? Someone needs to go in there and try to find Uncle Lawrence and Uncle Howard's wills and any other important papers. I certainly can't do it."

Ms. Hawk nodded. "We'll be happy to help."

I had the feeling this meant *I* would be happy to help, but kept my mouth shut. If Ms. Hawk wanted me to do it, I would do it.

"Just what is it you guys do, anyway?" Zack asked curiously. "Private-investigator work?"

"No," Ms. Hawk said in a tone that firmly closed the subject.

The police arrived then—two officers in a cruiser, followed by an ambulance. I faded into the background as best I could while Belinda and Ms. Hawk explained about the bodies, the booby traps, and the avalanche. The police didn't seem ready to call the place a crime scene quite yet—one uncle had apparently died in his bed, and the other by accident. The paramedics, meanwhile, looked nonplused.

"You want us to haul two corpses down from the second floor of a booby-trapped house?" one said. "You have to be nuts."

In the end, we called the fire department. I guided a firefighter named Frank through the house to Uncle Howard's room. Frank wore his breathing mask and oxygen tank, so the smell didn't bother him. I had to make do with one of Ms. Hawk's handkerchiefs tied around my face. It was still lose-your-lunch nasty, especially with my own lost lunch still on the floor. A few strokes of Fred's axe smashed out the plywood covering the window and revealed our location to his buddies outside. They raised a ladder to the room so Dr. Karen Wilewski, the medical examiner, could climb up and pronounce Uncle Howard dead at the scene. That done, I led her down the hall to Magazine Mountain and Uncle Lawrence's protruding hand. Dr. Wilewski, a middle-aged, rangy woman with graying hair pulled back in a bun, changed into a new set of rubber gloves and shined her flashlight on the hand. The attendant smells didn't seem to bother her at all. Carefully, she cleared away a few magazines to reveal part of an arm. I stood well away. Two close encounters with these corpses was plenty for me, thanks.

"Assuming there's a whole person under there," Dr. Wilewski said, "he's dead. We'll need an entire crew to clear away these magazines so we can get at him. And here I thought it was going to be a dull day."

"Do you need me for anything else?" I asked. "I can think of a thousand other things I'd rather be doing. Maybe two thousand."

"Sure, sure," she said with a dismissive wave. "Tell the paramedics to bring up a body bag for the first victim, would you?"

I exited the house through the basement again—the fire department doesn't let civilians climb their ladders—delivered the message, and went in search of Ms. Hawk. I found her holding court with Zack and Slava under the oak tree. Belinda was back in the car with the AC cranked up to high.

"There's no way we're going to find anything in there," Zack was saying in sour tones.

"You give up too easy," Slava said. "You must be part of American slacker generation."

"We?" I said, sitting down.

"Mr. Archer has kindly agreed to help us search the house," Ms. Hawk said.

"What?" I squawked. "After he let that guy get away?"

"Hey!" Zack said. "I almost broke my leg. A little sympathy would go a long way."

"In return," Ms. Hawk continued, "he can photograph the house and its contents, but not any of the people involved."

"But *why?*" I asked.

"My mother always say, 'Extra people make work go faster,'" Slava put in.

"Exactly," Ms. Hawk said. "The more people we have searching, the more likely it is we'll find what we need. It's also our client's hope that Mr. Archer can find whatever it was Mr. Peale intended to show him. She wants to know what it is."

"This is slavery," Zack growled. "Pure and simple. I'll spend more hours searching than shooting."

"Then leave," I said.

Zack set his mouth, and I started to wonder. Letters or no

letters, Zack's presence was damned coincidental. Was he telling the truth, the whole truth, so help him God? I had a feeling the answer was no.

On the other hand, if he found something, it would be better if he found it with me or Ms. Hawk looking over his shoulder. And the work *would* go faster with another pair of strong hands on the team.

"I still don't know how we're going to find anything in there," Zack said. "You've seen the place—it's a junkyard with an attitude."

"On the contrary, Mr. Archer," Ms. Hawk countered, "as Terry noted before you arrived, the contents of the house are surprisingly well organized. In theory, all we need to do is find the place where the uncles kept important papers and search through them."

"In theory, I could build an airplane," Zack said. "It doesn't mean it'll happen."

"It could be exciting," Slava said, brushing dust off her dress, now more gray than red. "There might be more booby traps. Or dead bodies."

"Fun," I muttered, sneaking a sideways look at Zack. Now that the condescending not-sneer had been wiped off his face, he was looking fine again. Maybe it wouldn't be so bad working with him. The view would be nice, if nothing else. I poured more water over my head and shook it free, then caught Zack staring at me.

"What?" I said.

"You look awful," he said.

I sighed and got to my feet. So much for a nice view. "Let's get this over with," I said. "Slava, are you coming?"

"Ha!" She crossed her arms. "I go home, take nice cool shower, and eat big piece of cheesecake, just for you."

Zack snorted. I glared at him, then strode wordlessly back toward the house. After a moment, Zack and Ms. Hawk caught up to me. We pushed aside bushes and trooped down stone stairs into gloomy darkness. The basement door gaped like the entrance to a dragon's lair.

"Dead bodies and booby traps," I said, and aimed a sweet smile at Zack. "You go first."

FIVE

ZACK CLIMBED THE basement stairs ahead of me, passing the microwave and side-stepping the stacks of cookbooks. We had decided that Uncle Lawrence wasn't likely to store important papers in a damp basement, so we'd start with the first floor and work upward. The thought of sifting through mounds and mounds of junk for something specific made me dizzy. What if Uncle Lawrence had decided to hide important papers by slipping them between the pages of a certain magazine? Or at the bottom of a box of Barbie dolls? We might never find them.

"This is awful," Zack said as he reached the top of the stairs. His flashlight bobbed around him, glinting gold off his hair. "I mean, I'm no Mr. Clean, but who could *live* like this?"

"Someone with a severe mental impairment, Mr. Archer," Ms. Hawk said behind me. "One that is not his fault."

"I know that. It doesn't change the fact that his impairment killed both him and his brother," Zack replied. He stepped carefully into the kitchen. I followed. The pile of foam trays that obscured the refrigerator looked like a miniature sled hill. Mrs. Biemer, my landlady, has a whole litter of conniption kittens if I leave a pizza box in my room overnight. What would she say to this mess?

"Let's look for some kind of study or den or something like that," Zack said as Ms. Hawk and I squeezed around the junk piled in the kitchen. "Start with the most obvious."

"No," said Ms. Hawk. She was toying with the hawk pendant at her throat, something she often did when she was thinking.

He cocked his head. "No? Why? Some sort of investigation technique I don't know about—start with the *least* obvious lead?"

"I am not an investigator, Mr. Archer. Besides, in this house we are more akin to archaeologists."

I couldn't help laughing at that. Indiana Faye was on the job! All I needed was a bullwhip. I gave myself a few moments to imagine myself whooshing around darkened caves, cracking my whip against cowering bad guys and using it to swing across open pits of molten lava. Zack would be tied up in a tomb somewhere, and—

Hmm. Probably best to put the brakes on that line of thought.

"So what's the first step, then?" Zack asked.

"We survey," Ms. Hawk replied primly. "Get an overview of the site. In this case, we should see what is stored in which rooms and, incidentally, clear out any other traps."

"That's why we brought you, Zack," I put in. "You can test the traps for us, being a big, strong man and all."

The last part of that sentence came out a little more seriously than I'd intended, and I flushed a little, bracing for his snappy retort. Rather than reply, however, Zack gave me a long, almost hungry look. My blush deepened, and I was thankful the room was dim so he couldn't see.

"So," Ms. Hawk broke in, "I believe the first thing to do is check the kitchen. We didn't set off any traps on our way in, but that doesn't mean none exist. Move carefully, please. And do remember, Mr. Archer, that my liability insurance does not cover you."

We set to work, carefully checking the clear spaces on the floor for traps and wires. The kitchen would have been spacious and well-appointed if it weren't for the trash. The cabinets—oak, if I was any judge—looked original to the house. Grime-encrusted tile countertops lay under mounds of paper. The refrigerator and stove peeked out from under piles of take-out bags, boxes, and trays. After some hunting, I found a porcelain sink. One side was filled with stacks of used

McDonald's cups. The other side was miraculously empty. I tried the faucet. Clear water flowed. I wouldn't have dared to drink it, though I suppose the uncles must have had *some* kind of water supply. Did the house have a hot-water heater? I didn't know. Hell, I didn't even know if the place had electricity, let alone gas. I hadn't seen so much as a light switch.

"Hey, look," Zack called from across the room. His voice was muffled, as if the trash around him was sucking up the noise. "I found another door."

The door in question was at the other end of a trail through the jungle of junk. Its hinges were on this side, which meant it opened outward. Zack cautiously tried the knob, and it moved under his hand. I couldn't see Ms. Hawk among the gloomy piles of stuff, though I could hear her moving around. I shined my flashlight beam full on the door. Looked like a pantry to me. What kind of trap could you hide in a pantry?

"Be careful opening that," Ms. Hawk's voice cautioned. I had a wild image of an anvil dropping on Zack's head like Wile E. Coyote and stifled a laugh.

"Ready?" Zack said. "One...two...three!"

He yanked the door toward himself, using it as a shield. I held my breath, waiting for something to smash outward or drop downward or do something else entertaining. Nothing happened. My beam flashed into the area beyond. I got a distorted view of shelves stacked with oddly shaped objects with occasional glints of metal or glass. The room was definitely a large pantry, with floor-to-ceiling shelves. Boxes stood knee-deep on the floor, and the shelves were crammed. My light wandered over the interior, and I stared.

"What?" Zack demanded. He was peering out from behind the door. "What is it?"

"Clocks," I said in wonder. "It's filled with clocks. Look at them all!"

Zack edged around to look inside. I moved my beam about so he could see. Every shelf in the pantry was piled with clocks. Round clocks, square clocks, cuckoo clocks, alarm clocks. A miniature grandfather clock lay sideways on one shelf, its pendulum forever stilled. All the clocks were dusty, but I caught glimpses of movement here and there—a few second hands were still ticking off forgotten moments in the dark.

"Wow," Zack said. "Kinda neat, too." He reached for the camera at his belt, then thought the better of it. "I'll wait until I can get some better lighting in here."

"What's in the boxes?" Ms. Hawk asked.

Zack leaned down and rummaged through a couple. "Broken clocks and clock parts. I'll bet the uncles figured they'd get around to some repair work one of these days."

"Back to work, then," Ms. Hawk said.

"Time's a-wasting," I added.

The rest of the kitchen survey turned up nothing of obvious interest—no booby traps, no boxes marked Seriously Important Papers—Read Now! We moved on to the dining room. The curtains Ms. Hawk had opened earlier allowed dusty sunlight to illuminate the place. Through the grimy windows I could just make out the fire truck with its ladder extended up to the third floor, where the bodies were. I stared at the huge mound of mail on the long dining-room table and wondered if anything was hidden at the bottom.

"Doubtful," Ms. Hawk said, as if reading my mind. "If Lawrence Peale wanted to show Mr. Archer something important, he wouldn't hide it beneath a pile of paper. He would put it where he could get his hands on it easily."

We found no traps in the dining room, either. Three doors led off the room—one to the kitchen, one down the back hallway that ended in the shoe-covered staircase to the second floor, and one to an enormous space that was probably a sitting room or parlor, though the only thing that was being entertained was more junk. Every piece of furniture sagged beneath piles of it. About half of the room was taken over by stacks and stacks of books—paperbacks, hardbacks, encyclopedias, dictionaries. One tall heap seemed to be made up of nothing but bibles, giving literal meaning to the phrase "swearing on a stack of."

Another section of the room was actually fairly tidy, considering. A huge set of bookshelves was faced with dozens and dozens of three-ring binders. In an actual clear space in front of them sat an ironing board. On it perched an iron and a small…microwave? I shined my flashlight on it. Yep—it was a microwave, one that looked like it actually worked. Well, why not? Who among us hasn't wished for a hot snack while doing the laundry?

Beneath the ironing board lay several long, narrow objects. I picked my way through the mess to get a better look. Boxes of waxed paper interspersed with rolls of paper towels. Weird, but what in this house wasn't? I pulled one of the binders off the shelf and opened it. Waxed paper crackled, and a bright red leaf the size of my hand looked up at me. It had been expertly ironed between two sheets of paper. A neat label beneath it said *Acer saccharinum: silver maple.*

"Leafing through the collection?" Zack said, peering over my shoulder. "Ha ha."

"You ruin the joke when you laugh at it yourself," I said, flipping a few more pages. *Quercus rubra: red oak. Betula alleghaniensis: yellow birch. Fagus grandifolia: American beech.* "This is what he showed you the first time?"

"Yeah. Like I said—second-grade collection."

"It's a standard way to preserve leaves, Mr. Archer," Ms. Hawk said. "Dry them in a microwave between paper towels, then iron them between sheets of waxed paper."

"The preservation method might be standard," Zack said, "but it makes for a boring photo shoot."

"Did he show you the collection in here, Zack?" I asked. "In this room, I mean?"

"Yeah, but this is as far as I got in the house."

"If the leaf collection was important to him," I said slowly, "he might have hidden other important stuff in it."

"We'll definitely examine the collection more closely once

we've finished our survey," Ms. Hawk said. "Meanwhile, we should keep moving."

My stomach growled and I felt the early pangs of a hunger headache coming on. I tried to check the time, but the face of my watch was coated with dirt, and I had to wipe it on my equally filthy shirt first. To my surprise, it was nearly six.

Before I could say anything, Zack spoke up. "You know, it's getting late, and I'm starving. Why don't we call it a day and come back bright and... Well, maybe not *early,* but sometime before noon."

Ms. Hawk pursed her lips, then nodded. "Nine o'clock," she said. "We'll meet here."

"Ten," Zack said.

"You may show up when you wish, Mr. Archer," Ms. Hawk said. "But if Terry and I find something when you are not here, I won't feel obligated to show it to you."

"Oh, all right," Zack said, making a face. "Have it your way."

"I usually do."

Zack stuck out his tongue behind her back, and I found myself trying not to laugh at him. We made our way outside. It was still hot and muggy beneath the trees. The fire department was still working up at the third-story window trying to figure out how to free Uncle Lawrence's body from the pile of magazines. I assumed they'd already removed Uncle Howard. Slava was long gone, probably already at home eating that cherry cheesecake. My stomach growled again at the thought.

Ms. Hawk, meanwhile, headed for the car to update Belinda, who had been waiting all this time. Or maybe she had been napping again. Zack sidled up to me. His face and body were streaked with dust, and his blond hair was gray with it.

"You didn't thank me," he said.

That caught me by surprise. "For what?"

"For getting you out of there." He mopped sweat from his forehead with one sleeve and only succeeded in smearing dirt around his face. "I heard your stomach growl halfway across the room. Now me, I was ready to go on all night."

His own stomach growled at that moment. I fluttered my eyelashes at him. "Really?"

Zack laughed. "Okay, you caught me. I'm hungry, too. Listen, how about—"

"No," I said.

"You don't even know what I was going to—"

"Yes."

"Yes, what?"

"Yes, I know what you were going to ask. No, I don't want to have dinner with you, even if it's your treat. I'm tired, I'm cranky, and frankly I don't trust you."

"I bet you like cheeseburgers," he countered, ignoring the trust remark. "You look like a cheeseburger woman. Ever eat at Blimpy's?"

"Cheaper than food," I said, reciting the restaurant's official slogan and feeling disgruntled that Zack was somehow able to spot this about me. I don't like cheeseburgers—I *love* them. And you can eat them all day at Blimpy's because their burgers are cheap, fast, and totally delicious. I could almost taste the first bite of salty, greasy burger, the onion and pickle creating tart taste bursts on my tongue.

"So," Zack said, "you want to meet—"

"No," I said firmly. "I repeat: I'm tired, I'm cranky, and I don't trust you."

"Fine." He sighed extravagantly. "See you tomorrow!" He trotted over to a patch of lawn, upended a black mountain bike hidden by the tall grass, and pedaled away with a little wave. I watched him go for a moment—it was worth watching—then turned my back. This let me catch Ms. Hawk's gesture beckoning me back to the car, where Belinda still waited. Time to go home.

The three of us rode in silence. We had to ride with the windows down because the mold and dust in our clothes was setting off Belinda's asthma, so I was covered in a wash of hot

air instead of cool AC. I was feeling grouchier by the minute.
My clothes were sticking to me in all the wrong places, dirt
and grit itched over my skin, and I was starving. Ms. Hawk,
who didn't look half as dirty as I felt, coolly negotiated traffic while Belinda stared thoughtfully out the window. Back
at the office, we dropped Belinda off at her car with a promise to keep her updated on our search tomorrow. Ms. Hawk
said she would lock up, so I retrieved my clothes from the
conference-room closet and trudged down the hot sidewalk
to the parking structure on First Street.

I drive a little brown Jeep Wrangler, the kind with a fold-
down roof. I like it quite a lot, actually. It's small enough to
zip around Ann Arbor's clogged, narrow streets and park in
Ann Arbor's small, clogged parking lots but powerful enough
to overcome Michigan winters, when sliding across the ice
becomes a way of life. Today, I wouldn't have minded a little winter. It took a while for the AC to kick in, and I left the
windows down as I drove out of the lot and struggled against
rush-hour traffic. Eventually I pulled up in front of a large
Victorian house, two stories tall with a little two-story tower,
painted light blue with white trim.

I parked in the gravel lot beside it, climbed the steps to the
wraparound porch, and entered through a side door that put
me in the dining room. A long trestle table ran the length of
the room, and it was already set for twelve. The hardwood
floor was polished to a warm glow, and I smelled pot roast,
potatoes and fresh bread.

"Honey," I called, "I'm home!"

"Supper's in ten minutes." Honi Biemer, my landlady,
poked her head into the dining room from the kitchen. "So
you'd better—good lord! What on earth happened to you,
young lady?"

"I lost a fight with a horde of dust bunnies," I said.

Mrs. Biemer—the only time you can call her "Honi" is
when you first get home—looked me up and down. She's a
plump grandma type with bright black eyes and silver hair

pulled into a grandma bun, complete with stickpins. At the moment she was holding a bowl of fluffy mashed potatoes. Even from across the dining room I could see little puddles of melted butter gathering in it like tiny gold lakes on a snowy mountain.

"Don't you dare track on my floor," she said. "Leave your boots on the porch. And hurry to supper. I have a surprise for you." She turned and bustled back into the kitchen.

"Yes, ma'am!" I saluted her retreating back, kicked my filthy boots onto the porch, and padded quickly out of the dining room, through the public living room, and down the hall to my bedroom. Mine is the last one on the right. It's one of the bigger ones, actually, and nicely furnished. I have a comfortable double bed (freshly washed comforter and sheets provided every Saturday), a nightstand, a bookshelf, and a small entertainment cabinet in the corner with TV, VCR, DVR, CD, and DVD. I'm wondering what kind of V or D will come next, but I'll add it, whatever it is. I have to keep a whole shelf just for the remotes. Buying DVDs is a waste—unless Orlando Bloom is involved—since you can rent them just as cheaply, which means I have space for books, which are not a waste, even though I love all three of my e-readers—they help me save even more space for print books. (Hey, it makes sense to me.) The stuff most people would call keepsakes are shoved under my bed, out of sight. They're no one else's business.

A sliding glass door opens onto the wraparound porch. The yard beyond the porch is shaded by a pair of oak trees, leaving it dark and cool in the summer and causing no end of trouble for Mr. Biemer, who spends inordinate amounts of time coaxing grass to grow in areas with permanent shadow. I see a thick lawn as a mowing headache, but since I pay rent not to worry about it, I leave it all to him.

I grabbed my bathrobe from its hook on the closet door and dashed down the hall to the bathroom. The Biemer Boarding House has three full baths—one on this floor and two upstairs—and although technically all the tenants can use any one of them, we each gravitate toward the one closest to our individual bedrooms. Luckily "my" bathroom was unoccupied. I peeled off my clothes—I swear my sports bra made a Velcro "ripping" sound as I pulled it over my head—and took the cool, refreshing shower I'd been fantasizing about for the last two hours, though I had to cut it a little short. The Biemer Boarding House has some strict rules about mealtimes. Mrs. Biemer lays out a hot breakfast at seven on weekday mornings and makes cold breakfast available until eight-thirty. Lunch is on your own. Supper hits the table at exactly six-thirty and is cleared away at seven sharp, even if you're in mid-bite. Mrs. Biemer makes up for the draconian rules by cooking great food you don't *want* to miss.

I wrapped my robe around myself and zipped down to my room, where I yanked on shorts, t-shirt, and sandals and pulled my wet hair back with a scrunchie. Major frizz coming on, but nothing I could do about it unless I wanted to miss ten precious mealtime minutes blowing it dry. Fat chance there.

I got to the table right on time and counted it a victory. Mr. Biemer, a wiry sixty-something with a gray buzzcut and tortoise-shell glasses, was standing behind his chair at the head of the table. The other boarders were taking their places up and down the long table. The Biemers rent to both men and women, and they seem to attract people from the ends of the age spectrum—we're all either in our twenties or over sixty. Only five of us live here long-term. The rest come and go, college students mostly, or people who need a place to stay for a month or two while they're between apartments or in town on long-term business. None of us long-termers pay them much attention, or even bother to remember their names.

Mrs. Biemer was setting a pitcher of ice water on the table just as I arrived and took up my usual place to her right. The longer you live at the Biemers', the closer you get to sit to them, and only Clara Boatwright, a rail-thin old lady who can do incredible things with a crochet hook despite her coke-bottle glasses, has lived at the Biemers' longer than I have.

Clara always sits across from me. Her eyesight is bad, but her hearing is perfectly good, and she nodded a greeting when I sat down. This end of the table is like having dinner with your mom and grandma, if you have them. Technically I have one of each, but I pretend I don't, so it's nice to eat with Clara and Mrs. Biemer.

Next to me sat Keshia Bishop, another long-termer. Tall, rangy, and very dark-skinned, she's one of the few black female veterinarians in the country. Farther down sat a couple of short-term women whose names I keep forgetting.

At the other end of the table sat the men. We have four right now. Kevin Baumgartner and Gary Kovak are long-termers, the other two are college guys whose names I also can't remember. There's no rule that the men have to sit down at Mr. Biemer's end of the table while the women sit with Mrs. Biemer. It just sort of happens that way.

By now everyone was sitting down with various murmured hellos and how-are-yous. The bowls and platters were heaped in front of us. Pot roast in thick gravy, mashed potatoes with cream and butter, fresh-baked rolls, a platter of sautéed vegetables. All of us were hungry, but we waited until Mrs. Biemer sat down and Mr. Biemer tapped his water glass with his knife. As one we all reached for the food.

Platters and bowls zipped clockwise around the table, then landed back in the middle. No boarding house reach at the Biemers'. If you want something, you have to ask someone to pass it to you. Conversation tends to be sparse until everyone's plate is filled and we've all had a few bites.

I gave a contented sigh as I picked up my fork. I like living at the Biemers'. Ms. Hawk recommended their place to me when I moved to Ann Arbor three years ago. The boarding house had initially been meant as a stopping point, a place to stay until I got settled at Hawk Enterprises and could look for a place of my own. But somehow, I never got around to hunting for an apartment. Living on my own would mean coming home to empty rooms and cooking for myself every day.

Here, someone else handles the domestic chores, and someone always greets me when I get home. In some of my more introspective moments, I think the Biemers' rules bring a little order to my otherwise chaotic life. That's what I tell myself, anyway. At other times I think I just couldn't handle being completely alone. Not yet.

"Long day at the agency, hon?" Clara asked me, her brown eyes magnified hugely by her thick glasses. Her plate was mostly bread and potatoes—easy to chew and digest.

"Very," I said. "Just once, it'd be nice to have an *easy* case."

"What kind of work do you do?" asked one of the short-termers. Marvin? Marty? Mark? I couldn't remember.

"She's a detective," Mrs. Biemer said proudly before I could answer. "Her cases take her all over the world."

"Really?" Marvin/Marty/Mark said. "So you're, like, a PI?"

My mouth was full, so I nodded. I have a PI license, so it's not technically a lie to let people believe that's what I do. The PI lie also makes long absences and odd hours easier to explain. Ms. Hawk likes to keep Hawk Enterprises low key, mostly because most of our clients need strict confidentiality, though I suspect it's also to lend Hawk Enterprises a certain exclusive cache. You have to Be Connected to have heard of us, even if the connection is your neighbor's daughter's best friend. I privately call it the Women's Underground.

"That must be so cool," Marvin/Marty/Mark continued. "You get to spy on people and shit."

"Not at this table, please," Mr. Biemer said with pointed mildness.

The kid flushed a little. "Sorry." He went on eating.

"Anything interesting at the clinic?" I asked, changing the subject.

Keshia shrugged. "The usual parade of spayings and neuterings and shots. I don't think anyone wants me to get more graphic at the table. We did manage to adopt out another of those kittens from that crazy woman's house." She gave our landlady a sidelong look. "You know, Mrs. B, this house could use a furry presence. Besides Mr. Biemer, that is."

"I heard that, young lady," Mr. Biemer harrumphed. Anyone under fifty is *young lady* or *young man* to Mr. Biemer.

"County regs, Keshia," Mrs. Biemer said. "No animals allowed if we have a commercial kitchen."

"Crazy woman's house?" asked a short-termer. "What's that about?"

"This woman was caught hoarding animals," Keshia said. "She had twenty-some cats in her house and who-knows-how-many cages of rodents—gerbils, hamsters, pet rats. The cages had wire floors and they were all stacked on top of each other, so the animals on the bottom were covered in—well, you can probably imagine."

"Sounds like a metaphor for our society," Kevin grumbled. "The ones on the top sh—er, dump on the ones below."

Greg Kovak set down his fork. "That's horrible! What happened?" Greg's a retired autoworker who once worked for Ford. He's a big, hearty old man who doesn't look like he harbors a soft spot for kitties and puppies, but he does.

"The neighbors had been calling social services and the police for months to complain about the smell," Keshia said. "They finally sent someone over to check it out. The humane society called the clinic for help when they saw the condition of the animals, and I came over to see what I could do. It was…pretty bad." Her voice shook a little, though with rage or sorrow, I couldn't tell. "The county is leveling charges of animal neglect. The house will probably be condemned, so the landlord is furious." She shook her head, her mouth set hard. "What's really horrible is that it's the second time the county's been called in about this woman. Last time it was an apartment. She lost her security deposit, moved to a different place, and started collecting animals all over again."

"Where does she get them from?" Clara asked.

Keshia spread her hands. "Who knows? The local animal shelters recognize her and won't give any to her, but you can find free animals in the classifieds every day of the week. In all other respects, she's a very nice lady, someone you'd happily give Fluffy's litter to—if you hadn't seen her house. It's an illness, of course. A compulsion she can't control. But the animals suffer for it."

I thought about the uncles and their horrible house. At least their hoarding hadn't hurt anyone but themselves.

"I'm majoring in psych," said the one guy, and I finally remembered his name was Marcus. "We've talked about this in class. Officially there are three kinds of hoarders—people who hoard animals, people who hoard paper, and people who hoard *everything*."

"Paper?" I asked, thinking of the piles on Uncle Lawrence's dining-room table.

"Printed material," Marcus clarified. "They can't even throw away junk mail, let alone stuff like newspapers and magazines. They're terrified they might need it someday. Haven't you ever had the feeling that you should keep those coupons or bank statements, just in case?"

"Oh, my, yes," Mrs. Biemer said. "With me, it's recipes. Whenever they do the food section in the paper, I keep thinking, 'That would be a nice dish to try,' but I never get around to it, and the clippings stack up until I give up and throw them away."

"Except compulsive hoarders *can't* throw them away," Marcus said, clearly enjoying the fact that he had something to contribute. "The 'just in case' feeling never fades, and they're stuck with all the junk."

At seven on the dot, Mr. Biemer rose from his place and helped his wife whisk the decimated food platters away. We boarders dutifully brought our plates and silverware into the kitchen and left them on the counter. The Biemers' kitchen is just big enough to qualify for commercial status. Two refrigerators and a dishwasher take up most of the space. One fridge is stuffed with the "touch this and die" food Mrs. Biemer cooks every day for us. The other is divided into sections, one for each boarder, with another section set aside for left-overs, which are community property. The dishwasher looks like it was built by NASA and is a requirement of the county health department. Thousands of people in Ann Arbor let the family dog lick their plates before putting them in a plain old Kenmore, but God forbid a spoon should pass human lips in Mrs. Biemer's house without first being scalded in boiling water surrounded by stainless steel.

Back in the dining room, Mrs. Biemer set a covered platter on the table. Dessert and coffee don't count as official supper time. This makes it easier for boarders on diets to slip away before temptation sets in. As it happened, all of the short-term female boarders had vanished, to which I say, "All the more for me." Mrs. Biemer whipped away the cover and revealed... a cherry cheesecake. Crunchy graham cracker crust lovingly surrounded smooth white cheesecake under a pile of home-made cherry topping that glistened like rubies. I made a low sound of ecstasy.

"I told you I had a surprise," Mrs. Biemer said with an impish smile.

I had two large, creamy pieces with three cups of coffee. After a day of slogging through dirt and grime, I deserved every mouthful.

After dessert, I headed for my room—my nice, clean, un-cluttered room—slotted a DVD into the player, and flopped onto my bed to fulfill the last piece of my fantasy for the day. I'd already had the cool shower and the cherry cheesecake; now it was time for some Orlando Bloom. *Elizabethtown* got rotten reviews, but it's sappy and gooey and totally the thing to unwind with after spending a day in gray grime and grit.

After a dose of Mr. Bloom, I went to bed at ten-thirty, my usual time, and got up at six-thirty to pull on sweats and stuff my *dobak* into my gym bag along with a set of khakis, a work shirt, baseball cap, and the boots I'd retrieved from the front porch. Mrs. Biemer serves breakfast buffet-style from the side-board in the dining room, and I helped myself to French toast, sausage, and coffee. Lots of coffee. I don't care what junkies on the street might tell you—no drug in the world is sweeter than caffeine. Wakeful, head-clearing, world-changing caffeine. Even the delivery is wonderful. Sweet black coffee in the morning and crisp diet soda in the afternoon with more coffee at supper. How can you top that with a syringe or a snort? I slugged down my first cup of Mrs. Biemer's best and felt perfection thrill through my veins.

Mrs. Biemer herself was at work in the kitchen, and the only other boarder at the table so far was Marcus, who was buried in a psychology course packet and didn't seem inclined toward conversation. Perfectly fine by me. For all that I'm an early bird, I'm not much of a talker in the morning. Even after several doses of coffee.

I drove downtown to Ann Arbor's spiffy new YMCA building, which conveniently straddles its own parking lot. Major plus in this town. They finished the building just a few years ago, and it's way better than the old one across from the library, which looked like a barrack and smelled like a kennel. Well, okay—maybe it wasn't *that* bad, but it's fair to say no one mourns the loss of the original place.

I changed into my *dobak* in the women's locker room, grabbed my padded sparring equipment, and trotted out to the section of a workout room, one with a matted floor. A martial-arts class was sparring in pairs in one half of the room, and their shouts echoed off the walls. Elaine Harker sat in the other half, stretching her way through a warmup. The instructor lets us advanced students use half of the workout room during the early bird beginner class. I greeted Elaine with a smile and sat down beside her to do some stretches of my own.

"Anything new down at the office?" she asked, reaching for her chest protector and padded helmet. Her equipment is all pink. Mine is green.

"New case came in yesterday," I told her as I climbed into my own gear. "Messy. And I mean literally."

Elaine slid her feet into the shin guards and pulled on soft, puffy sparring gloves. "Anything you might need some help with?"

Elaine is a single mother of two who came to Hawk Enterprises for the most common reason we get—to escape her abusive spouse. Her ex-husband pays alimony and child support on time, thanks to us, and Elaine herself got hired by a company that does freelance security work. She long ago paid off her favors to Ms. Hawk, and we now hire her from time to time.

"Not sure," I told her, straightening up. "We might need a hand later."

"Give me a call if you do," Elaine said, and punched me in the chest.

I evaded the blow and countered with a snap kick to her midriff. She swept it aside without hesitation. We went at it, blow and counterblow. Elaine knocked me on my ass twice, and I flipped her flat on her back once. We moved faster and faster, a blur of arms and legs. Elaine and I are both red belts, an even match, and I relished the adrenaline rush. I unhooked my mind and let my reflexes take over, a passenger in my own body. Block, lunge, punch, kick, duck, dodge, kick. At the end of an hour, Elaine was massaging her thigh, where I'd landed a solid kick, and I had a bruised shoulder where I'd failed a block and the protector didn't cover me. The pain was a penance—penance for letting myself get angry, for not watching my diet, for relishing a fight. Elaine and I bowed to each other, then realized the gym was silent. We turned. The early bird martial-arts class was watching us in silence.

"Observe and learn," the teacher said. "Observe and learn."

I flushed a little with pride. I don't cook, I won't clean, I can't do math, but I sure as hell can fight. The class turned back to their own sparring while Elaine and I hit the showers and dressed. Elaine dried her mass of dark brown curls while I slid into slacks and a blouse appropriate for office wear. I decided to forgo makeup: five minutes in the Peale house and I'd look like a weeping clown in a black-velvet painting. So I chatted with Elaine while she put on hers. Elaine, who is way prettier than I am, doesn't need much in the way of Maybelline. She has huge blue eyes and a cute little nose beneath all that hair, and her trim little body doesn't look like it can flip a two-hundred-pound man over it without breaking a sweat. The wide-eyed, harmless look has played well during some of the undercover work we've hired her to do.

I glanced at the clock and realized I was running late for my meeting with Zack at the Peale mansion. And there was no way I was going to let him root around in there by himself. I bid Elaine a quick good-bye, then retrieved my little Jeep from the open-air parking structure beneath the building and hotfooted it across town to the Peale house. At five to nine I was just pulling into the gravel driveway when my cell phone rang. It was Ms. Hawk.

"I have to investigate another case," she said. "I'm sorry to leave you alone like this, but I have little choice."

"I won't be alone," I said, swallowing my annoyance. Ms. Hawk owns Hawk Enterprises and she can do or not do as she likes. "Zack will be here."

"Of course he will," Ms. Hawk said with a hint of sarcasm. "Listen, Terry—I don't want you going in there by yourself. It's too dangerous. If Mr. Archer doesn't arrive, call Elaine Harker and see if she's available."

I acknowledged this would be a good idea, and Ms. Hawk clicked off. I got out of the car and faced the tall, moldering mass of house. The place looked sick and exhausted from holding in forty years of hoarded junk. Not a single leaf moved on the massive trees, and the crystal-blue sky promised another hot, humid August day. Great. And Ms. Hawk was probably right—Zack wouldn't show up. I'd have to call Elaine and go through the whole business of explaining the case and then wait until she arrived.

I got my equipment belt out of my trunk, clicked it around my waist—and realized I'd forgotten to stop at the Sweetwater Café to fill my thermos with its usual quart of morning coffee. Wonderful. I checked my watch. Five after nine, and no sign of Zack. Why was I not surprised?

Annoyed, I headed around to the back yard, feeling isolated and grouchy. Maybe I'd sniff around the basement before calling Elaine. The caffeine jonesing was already setting in, and it got worse the more I tried to think of something else. If I'd had the thermos with me, I wouldn't even have cracked it open for another half an hour, but because I didn't have it, I wanted it all the more. I could have ducked out to get some, but then *I'd* be late, and even though I had no witnesses, I didn't feel right running a personal errand on time Belinda was paying for. I'd just have to wait until lunch.

I was just about to call Elaine and tell her we needed her after all when I heard the distinctive clicking sound of bicycle gears and the rush of rubber tires over long grass. Zack sped around the corner, steering precariously with one hand while the other balanced a cardboard take-out tray that sported three foam cups. A yellow backpack was strapped to his broad shoulders, and his hair shone gold in the morning sun—the picture of athletic manhood.

He gave a cheery wave, shoved his bike into some long grass, and trotted over with the tray. My eyes went straight to his cups. They were so big. Huge. Whoever said size doesn't matter is a big, fat liar.

"Morning!" he said. "Sorry I'm late, but—"

"You brought *coffee?*" I gasped.

His face fell. "I'm sorry," he said. "Shouldn't I have?"

"Gimme!" I tore a lid open, mixed in two packets of sugar, and drank. Oh, yeah. Mama Caffeine worked her magic and I felt *fine.* Zack grinned at me, set the tray on the ground, and extracted a waxy paper bag from his backpack.

"Do doughnuts get the same reaction?" he asked.

I eyed the bag warily. "What kind of doughnuts?"

"Got a variety." He rummaged through the sack. "Devil's food, Boston creams, strawberry jelly."

"Any plain ones?"

He made a face. "No. What's the point of plain doughnuts? You notice they're always the last ones left? It's because everybody hates them."

"Okay," I said, reaching for the bag, "you can stay."

While I alternated sugary bites and magical sips, Zack took an equipment belt of his own out of his backpack and buckled it on. I automatically took note of what he had— photography paraphernalia, mostly, along with a cell phone and water bottle.

"Batman and Batgirl," he said, "utility belts at the ready."

"Why is she Batgirl instead of Batwoman, anyway?" I asked as we descended the stone steps. "It's not like she's nine years old."

"Not going there," Zack said. He put the bag into his backpack, zipped it shut, and left it on the stairs. "My main rule of life: never ruin good doughnuts with a discussion of social theory."

"That's your main rule of life?"

"It's gotten me this far. Where's Ms. Hawk? I brought coffee for three."

I smiled at that. I don't know anyone who refers to my boss by her first name, including me. Calling her "Diana" would be like calling the Queen of England "Liz." Something about her makes people fall into formal mode, even when she isn't present. I think most people don't even notice they do it.

"She's working on something else today," I said. "She didn't say what."

"Figures." Zack snorted. "Leave the dirty work to the peons."

Anger flared. "Hey! Ms. Hawk doesn't shirk anything. If she says she has to work on something else, she has to work on something else."

"Okay, okay." He put his hands up defensively. "I didn't mean anything by it."

"Yeah, sure." I opened the basement door and peered into the darkness beyond. Familiar smells of mold, mildew, and dust assailed me. Yay. Zack looked over my shoulder. I could feel the warmth from his body and smelled freshly shaven skin. My earlier anger mixed with newer, more fun feelings, which made me mad all over again.

"You first," I said.

"What? Why me?"

"Because I need someone to test for traps and cockroaches," I told him maliciously.

Grumbling, Zack led the way through the cardboard labyrinth, and a few minutes later we were on the stairs heading for the kitchen. Zack stopped at the top.

"Uh oh," he said.

"What? What's wrong?" I demanded.

"The kitchen's a mess."

I rolled my eyes. "No kidding. That's why we're *here*."

"No, I mean, it's a *mess*. A new one. Someone else has been in the house."

SIX

I PUSHED PAST Zack to see what he meant and let out a low whistle. The kitchen had been pulled apart. The neat stacks of foam trays were scattered all around the room. Cupboard doors hung askew, their papers and dishes pulled down to the floor. The pantry stood open, and the clocks inside had been yanked off the shelves and shattered. Broken bits of wood and dented metal looked accusingly back at me. For some reason, that particular piece of vandalism made me both angry and sad. The clocks had just been lying there, counting to themselves in the dark, bothering no one, and someone had smashed them down.

"I don't suppose you and Ms. Hawk came back last night and did this?" Zack said.

I whirled on him. "What do you take us for? Vandals who'd victimize an old man's house?"

"Touchy, touchy." Zack took a digital camera from his belt and took several photos of the wreckage. "You were going to ask me the same question, admit it."

I was, but sure as hell wasn't going to admit it. I was also wondering if there was a connection between the scratches on the basement lock from yesterday and our mystery intruder, the one who started the pan avalanche. "Let's see what else they've done. Maybe whoever it was set off another trap."

We moved into the dining room. A huge gouge had been taken out of the mountain of mail on the table and the room was now ankle-deep in old paper. Someone had flung the books all around the sitting room, pulling entire sets of volumes from the shelves. Even the stack of bibles had been reduced to rubble. Zack and I were forced to climb over slippery, shifting piles. Dust hung thick in the air, and we both sneezed.

"Someone else definitely wants whatever is in here," I said when we reached the leaf collection. The intruder had pulled several notebooks from their shelves and ripped them open. Wax-encased leaves lay scattered all over the floor in a preserved parody of autumn. "Who the hell could it be?"

"Belinda, for one," Zack replied. He set the iron back upright, a futile gesture amid the chaos around him. "She wants the will, but maybe she didn't want anyone—including you—to find the other thing, whatever it is."

"She can't even come in here," I reminded him. "Asthma."

"Maybe she's faking that."

"That would make no sense," I said, sniffling. Dust caked in my throat. "If she didn't want us to find anything, all she'd have to do is thank us for our help to date, wave good-bye, and we're done."

"True. Aw, no!" Zack leaned down and fished a book out of the chaos at his feet. "This is terrible! How could anyone do this?"

"What?" I scrambled closer. "What is it?"

"It's *The Secret of the Old Mill,*" he said, holding up a tattered book. Pages hung half-torn from the binding. "Hardy Boys."

I shined my flashlight on the cover. Frank and Joe Hardy peered through a limned crack in the floor of an old building. Cobwebby gears and gear shafts loomed behind them. "Wow. I haven't thought about these books in years."

"This was the first one I read," Zack said, trying to put the pages back in. He looked like a little boy trying to fix a broken toy, for all that he was over thirty. "My mom bought a copy at a garage sale, and I spent a big part of the summer at the library reading my way through the rest of the series."

"I did the same thing." I laughed. Then I sneezed. The dust was thick as Los Angeles smog. "I always thought Frank and Joe were so grown up, you know? Nancy Drew, too. They could drive, they had girlfriends and boyfriends. But now—look at the cover. They're just kids."

"When you're nine, sixteen and seventeen seem so grown up," Zack agreed. "Hell, Nancy's boyfriend was in college. Nowadays they'd haul out the tar and feathers if a college freshman dated a high-school junior."

"You read Nancy Drew, too?"

"Sure. Why not? The stories were fun. Besides, if girls can read about boy detectives, why can't boys read about girl detectives? You're the one who brought up the whole Batman/Batgirl thing."

I laughed. "Point." I peered down at the book he was holding. The cover looked like it had been chewed by a dog. "You know, I always thought it would be cool if the Hardy Boys and Nancy Drew teamed up. But they never did."

"Not true." Zack sneezed into the crook of his elbow. "Some publisher restarted both series with new plots and updated characters and crossovers and all that. The new Hardys have teamed with the new Nancy lots of times. I've seen them at the bookstore."

"Really?" I hadn't heard about this. Nancy Drew was one of my childhood heroes. Not only did she solve mysteries and save her friends from kidnappers, she had a way cool dad. Nancy's dad didn't drink, unlike some dads I could mention.

"Sure. I haven't read any of the new ones, but they look interesting. We could go down to the bookstore this evening and check them out, if you want."

I cocked my head, giving the idea serious consideration. That might be kind of fun, paging through one of the few happy pieces of my childhood with Zack at my elbow. We could—

"Wait a minute," I said. "Are you asking me on a date?"

"Heaven forbid," Zack said. He gave a dusty cough and slid the book into his back pocket. "I don't think the old man would mind if I kept this."

I sneezed hard, then sneezed again. "God, it's worse than

yesterday. I should have brought dust masks, or…or…" I trailed off as my stomach went cold.

Zack cocked his head. "Or what?"

"The dust," I said. "It's still hanging in the air. If someone had come in last night, it would have settled by now."

It took Zack a moment to catch on to what I meant. He blinked, then his eyes widened. "So this—" Zack gestured at the mess "—is new. As in 'ten minutes ago' new."

"Yeah."

We both stopped talking and listened. I didn't hear a thing at first. Then I thought I caught a faint creaking deeper in the house. Footsteps, or the house settling? Zack and I exchanged glances.

"Do you have a gun?" he murmured.

My hand went to my belt. Shit. I had been in such a hurry to beat Zack here that I had not only forgotten my morning coffee, I had forgotten that my pistol—a Glock nine—was currently locked in a wall safe at Hawk Enterprises, along with some highly illegal stun guns. Yes, it's true—Michigan law lets you conceal a cannon that can blow a hole through an engine block but balks at allowing you to own a non-lethal stun gun.

"I don't have my gun," I admitted.

"Why the hell not?" Zack asked.

"What was I going to shoot, rabid dust bunnies?" I hissed, going on the offensive.

"We chased that guy yesterday. Didn't it occur to you he might come back? Maybe he did all the trashing."

I was starting to get pissed at him. Forgetting my weapon was a rookie mistake and that was bad enough. I didn't need Zack rubbing my face in it.

"What about you?" I countered. "Don't *you* have a weapon?"

"I shoot pictures, not guns."

Great. I listened again but heard only my own breathing.

The still, dusty air was completely silent. "Maybe we should call the cops."

"Sure. They just rushed right in all those other times they came out here."

He had a point. The cops wouldn't enter a dangerous, booby-trapped house unless someone's life was in danger. I listened one more time. Dusty silence. The furniture and bookshelves loomed like lethargic ghosts. Zack put a hand on my shoulder just as I heard the faint creaking again.

"Hear it?"

"Yeah." My mouth was dry, though from unease or Zack's hand on my shoulder, I couldn't say.

He dropped his hand. "Let's go."

It occurred to me that we could just leave the house entirely and wait outside for whomever it was to come out. But then I realized that Zack and I would never be able to cover the entire house, and the basement might not be the only exit. I also didn't want to hear whatever jibe Zack came up with about women chickening out.

Zack and I threaded our way out of the sitting room and down a dark, cluttered hallway. We tried to move quietly, but it wasn't easy in an unfamiliar environment. The floor groaned beneath our feet, our shoes scuffed against the grimy floor. I realized belatedly that the floorboards were actually covered in a carpet so old that it had rotted through to the wood beneath. The ever-present smells of mold and dust assaulted me, and my face hurt from holding back more sneezes. Every few yards, we stopped to listen for more creaks.

The hallway opened into an enormous space. I think it was a ballroom. Most of the floor was taken up by boxes and crates stacked head-high, though a few open areas cropped up like glades in a murky forest. Over the forest and to the right, just visible in the gloom, I could see the top of a massive oak door that I realized was probably the main entrance to the house. To the left lay the grand staircase, the one buried in bundles of magazines. I had seen it from the top, now

I was seeing it from the bottom, though the lower half was obscured by the cardboard forest. A magnificent chandelier hung in the shadows of a two-story ceiling. I eyed it warily. I'd seen *The Phantom of the Opera* and resolved not to walk beneath the thing.

I found a set of light switches, but they didn't work. The area was so dimly lit that Zack and I were forced to use our flashlights. I didn't like it—flashlight beams would tell an intruder right where we were. I felt nervous and exposed, but it was either that or blunder around in the dark.

"Do you hear anything?" Zack murmured.

I listened. Quick heartbeat, raspy breathing, creak of boot leather. All the sounds belonged to me. I shook my head and told Zack to head for the stairs as best he could.

With me in the lead, we moved carefully through the open places between the boxes, trying to keep the staircase in view and not always succeeding. Piles of boxes, some squashed down like stunted trees, often got in the way. The pathway abruptly changed direction or split in two, forcing us to guess which way to go. Every few yards we stopped to listen but always heard nothing. Sweat dripped slowly down my face and I swiped at it with a grubby hand. Zack's blond hair was dark with dust.

Abruptly we came on a large open area. I played the beam around ahead of us and saw a pile of corpses stacked to one side. I squeaked and jumped back, bumping against Zack hard enough for me to feel the muscles move under his clothes. A second later, I realized the corpses were nothing but rolled-up rugs.

"Don't blame you," Zack said, nudging me carefully forward with one hand at the small of my back. "Some of those Persian patterns are really horrific."

"Shut up," was the best I could come up with.

I let my light play over the rugs and saw they lay stacked against a wall. Next to them was the huge front door. I swore, realizing I had gotten completely turned around. We were nowhere near the staircase. The boxes loomed around us. One of the rugs lay unrolled in front of the door like a dusty carpet of leaves. Zack moved around me and headed for it.

"I wonder," he began, "if we could unlock this thing from the—"

And then he was gone. I stared at the spot where he'd been standing, my flashlight beam showing empty space. I blinked, not understanding what I was looking at. One second Zack had been heading for the door, the next he was just…gone.

"Help!"

I shined my flashlight downward. Two pale hands clutched the side of a rectangular hole that had been sawed into the floor directly in front of the door. Comprehension flashed. The rug had been covering a hole. Zack had stepped on the rug and fallen straight through, though he had managed to catch the edge. Heart pounding in my throat, I dropped the flashlight and sprinted over to help. When I knelt by the hole, Zack's pale face looked up at me. His legs swung uselessly below him, trying without success to find some kind of purchase.

"I can't see what's below me," he said hoarsely. "I don't think it's good."

I shot a fast glance downward. Blackness dark as a dragon's throat filled the space below him. A tiny spot of light gleamed in the darkness. Zack had dropped his flashlight and it had fallen down the hole. Way, *way* down the hole. The basement floor wasn't *that* far away, was it? I gave myself a mental shake—this wasn't the time to figure it out. I grabbed Zack's forearms and heaved.

Have you ever tried to haul someone who has thirty-odd pounds on you over the lip of a pit? Me, either. It was fucking *hard.* I felt the muscles in my arms and shoulders stiffen. Tendons stretched and joints popped. Zack's feet couldn't get purchase on anything, so he couldn't help me. I pulled. His wrists came clear of the pit's edge. I realized at that moment that I had his full life in my hands. If I let go, he would fall into hungry darkness. My hands were sweaty and I felt his skin cold on mine. My stomach had tightened up so bad I was afraid of losing all the coffee I'd drunk. I leaned back and pulled. Pain stretched over my shoulders, but I didn't even think about letting go. Zack pulled with his own arms and shoulders, as if he were doing pull-ups. His forearms came up. One of them cleared the rim of the pit and Zack planted his elbow on the solid wood floor. Using his elbow as a bracing point, we got his other arm forward and his other elbow planted.

After that, it became much easier. The two of us were able to get Zack far enough out of the hole so he could roll onto solid flooring. We both lay there, panting like dogs. After a moment, I sat up and handed Zack my water bottle. He accepted it, though he had his own, and took a drink. Then he doused his hands. The palms were scratched. I winced in sympathetic pain at the angry red marks and took the tiny first-aid kit from my belt.

"Why is it always me?" he complained. "Why am I the one who falls through the stairs or into a hole?"

"Maybe the house hates you," I said.

"Don't say that." Zack looked around with a shudder. "It already feels like this place is alive."

"You're being silly," I scoffed, though a cold finger ran down my spine. "Let me see your palms."

We were still sitting on the floor. I took one of his hands in my lap and examined it under the beam of my flashlight. His arm lay warm and heavy across my thigh. Zack sucked in a breath when I plucked out a splinter but he didn't yelp. I rinsed his palm, spread antibiotic ointment on the scratches, then did the same for his other hand. I had to admit I felt a little guilty. The jokes I'd made about using him to test for traps sounded harsh, even mean, in retrospect. Zack wasn't all bad. He could be funny when he wasn't being a jerk. And any guy who could admit without a trace of embarrassment to reading Nancy Drew had to have *something* going for him.

"That should do it," I said, putting the ointment back into its compartment.

Zack's hand remained in mine, palm up, for another heart-beat. Then he withdrew it.

"Thanks," he said. "For the medicine and the save."

"Uh, yeah," I said, feeling suddenly embarrassed. "No problem. What the heck do you think is down there, anyway?"

I edged over to the hole and shined my flashlight down-ward. Zack scooted up next to me. A few fibers from the car-pet clung to the rough edges. Below, Zack's flashlight was nothing but a peep of light in the distance, a star that had fallen down a well. The light wavered a little bit. Weird.

"It's almost as if the light is…underwater?" I said.

Zack snapped his fingers, then winced. Sore palms. "It's a cistern," he said. "I used to live in a house that had one like it. Rainwater drains from the gutters into a pit in the base-ment and you use it for drinking and washing. Or maybe it's an old well. Lots of old houses had them."

I pulled a penny from my pocket and dropped it. A faint splash followed, and the flashlight rippled again.

"Wonder how deep it is," Zack said.

"Deep enough to drown in. Especially if you broke some-thing while falling in. We need to keep being careful."

More shuffling noises sounded overhead. Definitely foot-steps. We both froze and a little thrill of fear trilled through me.

"Do you think they heard us?" Zack whispered.

I considered. "You shouted for help, but all this junk muf-fles noise. Hard to say."

"I think the stairs are over this way. Come on!"

Zack drew a second flashlight, a smaller one, from his belt and tiptoed back into the forest of boxes. I followed, keeping an eye out for tripwires, loose boards, suspicious rugs, any-thing that looked like it might turn injurious or deadly. Some-thing metallic rattled in the distance.

"He's on the pan stairs," I said. "Come on!"

We tried to hurry, but in the end fell back to going slowly, for safety. Zack swept his flashlight beam across the floor in front of him and I played my beam over the head-level spaces in front of us. The passageway within the boxes twisted and turned, forcing us to make detours. In the distance, I would see the staircase, then some boxes would obscure it, forcing us to detour. A few minutes later, the stairs would show up again, always in the wrong place. It was like chasing a fairy ring. There seemed to be no way to get to the damned staircase. Any moment I expected another trap, something to crush us or drop us or skewer us. I was sweating and my stomach muscles were stretched tight as a drum. My legs were getting sore from maintaining constant readiness to jump.

After several more twists and turns, Zack halted. I almost bumped into him from behind.

"What?" I demanded. "What is it?"

"We've been here before," he said, playing his beam around.

All I saw were blank walls of aging boxes. "How do you know?" I asked.

"Look." He shined his light on a cardboard wall at shoulder level. Thick dust coated the surface except for a long swipe, freshly made. "I've been marking our trail."

I spun around. The narrow passage behind me was a crack through unmoving mountains. And then it hit me. "Oh, my God," I said in awe. "It's a *maze*. Uncle Lawrence built a fucking maze!"

"Jesus," Zack breathed. He craned his neck to look upward. "I don't know whether to admire the old guy or shoot him."

"He's dead, so there's no point in either one," I pointed out tensely. "But, yeah, I know what you mean. We were caught in a trap and didn't even realize it."

"How do we find our way out?" Zack asked. "I don't suppose you have a ball of string in your Batbelt."

"Not today," I said, trying to stay calm. "We do have options." Boxes and crates seemed to lean inward, as if they wanted to devour the feeble light of my flashlight beam. The thin passageways were just wide enough for one person, but hovering dust and hot air made them feel narrower by the second.

"Options such as?" Zack whispered.

"We can follow one wall," I said. "That will get you out of most mazes. We could try to climb over the top. Or we could try to dismantle the maze by pulling the boxes down."

"Veto the last idea," Zack said. "No place to put the boxes we pull down. And the climbing one's risky. Lots of dangerous stuff you can put in a box. Why do you think no one wants to hit one on the highway?"

I nodded. "Let's follow the right wall, then."

"Hold on." Zack wrote his initials in the dust on one wall with a finger. "Okay."

We followed the right wall. The air grew hotter and sweat made my shirt stick to my back. After several minutes, Zack stopped again. His flashlight beam picked out the initials ZA on the cardboard wall.

"We're right back where we started from," he said hoarsely.

I took a swig of warm water from my bottle. "Left wall, then."

The world narrowed to the dusty brown blur at the end of my flashlight beam. The staircase flitted in and out of view, but I ignored it. I just wanted to find the way out. The heat and dust made me think of the cistern Zack had almost fallen into. Death by drowning in cool, delicious water was starting to sound pretty good.

"Dammit," Zack breathed.

I grimaced. Ahead of him, his flashlight picked out the initials ZA again. Panic burst inside me, and I was seized with the desire to claw my way up to the top of the boxes, not caring what might be in them—or under them. My breath came faster and my heart pounded.

Zack put his hand on my shoulder. "Don't," he said in a surprisingly soothing voice. "We'll be okay. We have our cell phones and can call for help if we really have to."

Relief flooded me. How could I have forgotten? I snatched my cell off my belt and checked the display.

No Service, it read. So much for roaming.

Insane laughter bubbled up, and I swallowed it down. "All the junk must be blocking the signal."

"Okay, okay." Zack checked his own phone, with the same result, and passed a hand over his face. "Maybe we should split up. We'll cover more ground."

"What do you think this is, an episode of Scooby Doo?" I snarled. "That's the stupidest idea yet."

"I don't hear you coming up with anything," he shot back.

"Right. Okay. Think," I said, keeping the panic away by sheer force of will. "There's a way in, so there must be a way out. We must have missed a passage somewhere, a narrow one or one that's in shadow. Let's go to the left again, but slower."

We did, forcing ourselves to stay at a slow, careful pace. I was in the lead this time. Dusty cardboard brushed against my shoulders and gloom pressed in all around me. The path wound crookedly through the piles. Left, left, left, straight ahead. The sound of Zack's breathing stayed right behind me. Stay with the left wall, always the left wall. It felt as if we'd been in this maze of dead trees forever.

And then I saw it—a narrow path between two stacks. It was just wide enough to pass through sideways. I pointed it out to Zack.

"Did we come in through that?" I asked. "I don't remember."

"Let's check," Zack said.

He slid sideways into the opening and vanished, as if it had swallowed him alive. I swallowed hard and followed. Blackness closed around me, eating at my flashlight beam. The boxes pressed against my nose and my shoulder blades. I gritted my teeth and kept going.

And then we were in open space. I faced forward again and barked my shin on a pile of magazines. A staircase, piled waist-high with more reading material, rose ahead of us. Relief washed over me, and I felt as if I had stepped into a cool, shady meadow instead of a gloomy, dust-laden foyer. I unhooked my water bottle and took a long drink. Dust washed out of my throat.

"Man," Zack said. "What a trip."

I held up a hand and listened. Nothing. Which didn't say much.

"Come on," I said, and pulled Zack by the hand toward the stairs.

Another narrow trail led among the magazine piles and we climbed carefully, checking for trapped steps along the way. All the constant checking was making me tense. People aren't meant to be on high alert every moment, and I was getting tired of concentrating all the time. It was easy to get distracted.

Dusty magazine covers criss-crossed with rotting twine kept shouting for my attention. The McCarthy hearings made the cover of *Life*. John F. Kennedy's picture graced *Time*. *National Geographic* visited Africa yet again. *Highlights* promised kids and their parents "fun with a purpose." The Fonz lifted both thumbs on *TV Guide*. Halfway up the stairs I realized I was still holding Zack's hand. He hadn't said a word about it. It made me feel better, being able to touch another person in this weird and hostile environment, but I pulled away anyway. He didn't comment.

At the top of the stairs we had the choice of traversing a short balcony and entering the second-floor hallway or continuing on upward to the third floor. Pots, pans, and lids still made a knee-deep iron waterfall on the steps. I swept them with my flashlight. The path Ms. Hawk and Zack had cleared was still there, mostly.

"Our housebreaker didn't go all the way up," Zack murmured. "If he had climbed over those pans or cleared a path, we'd have heard a lot more clanking."

"You're thinking just what I am," I whispered back, "which scares me more than I can say."

I shined my light down the hallway. Another forest of boxes

with a single narrow path looked back at me. I was getting so tired of staring at stupid boxes. The guy we'd chased last time had tipped over several of them, and they were still there, clogging part of the way with mangled cardboard and twisted clothes. It looked like a pile of dead scarecrows.

If we hadn't been hearing things, and *if* there was an intruder in the house, and *if* he hadn't come back down the main stairs while we were bumbling around below, our visitor had to be on the second floor.

"That's a lot of ifs," Zack muttered when I voiced this line of thought.

"We have to start somewhere," I pointed out. "May as well be here."

Zack had no answer to this, so we moved forward. Now that we weren't chasing someone down it, I took more time to check out the hallway. The corridor was wide, with a vaulted ceiling. Occasional cracks in the stacks showed that a waist-high molding of dark wood ran the length of the walls above a hardwood floor. In its heyday, it must have been breathtaking. Today, however, the wide way was clogged with box after box, crate after crate, all the way to the ceiling. Only a narrow path allowed us to squeak through.

I sniffed the air. Rot. The medical examiner and the firefighters had removed the bodies, but the smell hadn't entirely gone away. It would take some serious cleaning to get rid of it, and that didn't seem a too-likely event.

Zack and I made our way down the path. As upstairs, several doors faced the corridor. Some were partially or completely blocked by boxes, others were readily accessible. Each time we passed a reachable door, Zack tried the knob. All of them were locked. One had an old Stop sign hanging on it. Taped below this was a hand-lettered card, the letters faded with time. I paused and gave it the full beam of my flashlight. In firm, teenage script, it said:

BEEBO'S PLACE
STAY OUT!!!

"Beebo?" Zack said, reading over my shoulder.

"Sounds like a pet bear," I said, and tried the heavy, old-fashioned knob. Locked. "I wonder if we can find any keys around."

Zack laughed at that, the sound hushed by the boxes surrounding us. "Find? In this place we'd be lucky to find our own...elbows."

"You were going to say 'asses' and then changed your mind," I said with a grin.

"I can't help it if I'm a proper gentleman," he sniffed. "Even to a clearly improper lady."

When I turned to give a response, my flashlight beam shined down the hallway and picked out a ghostly face in the gloom. I froze in surprise. The face turned and disappeared.

"Hey!" I shouted, and vaulted after it. Boxes slapped my shoulders. "Wait!"

Ahead of me, light flooded part of the hallway as a door slammed open, then shut. I leaped over some dead clothes and lunged for it. No boxes stood in the way. I twisted the knob, expecting it to be locked. It turned easily, however. I flung the door open and found myself momentarily blinded. The room beyond was brightly lit. Blind and exposed, I flung myself back into the dark hallway, but this only catapulted me hard into Zack, who had rushed up behind me. We went down in a heap. I couldn't move, couldn't maneuver. An odd *thump* sounded inside the room, and for a horrible moment I thought it was a gunshot. My skin prickled, expecting to feel a tearing pain. None came. I finally managed to roll away from Zack and get to my feet in a fighting stance.

Nothing. No attack, no sign of an intruder. Just an open door spilling sunlight and dust motes into the hallway. The bright yellow light felt unnatural after all the gloom. Cautiously, I peered into the room beyond.

"What is it?" Zack asked, getting to his feet behind me. "What's in there?"

I couldn't make it out at first. Jumbled shapes, round ones, swooping ones, wires and frames. A split-second passed and I realized I was looking at bicycle parts. Spoked wheels hung from the walls and made rusty piles on the floor. Clumps of bike frames, their colors muted by rust and dust, made weird sculptures all over the floor. Several bikes hung upside-down from the ceiling, their ancient tires hanging in rotted strings. A tool bench ran across the back of the room, and it was piled with more bicycle parts and even a few ancient tools. A large window at the back was actually uncurtained, and it let in hot August sunlight. I scanned the room—once a large bedroom, I guessed—for the intruder. No sign. What the hell?

"What happened?" Zack demanded. "What did you see?"

"A face," I said, though now I was starting to wonder if I'd somehow imagined it. "In my flashlight beam. Only for a second. Then it disappeared and I heard this door slam."

"I saw the light," Zack said. "There must be someone in here. Hello?"

No response. We fanned out and checked the room. It looked like a bicycle butcher shop. The Wright brothers would have been horrified. I saw no sign of a human being, however.

"Shit," I said.

"Not exactly ladylike," Zack said. "All those curse words."

"Fucking A," I agreed. "Now what do—"

"Here," Zack interrupted. "Over here."

I skittered between a pile of Schwinns and a stack of wheels until I could stand near him. He was pointing at a clear section of floor. An iron ring lay flush with the wood, and I made out the shape of a trapdoor about two feet by three feet. The ring was free of dust. I remembered the odd slam I had taken for a gunshot.

"He went down there," I said.

"No kidding." Zack grabbed the ring and pulled. The door came up with a creak of protest, revealing a black space beneath. I shined my light downward. A ladder descended into darkness. Bizarre. I stepped toward it, but Zack grabbed my biceps. He had a strong grip.

"You're not going down there."

"The hell I'm not," I snapped, trying to shake him off.

Zack didn't let go. "Are you nuts? You're going to climb down, feet-first, into an unknown black space to chase an assailant who may have a gun, in a house with more tricks and traps than Houdini's basement. What if Uncle Lawrence sawed halfway through certain rungs? You'd break your neck. Not to mention expose yourself to a few dozen bullets."

I started to protest, then stopped as one of Ms. Hawk's main axioms popped into my head. *Women can take risks just like men,* she always said, *but they don't need to take* stupid *risks.* Zack was right. Reluctantly I stepped away from the trapdoor.

"All right," I said, surprised at how tightly my teeth were clenched. "What do we do now?"

Zack closed the trapdoor with the same *thump* I had heard earlier. "I think we have to let him go, though maybe you should tell the cops that someone's been in here. And then we go back to looking for the will and whatever it was Uncle Lawrence wanted to show me. I just wish I knew what it was."

"There's definitely something important in this damned house," I groused. "Someone's going through a lot of trouble to find it."

"Did you get a good look at the person's face?"

I shook my head. "Couldn't even tell if it was a man or a woman. At least we know whoever it is hasn't found what they're looking for yet."

"How do you know that?"

"They wouldn't have stuck around." I suddenly wanted more coffee and another doughnut. The morning had been long and the situation felt hopeless. The uncles had been piling up junk for decades, and it would take just as long to sort through it all. We didn't even know what we were looking for, let alone where to find it in this mess. And then another of Ms. Hawk's axioms came to mind: *Your action is only as good as your information.*

"I think," I said slowly, "that I need to look somewhere else."

Zack cocked his head. "Explain?"

"I need to know more about the uncles," I said. "Learning something about their backgrounds might give me a clue to what I'm looking for and maybe even where to find it. I should hit the library and the courthouse, see what I can learn."

"You keep saying *I*," Zack said. "Shouldn't that be *we*? Nancy Drew and Frank Hardy—we can team up."

"Confidentiality issues," I said smoothly. "I might find something our client would want kept confidential, and you don't work for Hawk Enterprises." I headed for the door, expecting to hear a protest. When none came, I glanced back at him. Zack was standing by a stack of warped bike rims. We were both sweating in the hot, stuffy room. Zack's blond hair had darkened and was curling into ringlets.

"What?" he said.

"No 'Aw, come on'?" I said. "I'm surprised a big photographer like you gives up so easily."

"You've clearly made up your mind," he said airily. "Far be it from me to try and change it."

My eyes narrowed. "What are you up to?"

"Nothing!" he protested. "Why are you always so suspicious of everything I do?"

"Because everything you do is suspicious." Then it came to me. "You're planning to stay here and search while I'm gone, aren't you?"

"Nope." He headed for the door himself. "Actually, I'm planning to go outside and have another doughnut."

We threaded our way cautiously back through the house. We took the by-now-familiar route down the shoe stairs, through the messed-up kitchen, and out the basement. Outside, I inhaled fresh summer air, enjoying the total lack of dust. My skin was itchy beneath my clothes and I wondered if I was going to spend the entire case covered in the stuff. I read somewhere that most household dust is actually human skin cells shed by a house's inhabitants. The thought that I was covered in a layer of someone else's dead skin made me shudder.

Zack, meanwhile, retrieved his backpack from the stairs where he'd left it and pulled out the doughnut bag. I was expecting him to pointedly eat one without offering any to me, but he surprised me by waving the waxy sack in my direction.

"Want one?" he asked. "They're still pretty fresh."

I did, but said, "No, thanks," partly out of principle and partly out of respect for my thighs. Cherry cheesecake last night and doughnuts this morning—I'd been pushing it.

"Suit yourself," he said, and sank his teeth into a round pastry that oozed red jelly. "You gonna call Belinda and the cops? They'll both want to know about this, even though the cops probably won't actually do anything."

To my chagrin, I realized he was right. Even if the police did nothing but file a report, they had to be alerted. And Belinda needed an update. I'd already entered the number of her hotel into my cell phone, and she picked up almost immediately.

"Thank heavens you called," she said before I could launch into an explanation. "I just heard from the medical examiner's office, and the police are on their way to the house right now."

I blinked at that. "How did you know?"

"Know what?"

"That someone broke into the house early this morning."

"Someone broke *in?*" Belinda squeaked.

"Isn't that why you called the police?"

"I didn't call the police. They called me. Who broke in?"

We were repeating questions to each other without answering them, and both of us were just getting more confused. "Let me go first," I said, and told her what we'd found in the house, including the fact that we'd chased the intruder and lost him— or her. Belinda greeted this news with momentary silence.

"Oh, dear," she said at last. "I wonder if the intruder killed that poor man."

"What poor man?" I asked. "Ms. Harris, please explain."

"Of course, of course." I imagined her sitting in her hotel room, an inhaler on the nightstand, her sun dress neatly pressed by a hotel iron. "The medical examiner put the autopsies on the fast track because of the advanced decomposition of both bodies. Uncle Howard was pretty…pretty far gone, you understand, and they're still working on a cause of death for him."

"All right," I said, trying not to show my impatience to a client. "And Uncle Lawrence?"

"That's the main reason the medical examiner called me," Belinda said. "The medical examiner told me the man crushed under all those magazines was definitely not my uncle."

SEVEN

BELINDA GAVE ME what details she had. Once the medical examiner, Karen Wilewski, had gotten the body into good light at the morgue, she had instantly realized it didn't belong to Uncle Lawrence. The dead man was far too young, in his midforties or so. He had no identification on him, so they had no idea who he was, yet.

This revelation opened up a whole mess of possibilities, and my mind tore through them like a weasel ripping through a chicken coop. If the body wasn't Uncle Lawrence, that could mean the old man was still alive somewhere. Maybe he was the intruder Zack and I had almost caught. It would certainly explain how he got around the traps and knew there was a trapdoor in the bike room. On the other hand, why would he ransack his own house? Or sneak around inside it? Maybe Uncle Lawrence had been kidnapped by someone who wanted the same thing Zack was looking for. Or maybe they were looking for something else entirely.

All this flashed through my mind as Belinda's voice continued over my cell phone.

"Dr. Wilewski said the man—whoever he is—hadn't actually been crushed to death, you understand. He had died of suffocation. The magazines were so heavy that he couldn't inhale. Can you imagine?" Belinda paused, and I got the impression she was shuddering. An asthma sufferer probably had more nightmares about suffocation than your average person. "Dr. Wilewski wouldn't tell me more than that, since I'm not related to the dead man." A note of hope suffused her voice. "Do you think Uncle Lawrence is alive somewhere?"

"We need to keep our minds open." I learned long ago that it's a bad idea to say you think something might be possible. Clients usually take that to mean "Yes, definitely."

Zack, meanwhile, was dying of curiosity. He danced back and forth as if he had to go to the bathroom. I waved at him to calm down. He made a face. At that moment, sirens ripped through the quiet air. Cops on the way. Zack whipped his head around, startled. I plugged my free ear with a finger and turned my attention back to the phone.

"Would you keep looking, then?" Belinda was asking. "I need to know what's going on."

"Of course, Ms. Harris," I said. "We'll stay on this as long as you like."

"I have to go get my bike," Zack said.

I waved him off and asked Belinda if she had gotten any other information from the M.E.'s office, and Belinda told me she hadn't. We clicked off just as a black-and-white came cruising down the driveway, lights flashing like a rock-concert stage. At least they had shut the sirens off. A plain blue sedan followed. Four doors swung open and four people got out—two uniformed cops and two plainclothes detectives. I gave them a cheery wave. The cops were the same ones who had responded yesterday, when we had found the bodies. I never did catch their names—Ms. Hawk had dealt with them. The two detectives, however, I knew well. The first was Henrietta Flinch, a former client. Her ex-husband had fallen behind on the child-support payments, and Hawk Enterprises had... arranged for him to catch up. Henrietta had already paid back the favors she owed Ms. Hawk, but we remained on friendly terms. The same couldn't be said about her partner, Carl dela Cort. My jaw tightened when I saw him.

Henrietta and Carl headed in my direction while the two officers got out big rolls of yellow tape. They started unrolling the stuff, setting off a boundary around the house. Frustration pulled my eyebrows together. Great. Now that the place was a crime scene, I wouldn't be allowed back in. I felt sorry for whoever was assigned to gather physical evidence inside, though.

"Terry!" Henrietta sang out as she approached. Her blue pantsuit complemented her whipcord figure and fair skin, and she wore her shiny black hair in a twist. "What are you doing here? I thought you and Ms. Hawk had cleared out yesterday."

"Our client wanted us to examine the house some more," I replied. "So I came back this morning."

"Coroner says the poor bastard who died in all those magazines wasn't one of the old guys who lived here," Carl said. He was a powerfully built man who clearly spent hours in the gym, and his starched white shirt bulged like a sack of footballs. Henrietta had once told me Carl had his work clothes tailored to show off every contour. That seemed to be the case—I could almost tell his religion by glancing at his crotch. His face might have been handsome in a blocky, square sort of way if it weren't screwed into a permanent sneer. "How are you involved in this shit?"

I shook my head. "I wasn't involved in the guy's death, if that's what you mean."

"Oh, ho!" He looked me up and down, and his gaze stopped at my chest. "What makes you think I was talking about the dead man—what was his name again?" I rolled my eyes. The guy's interview technique was as subtle as a barrel of toxic waste.

"I have no idea, Carl," I said. "My boobs don't know, either."

He flushed red at that. "Listen, girlie—all I know is that whenever there's some kind of trouble in this town, you and that Hawk lady are Janie-on-the-fucking-spot. Looks damn suspicious, you ask me."

"Yeah, sure," I said vaguely, knowing full well I wasn't going to be a suspect anywhere except in Carl's piggy little mind. "Look, Henrietta, our client—"

"Belinda Harris," she supplied. "The M.E. told us."

I nodded. So much for confidentiality. "Right. Anyway,

back when we all thought that both Howard and Lawrence Peale were dead, Ms. Harris—next of kin—asked Hawk Enterprises to go through the house and look for various legal documents. Zack and I went in this morning and saw the place had been ransacked."

"Zack?" Henrietta said.

"You got a boyfriend?" Carl said. "Good God. I thought Diana Hawk had you batting for the other team."

"He's more your type than mine, Detective," I said before I could stop myself. "Don't you go for blonds?"

Carl's reaction rather surprised me. He clamped his lips into a white line and said nothing. Hmm. I filed that one away for later.

"Who's Zack?" Henrietta asked.

"Zack Archer," I said. "He's a photographer." I sketched out a brief explanation of his involvement and how we knew the house had been ransacked.

"And where is this Zack guy now?" Carl asked.

I was wondering that myself. "He said he had to go get his bike."

"Anything else you can tell us, Terry?" Henrietta asked. "Either from today or from yesterday, when you found the body?"

"No, nothing," I said, shaking my head. "Have you ever been inside?"

It was Henrietta's turn to shake her head. "Never had the pleasure. I've heard rumors about booby traps, though. Looks like they were true."

"Yeah. I'm guessing it's what killed that guy." A thought struck me. "How did the owners pay their property taxes and stuff like that? I can't imagine either of them had jobs."

"Oh, this place has been on the department's crapola list forever," Henrietta said. "Twice in the last year we've gotten court orders to seize the house for non-payment of debts, but no one was able to get inside to evict the owners. And then they came up with enough money to hold off their creditors. Last-minute stuff, you know."

"Weird. So where'd they get the money from?" I wondered aloud.

"We'll ask the questions here," Carl said.

Just to annoy him, I said to Henrietta, "How long will this place be a crime scene? I'll need to tell Ms. Harris how long it'll be before I can go back in."

"It'll stay a crime scene as long as we say it does," Carl growled.

"Well, back when we thought the body belonged to Lawrence Peale, we figured he had died by accident. Now we have to look a little more closely, check for foul play," Henrietta said. "It may take a while. And if Lawrence Peale is still alive somewhere, we'll want to talk to him. You wouldn't know where to find him, by chance?"

"Sorry," I said. "I do wonder if he was the intruder—I never did get a look at the person—but that raises more questions. Why would Uncle Lawrence sneak around his own house? Or trash the place?"

"I told you," Carl said. He hawked and spat. "They were fucking loony."

Henrietta shot me a sympathetic look that said, *He may annoy you, but I have to work with him every day.* She definitely had the short end of the deal.

We exchanged cards, and Henrietta told me to call night or day if I thought of anything else.

"And don't leave town, lady," Carl said.

My annoyance blew into outrage. "Am I a suspect in a crime, Detective? Are you planning to charge me with anything? If the answer is 'no,' then I'll go where I damn well please, and no petty pin-dick dictator with a badge is going to tell me otherwise. You got that?"

"I think we're all set here, actually," Henrietta put in loudly before Carl could reply. "You can head on home, or wherever you need to go. Thanks, Terry."

I stomped away, feeling Carl's eyes on my back—and probably my ass. I hopped into my Jeep and drove home, still fuming. All the other boarders were out for the day, and the Biemers were both cleaning upstairs, so I had the first floor to myself. For the second time in two days, I peeled off sweaty, dust-laden clothes and took a cool, refreshing shower. Anger at Carl dela Cort's attitude continued to bubble inside me. I took a deep breath as the water washed over my body and imagined the anger as dirt that swirled down the drain. Carl was an idiot, not worth the energy. He would love it if he knew I was thinking about him, so I wouldn't give him the satisfaction. Nor would I wonder where Zack had disappeared to. Water, dust, and anger went down the drain with little sucking sounds, and I emerged from the shower feeling much better. The comfortingly domestic drone of a vacuum cleaner running upstairs calmed me even further.

A bit later, I was dressed in fresh khakis, a polo shirt, and tennis shoes. I snagged my phone and my laptop—both indispensable on any research trip. The next stop, however, would be lunch, and I knew exactly what I wanted.

Blimpy Burger is situated a little ways north of State Street and is actually in a mostly residential district. The blocky little building is partly brick and partly painted homey yellow. Two big picnic tables occupy a front porch shaded by an enormous maple tree. Since it's so far away from downtown, it's usually easy to grab a metered parking space on the street, and that's what I did. The sign out front says Blimpy Burger: Cheaper Than Food, and you can smell the burgers frying before you even hit the door. I inhaled appreciatively as I stepped inside.

The inside of Blimpy's hasn't changed in nearly sixty years. It's furnished with fifties-style Formica counters and chairs, chipped and battered but clean. One wall is taken up by the grill, in front of which runs a long counter. During lunch rush, they'll have as many as three people at the grill, all dressed in spotted white aprons, but by now the last of the lunch crowd had faded away. Only four people waited in line, and six sat at the tables. Hamburger hissed on the grill, and fries sizzled in hot oil. I smelled melting cheese and onions, and my mouth watered.

As an experienced Blimpy Burger–eater, I knew the drill. I grabbed a tray, put a bottle of Coke on it from the nearby cooler, and glanced at the whiteboard menu above the grill. Blimpy's has never heard of a single—the smallest burger is a double, and they'll pile up to five patties on your bun. I usually opt for just a double, but I deserved a treat after this morning. When it came my turn to order, I said, "Fries, please. Then hit me with a triple."

"You got it," said the cook, a woman with a Jamaican accent and her hair all in braids. She dropped a basket of fries into the fryer, then plucked three balls of ground beef from a pan and squashed them flat on the grill. They hissed deliciously.

While I waited for my burger to cook, my mind wandered inevitably back to the mansion. If Uncle Lawrence hadn't been crushed under Magazine Mountain, who had been? And how long had he been there? Long enough for the body to start decaying, obviously, but that wouldn't take long in summer heat. Was the guy a trespasser who had fallen victim to a trap or an invited guest who had met an accident? The latter possibility intrigued me. Uncle Lawrence had invited Zack into the house. Who was to say he hadn't invited other people? Zack might not be the only one Uncle Lawrence wanted to show something to.

I shook my head. That didn't feel right. I got the distinct impression that talking to Zack had been a major step for Uncle Lawrence. Someone who had lived as a recluse for decades wouldn't break that pattern easily or lightly. But that left the question of who the magazine guy was. Had he been working with whomever had tossed the house this morning? Or the intruder we had chased? It was still too hard to say.

"What kind of cheese you want, hon?" the cook asked over her shoulder.

"Provolone."

The cook skillfully alternated slabs of meat with slices of cheese and passed the stack down to the sandwich station, where another worker added ketchup, mustard, and pickles at my request. In a few seconds, I had a paper-wrapped cheeseburger and a pile of hot fries on my tray beside the bottle of Coke. Breakfast, and Zack's doughnuts, were a fading memory, and the food smells made my knees weak.

I paid and got a fifty-cent piece in my change. The Blimpy cashiers are notorious for handing out weird money—fifty-cent pieces, Canadian quarters, two-dollar bills—and I suspect it's to encourage customers to drop it into the tip jar by the register. I tossed the coin into the jar with a clank. The cashier, a young man, nodded thanks and turned to the next customer. I selected a table, inhaled the mouth-watering aroma of a fresh cheeseburger, and leaned in to take a succulent bite.

"I knew it."

I dropped the cheeseburger. My elbow thrust sideways and connected before I could register who was standing beside me. I heard a squeak and a *thump* as I spun in my chair, combat reflexes at the ready. Zack was kneeling on the floor, both hands buried in his groin. His face was contorted with surprise and pain.

"Oops," I said.

"What'd you do that for?" Zack gasped. He was dressed in fresh clothes, and his hair was still damp from a recent shower. "Jesus."

"Sorry. I would have gotten your stomach if the chair was a little higher."

"Don't sneak up on a woman, hon," the cook called from the grill.

Everyone in the place was staring at us. The women looked faintly amused, and the men, including the cashier, wore expressions of sympathetic pain. Zack gave several gasping breaths. I've always wondered what it must be like to have such vulnerable little thingies just hanging there, waiting for something to whack them, and what the pain might feel like.

My curiosity is purely academic, of course—I don't *really* want to know.

It wasn't academic for Zack. I finally reached down and helped him into a chair. His big yellow backpack was on the floor beside him.

"You want some ice, hon?" the cook asked him.

"No, thanks," Zack said hoarsely. "Just a triple with cheddar and an order of fries. She's paying." He cocked a thumb at me.

"I am?" I said.

"Damn straight. Come to that, make it a quadruple, with a whole bunch of those expensive mushrooms on it."

I waved acquiescence to the cook and finally took a bite of my own burger. Oh, yeah. Salty meat, tart pickle, tangy mustard. Heaven on a bun!

"So what do you want?" I asked with my mouth full.

"Lunch," he said. "Us he-man photographers get hungry, too."

"Uh huh. I take it you found your bike. Why did you take off?"

"I don't get along with cops. They ask too many questions and they don't like reporters."

I selected a fry so hot it singed my fingertips and dipped it in ketchup. "You ever been arrested, Zack?"

He gave me a long look. "Yeah. Back when I was young and stupid. A friend dared me to break into a house and I did. Got caught, got cuffed, end of story. You figured it out, hooray for you. I don't like cops." He paused. "So what did Belinda say? And what did the cops want?"

"Nothing you need to know about."

He gave an easy smile. "Belinda will tell me if you don't. Why not save me the trouble?"

"If she wants to tell you, she can," I said. "My lips are sealed."

"Sealed around that cheeseburger."

"You're awfully mouthy for someone who just took an elbow in the groin."

The cashier set a tray piled with food in front of Zack and clapped him sympathetically on the shoulder. "Dude," he said. I paid him, and he went back to his station.

"Tell you what," Zack said. "I'll tell you mine if you tell me yours."

I eyed him warily. "What's that supposed to mean?"

"I met Uncle Lawrence long before you came along." Zack picked up a fry, swore, and dropped it. Too hot. He picked up his heavy mushroom burger instead. Cheese oozed between the layers and mushrooms peeked out from under the bun. "I did a little background work of my own, you know. I'll tell you what I know if you tell me what you know."

I considered this while I chewed. Research was always iffy—you never knew if it'd take five minutes or five days. Another set of eyes would be useful. Finally I swallowed and said, "Only if Belinda says it's okay. It's all about—"

"Confidentiality," he finished. "I know. So call her already."

I did, and Belinda was delighted to hear "that nice young man" still wanted to be involved.

"You can tell him anything about the case you want," she said.

"I don't know if full disclosure is such a great idea," I replied. I was outside the restaurant under the maple tree. Zack was inside, eating, and my cheeseburger was getting cold. "I'm not quite sure if we can trust him."

"Do whatever you feel is best, then," Belinda said. "You have my permission to share whatever information you feel is relevant or necessary."

Back inside, I sat down again. Zack had finished most of his burger. "Well?"

I sighed. If Zack had information, I needed to at least pretend to trust him so I could worm it out of him. "Belinda said it's okay. Let's trade info."

"I'll even go first as a good-faith gesture," he said magnanimously. "I looked into the Peale family history and I learned there are two main branches—one in Chicago and one here in Detroit, which includes Ann Arbor."

I remembered Belinda mentioning that she had distant relatives in Chicago but didn't know how to contact them. I nodded and dipped another fry in ketchup.

"The family has a weird history of crime," Zack continued. "They seem to be victims of it a hell of a lot. I found several old newspaper articles and police blotter reports about burglars breaking into Peale family residences, both here in the Detroit area and out in Chicago. The Chicago Peales have a family estate complete with mansion, and it's been in the family for generations."

"The Peales seem to like big houses," I mused.

"Yeah. But here it gets really interesting. In every single case—and I found references going back to the twenties—the Chicago Peales claimed nothing had been stolen and they had no idea who might be breaking in. The police never caught anyone, as far as I could tell."

I thought back to the magazine guy and the intruder Zack and I had chased. "So people have been breaking into Peale houses for decades. Why?"

Zack shrugged. "Couldn't tell you. All I had to go on were microfilmed newspaper stories. And it gets better." He opened his backpack and pulled out a piece of paper. "I copied this article from a 1938 *Detroit Free Press*. A certain Edmund Peale of Chicago was arrested for breaking into the house of Victor Peale in Detroit. A beat cop was in the right place at the right time and arrested Edmund as he was sneaking out of Victor's house. But check it out—Victor didn't press charges."

I skimmed the fuzzy print. Zack was right. Victor had let Edmund go. The newspaper didn't say why. Familial regard? As an aside, the article also mentioned Victor's two sons— Howard and Lawrence. No mention of a daughter—Belinda's mother—but I realized that if Belinda's mother was barely sixty at her death, she wouldn't have been born yet. I looked at the story again.

"If Edmund Peale of Chicago broke into the house of Victor Peale in Detroit," I said slowly, "that seems to hint that other Peales were behind the other break-ins. They were breaking into each other's houses, back and forth."

"That's what I'm thinking," Zack said. "But it seems to have stopped in 1947."

"Why's that?"

Zack pushed another sheet of paper to me. The microfilm copy was a little blurry, but the headline was clear enough: Peale Home Burns to the Ground. I read quickly. The Peale house, located in what was then a wealthy, riverside section of Detroit, had mysteriously caught fire in the middle of the night. No one had been hurt, but the house had been a total loss. The police were suspicious, of course, but back then there wasn't much going in the way of arson investigation methods.

"When asked if it were possible that someone in the Peale home had set the fire," I read aloud, *"police investigator Tom Flugel said, 'We're investigating all possibilities.'* Huh."

"Yeah. A couple weeks later, the paper must have had a slow news day because they did a follow-up. The article said no one had been arrested or even charged yet, and the police had no suspects."

"Assuming it was arson," I said slowly, "did the Chicago Peales set the fire, or did the Detroit Peales burn their own house down? Was the house insured?"

"Papers didn't say. I would guess so. Fire insurance was fairly common by the forties, especially for the rich. Notice, though, that Victor moved to Ann Arbor after the fire. That was when the junk mansion got its start. *The Ann Arbor News* ran several articles about Vincent Peale building his new home and moving in with his wife and with his sons Howard and Lawrence. They were almost teenagers by then. The main thing is that I couldn't find any more references to break-ins, not here and not in Chicago. They stopped after the house in Detroit burned down."

"Or you missed the references to the break-ins," I said, "or the paper didn't report on them. Or the Peales stopped calling the police about them."

"All possible, but not likely," Zack said. "I did catch the other break-in articles, and it doesn't seem likely the papers would have ignored the other ones. Reporters read the police blotter, after all. And you're saying the Peales in both cities alerted the police after every break-in before the fire, but not after it? It seems way more likely that the break-ins just stopped."

"That's the most likely explanation," I admitted. "I'm just saying we have to keep an open mind."

"Sure. Right." He popped the last bite of burger into his mouth. "Anyway. I'm trying to put the pieces of all this together. I'm thinking the Chicago Peales and the Detroit Peales had some kind of feud going, and they were breaking into each other's houses. But why? And why did they stop?"

I drummed my fingers on the Formica table. Thoughts coalesced in my mind like gathering thunderheads. "Because," I said, thinking as I went, "there was no longer a reason to break in. What if the break-ins were to look for something in particular? Something valuable to the families? Something that got stolen back and forth between the two branches of the family?"

"Something like what?"

"Not sure. But I'll bet the fire destroyed it back in forty-seven. That would explain the end to the break-ins."

"And maybe it wasn't destroyed after all. Maybe Uncle Lawrence wanted to show the thing to me." Zack took a swig of pop. "Okay, your turn."

"My turn?"

"Spill. What was Belinda calling about back at the mansion and why did the cops show up?"

I sketched out what the medical examiner had learned about the dead man. Zack listened carefully, without interrupting.

"Looks like the break-ins are starting up again," Zack said. "I wonder…do you think the dead guy might be a Chicago Peale?"

"Dunno. It's a good possibility. I'll let the cops know."

"Better you than me, babe."

"Don't call me 'babe,'" I said. "Unless you want another jab in the groin."

"Only if you promise to call me…" he trailed off.

"Call you what?"

"Just call me." He grinned rakishly—Jesus, he had a cute smile—and I couldn't help the little laugh that burst out. "Oh, good. You *do* have a sense of humor."

In response, I emptied my tray into the trash and headed for the door. "You coming?"

He was right behind me. "Not yet. What do you have in mind?"

I paused for a moment, trying to decide if his answer had been an innuendo, then decided to let it slide. "The library. It's where I take all the hot men I meet."

"I was just there. Why should we—did you say 'hot men'?"

Had I said that out loud? Oh, shit. I could feel the blush begin. To cover, I put a winsome little smile on my face. "I'm making an exception in your case."

Now *he* looked confused about potential innuendo. Good. I led him outside.

Zack's bike was chained to my parking meter out front. We wedged it into the back of my Jeep with the front tire hanging out over the bumper and drove to the public library, a long, low building made of brick. They keep reference on the top floor, and I was glad to see Marge on duty behind the desk. Marge isn't a former client, but like most librarians, she loves serious researchers who don't abuse the library's equipment or materials. I approached the reference desk with a smile, and Marge looked up.

"You're back," she said with a smile that took ten years off her face.

I blinked at her. I hadn't visited the library in several days. Then I realized she was smiling at Zack, not me.

"I just can't get enough," he said, casually leaning on the desk with another rakish grin. The remark dripped with implications. I would have whacked his wang for it, but Marge actually simpered. I didn't think women did that anymore.

I none-too-gently elbowed Zack aside. "We need to look at *The Ann Arbor News* starting in 1947."

Marge handed me a form to fill out without taking her eyes off Zack. Annoyed, I scribbled my request on it. Marge bustled back to the enormous cabinets behind the reference desk and returned with a white box of microfilm spools.

"These are for 1947," she said. "Come back when you're done and I'll get you 1948."

I thanked her, but Zack had to go one further. "You're a wonder, Marge," he said over his shoulder as I towed him to the film readers and all but shoved him into a seat.

"What's with you?" he demanded in a low voice, though we had the readers to ourselves.

"Turn off the charm, Mr. Prince," I growled. "We're not impressed."

"A little social grease goes a long way in getting some help." He lifted a spool from the box and fed the film into the reader. "No reason to get jealous."

I gave a superior snort that said I felt no need to answer that, then fed my own spool into the reader and started skimming. Text slid slowly sideways on the screen in front of me as I rotated the wheel.

"What are we looking for, anyway?" Zack asked. "I told you I already checked the newspaper."

"All the stuff you told me about came from hard news," I said. "Did you check the society pages and the gossip columns?"

There was a pause. "No," Zack said in a small voice.

"Then let's get started," I said sweetly. "And this time be thorough, Mr. Prince."

He made no response. I plugged my iPod into my ears and settled into the Zen of research. Reading old newspapers on microfilm isn't easy. Text slips sideways, and it's easy to lose your place. After a while, headaches set in, if you aren't careful. Rather than read every word, I set my internal search engine to scan headlines for terms like "house," "mansion," "fire," "recluse," "burglary," "break-in," and "Peale." I also checked the gossip columns. They rarely had informative headlines, though, and I had to read them carefully. Zack worked in silence beside me. I was glad he didn't try to talk. Some people feel the need to fill the silence with chatter in these circumstances, even though talk is a distraction.

After two hours of eye-watering work, I came across a gossipy little item on the society pages. The date was June 15, 1949.

Can it be true? Have the Peales renounced society forever? A little bird says that Darlene Peale, the darlin' wife of Mr. Victor Peale, has flown the coop, taking daughter Nell with her. Can it be that Mr. Peale's eccentricities finally drove her away? Or maybe she couldn't find the legendary Peale family treasure? Everyone knows that dear Darlene married up, after all. Their two sons elected to stay with Dad, who hasn't been seen in public for months now. Even the help never see him, and rumor has it he wanders the hallways only at night. Exactly what goes on behind the walls of that mansion? And is the treasure still there?

Peale family treasure? My heart quickened. What kind of treasure? My imagination tossed up an image of a one-eyed pirate standing with a booted foot on a wooden chest, an image the rational side of my mind quickly dismissed. "Treasure" didn't have to be gold or jewels. It could be anything of value. But what? Belinda hadn't mentioned a family treasure. Maybe she didn't know about it. Or maybe she didn't want *us* to know about it. I read the column three times, but it didn't have anything else to say on the matter. Finally I shut off my iPod and showed the item to Zack. Fascination spread across his face like a sunrise.

"Treasure," he breathed. "Wonder what it is. Or was. Do you think it was destroyed in the Detroit fire?"

"Whoever wrote this column didn't think so," I pointed out.

"Okay, okay." Zack stood up and started to pace. "Let's go through this. There's a—"

Across the room, Marge pointedly cleared her throat and looked hard at Zack over her reading glasses, clearly reminding him he was in a library. He blushed boyishly, then gave her a sheepish little wave and lowered his voice, though he continued to pace a little.

"The Peales have some kind of treasure, but no one knows what kind."

"What makes you say that?" I said.

"If the gossip columnist had known, or even suspected, she would have said so."

"True," I conceded. "Can we assume the treasure is the reason the families kept breaking into each other's houses?"

"What do you mean?"

I gnawed a thumbnail. "Suppose both the Chicago Peales and the Detroit Peales felt…entitled to the treasure. Maybe the break-ins were attempts to steal the treasure back and forth. The Detroiters would steal it from the Chicagoans, who would then steal it back. Family rivalry. It would explain why Victor Peale didn't file charges against Edmund."

"I'm not sure I follow," Zack said, sitting down again. "Why not arrest the bozo who breaks into your house?"

"Because both sides wanted to keep the whole thing quiet. If you press charges, he's likely to blab about what it is he was trying to steal, and that would be entered into the police report."

"So why did they call the police at all?" Zack countered. "It looks like every time there was a break-in, someone notified the cops."

"I'm guessing the families either wanted to show the other side that they meant business, or they called the police before they realized the burglar was a family member. It's also possible that the servants called the police."

"The Peales could leave standing orders about that."

I rolled my eyes. "Right. 'Jeeves, if someone breaks into the house, don't call the police.' 'Why not, sir?' 'Because the person might be after our super-secret family treasure. Oh, and keep that to yourself.' Sure."

"Good point."

"So the two branches kept stealing the treasure back and forth until 1947. I'm betting Victor had it at the time his house caught fire, and everyone assumed the treasure was destroyed. That's why the break-ins stopped."

"But maybe the treasure *wasn't* destroyed," Zack finished.

"Exactly. I wonder if that's what the intruder was looking for—and what Uncle Lawrence wanted to show you."

"If everyone thought the treasure was destroyed," Zack said, "why would they be looking for it now?"

"Don't know. Someone may have found out about it just recently. Or we could be barking up the wrong tree and they might be looking for something else entirely." I knuckled both eyes. "Let's keep reading and see if anything else turns up."

Another hour went by. A headache knocked at the back of my eyeballs like a Jehovah's Witness on caffeine. Caffeine. When was the last time I'd had any? Lunch. And that had been hours ago. No wonder. Now that I was aware of it, the caffeine jones settled in for real. It felt like an emptiness, a very strange thirst that wouldn't be slaked by water or juice, and I knew the more I tried to ignore it, the worse it would get. Text blurred past me on the reader, and I decided I was likely to miss something important if I kept it up. I was just about to tell Zack I was knocking off for the day when he paused his reader.

"Here's something," he said. "Another gossip column. Says

a woman named Mary Bentwick has been putting the make on 'young, handsome Howard Peale.'"

I thought about the corpse with the coke-bottle glasses, the squishy one I had sunk my hand into. Not what you'd call handsome.

"The column also wonders," Zack continued, "if Miss Bentwick is just trying to get her hands on the 'legendary' Peale family papers."

"Papers?" I leaned over to look. "Is that a reference to the treasure or to something else?"

"Dunno. Paper burns, though, and that would explain why people might believe the treasure was destroyed in the Detroit fire."

"What kind of papers could be valuable enough to cause this kind of brouhaha?"

"A diary of a famous person," Zack hazarded. "Abraham Lincoln or Ulysses Grant or something. Or maybe it's a famous document. An original copy of the Declaration of Independence turned up a few years ago and went for something like eight million bucks at auction." His green eyes tracked farther down the microfilm page. "It also has a little history on the Peales. Not much, though. They probably just needed to fill some column space."

I tried to read it over his shoulder, but my eyes rebelled. "What's it say?"

"Just that the family originally came from Philadelphia and was there long before the American Revolution. The Peales are quite the old American family, then."

"Huh." I straightened, and the caffeine monster roared for attention. "Let's make copies of all this and call it a day. I need coffee."

Zack agreed, and we were outside in the harsh August sunlight a few minutes later. The air had gotten muggier, pressing down like a hot, wet weight. Leaves hung limp from the little sidewalk trees in front of the library. The effort of breathing was enough to make me sweat.

"Do you think Belinda knows about the treasure?" Zack asked as we walked slowly to my Jeep.

"I'll have to ask."

"Let's call," Zack urged.

I shook my head. "Much better to talk to her in person. Easier to tell if she's holding something back."

"Got it." He wiped sweat from his forehead with one sleeve. "We heading over there now?"

"*We* aren't doing anything," I said, pointing my remote key ring at the Jeep. It chirped like a baby bird and unlocked itself. "*I* am getting something caffeinated. *I* was thinking iced coffee. And then *I* have a few other leads to follow, including talking to Belinda."

Zack opened the passenger door and jumped in before I could say anything further. "I thought we were a team."

"We're a team only on my terms. Get out of my Jeep."

"I'll buy the iced coffee. How about that? And then, if you don't want me to come along, I won't."

I opened my mouth to refuse, order him to get his bike out of my Jeep, say I don't work with someone looking over my shoulder—unless it's Ms. Hawk.

What I said was, "Okay."

EIGHT

To MAKE MYSELF feel better about my runaway mouth, I chose the most expensive coffee shop in downtown Ann Arbor. It's on State Street near the University, a marble-walled place furnished with spindly wrought-iron furniture. I privately call it "Café Pretentious" because a thimbleful of coffee costs more than a gallon of gasoline. I ordered an iced latte, extra sugar, while Zack got an iced tea. For what he paid we could have bought dinner in a mid-priced restaurant, and I gave him a mean smile which seemed to go totally over his head. We found a table in the rear, and icy air from the air conditioning turned the sweat on my back into a clammy second skin.

"So what's a nice girl like you doing in a job like this?" Zack asked.

"Oh, man," I said. "What's a nice boy like you doing with a pick-up line like that?"

"I'm terrible at pick-up lines," Zack sighed. "I have to rely on my dazzling good looks instead."

He gave a wide, sexy smile that went all the way up to his enormous, sea-green eyes, and any appropriate retort I might have had sailed straight out the plate-glass window. Suddenly the AC didn't seem quite so cold. A little flush started at my cleavage and worked its way upward—and downward. I snorted in completely fake disdain and took a long pull from my iced coffee. Good move, as it turned out. Mama Caffeine worked her magic again. The jonesing instantly stopped, and revitalization flooded me down to my toes. Flush? What flush?

"Oh, yeah," I said huskily, licking milk from my upper lip. "That's what I need."

Zack gave me a long, peculiar look. "You're a real addict."

"Yep. I'd sell your mother for a good cappuccino." I took another drink. "So where'd you grow up, Zack?"

"Small talk?" he said. "That mean you like me enough to find out about my past?"

"Talking about you is a way to stop you trying to weasel my background out of me," I told him.

He rested his chin on one hand. "I love a mystery woman."

"So where'd you grow up?" I repeated. "No—let me guess. 'Here and there.'"

"You guessed!"

I saluted him with my coffee but didn't answer, deciding to see if he would fill the silence. An old trick, but people still fall for it.

Zack was no exception. "It didn't start off that way. I was actually born into a hippie commune."

I set my glass down with a click on the iron tabletop. "Get out."

"Absolute truth. Late seventies, and my parents were still totally into the hippie thing. They'd joined with a bunch of people who had a farm in Indiana. They grew their own food, as much as they could, and sold organic produce for what they couldn't. I grew up running around bare-ass naked among the tomatoes."

"Naked?" I laughed. "You didn't really."

"I did. The whole place was clothing optional. During summer I'd go days without wearing a stitch. So did most of the other kids."

I tried to imagine a troop of children rampaging through a vegetable patch while adults dressed in fringed ponchos pulled weeds and passed lit joints from hand to hand. "What about school?"

"We were home-taught. Mom told me later that she and the others took a lot of flak from the locals, actually. I remember the cops showing up a couple times. We kids were told to hide in the woods. We thought it was a kind of adventure, but I remember being scared they'd arrest Mom or Dad. They never did, though."

"So it really was a commune," I said.

"Yep." Zack sipped his tea, made a face, and stirred in several packets of sugar. "It didn't last, though. Eventually infighting started and people started leaving. I kind of suspect the free-love thing works better on paper than in practice. When Alice slips out of Ben's bed and into Charlie's, Ben can't help feeling jealous, you know? And you have the people who get high all the time instead of working the farm but still show up at every meal. Puts a strain on relations. When I was about nine, my parents put their few possessions into a VW bus and we took off."

"A VW bus?" I said. "Now you're going to tell me you followed the Grateful Dead around."

"Well, yeah. Mom and Dad lived by selling beadwork and stuff to Deadheads. We drifted around for three or four years, actually. Finally, though, Mom had enough. I remember the night she and Dad had it out. I knew it was serious because she called him Arthur instead of Stardust."

"Nooooo," I said. "You can't mean it. They used actual hippie names? It must've been the eighties by then."

"Not to the Deadheads. I was eight before I found out Dad's real name."

"What was your Mom's name?"

"Her real name is Eileen, but she went by Greenflower."

"And your name?" I asked, blinking coquettishly.

"Not important." His face went a little pink.

"You're blushing," I said, quick to press my advantage. "I don't believe it! Come on, come on. Give! I saved your life twice, so you owe me."

Zack picked up his iced tea and muttered something into it.

I leaned forward. "What was that? I didn't quite hear you."

"It was...they called me...Rainbow Sunshine."

Okay, I tried. I really, really tried. But the laugh burst out before I could stop it. Zack's blush deepened even farther. I laughed again and dabbed at my eyes with a napkin.

"Rainbow Sunshine," I said. "That's some fine blackmail material there."

"That's right—make fun of my childhood tragedies, including my broken home and rootless upbringing."

"I'm sorry," I giggled, and reached across the table to pat his hand. "I'm imagining your mother calling you in to dinner. 'Rainbow Suuuunshiiiine! Time for dinner! And the cops are coming later, so put some clothes on!'"

Zack gave a small laugh at that. "Yeah, yeah. Fine."

"So what happened that day your mom called your dad Arthur?"

"Mom said that they couldn't raise a kid in the back of a bus anymore. Dad said I was turning out just fine, but Mom wouldn't hear it. Either Dad had to settle down and get a real job or she would get a divorce. In the morning, Dad was gone. I never saw him again."

"Oh, God," I said, feeling suddenly contrite. "I'm sorry."

"It was a long time ago," Zack said with a shrug. "Mom got a waitress job and then a secretarial job and I went to a real school for the first time. Eventually I grew up and I became a photographer. So it's really true—I *did* grow up here and there."

These last sentences came out in a rush. Zack was leaving out quite a lot, that much was obvious. On the other hand, how much detail could you go into over iced caffeine?

"Does this place have a restroom?" he asked, intruding on my musing. "I'm starting to realize I didn't go once the whole time we were in the library."

I know all the caffeine joints in Ann Arbor like I know my own bedroom, and I jerked a thumb over my shoulder. "Back that way."

While he was gone, I pulled out my phone and called Ms. Hawk's cell. She answered on the first ring.

"Don't we have a favor coming from a police detective in Chicago?" I asked.

"We do," Ms. Hawk said. I heard birdsong behind her and figured she must be outside somewhere. "Why?"

I glanced at the restroom door. Still shut, but how long would Zack be gone? "I don't have time to give details now," I said. "Can I call her up? I need some information for the Peale case."

Ms. Hawk paused only a moment. "Of course. Let me put you on hold and I'll check my phone records." She clicked away, then came back to read me a name and Chicago phone number. I thanked her, promised again to explain later, and hung up. Still no sign of Zack, so I dialed the number. Two rings later, a woman picked up.

"Is this Jackie Gold?" I asked.

"It is," she replied. "Who's calling, please?"

"My name is Terry Faye, and I work for Hawk Enterprises. We helped you with a personal problem several months ago? When your daughter was dating that drug dealer?"

"Oh, right." Jackie gave a little laugh. "I think that guy is *still* running. How are things in Ann Arbor?"

I did the small-talk thing, then said, "I wanted to know if you could help me with a little favor."

Most clients get a little quiet at this point, and Jackie Gold was no exception. I think they're afraid we're going to demand more money or ask them to do something dangerous.

"What sort of favor?" she asked at last. I heard a chair creak and imagined she was at her desk, leaning backward.

"I want to know if you have anything on a family named Peale. They're out your way."

"The Peales?" She sounded startled. "Why do you want to know about them?"

"It's for a case," I said. "I take it you've heard of them."

"Of course I've heard of them. Everybody in Chicago has heard of them."

I cocked an eye toward the bathroom door. "What can you tell me?"

"They specialize in…imports," Jackie said dryly. "Have for generations, near as we can tell. It's a family business that goes all the way back to the Civil War, when they brought in illegal rum. Once Prohibition started, it was alcohol of any kind. From there they got into drugs. The current head of the family is one Quentin Peale, and he's a right bastard."

Interesting. "Any busts?"

"Small-time stuff. Possession, usually. We've never gotten proof of anything worse than that, hard as we've tried. They just keep bringing stuff in, and we keep missing them. They probably have eyes and ears in the force, but no one's been able to prove that, either." She paused. "It's funny you should call me about them just now."

"Oh?"

"Yeah. Rumor on the street has it that Quentin Peale's usual customers haven't been getting their regular shipments lately. Coke, heroin and crack supplies—all running low. The dealers are getting antsy, and prices are going up."

"Really."

Zack emerged from the restroom and headed back to our table. I gave him a little smile but kept my attention on the phone.

"Yep," Jackie said. "We're hearing from the usual sources that the Peales are importing something new these days, but no one seems to know exactly what it is."

"Is anyone speculating?" I asked. Zack cocked his head at me, silently asking who I was talking to, but I ignored him.

"Oh, sure. Weapons. Terrorists. Cuban cigars. You name it, someone's brought it up. But come down to it, we don't have a clue."

"Can you e-mail me some names and addresses for these people?" I asked.

"The Peales?" Jackie said. "Sure. It's public information,

so that's no problem. Is that all you wanted to know? I mean, it's not like this was privileged or anything."

"Maybe not, but the information helps me a lot. If there's anything else you can think of, give me a call or send me an e-mail."

"Sure. No problem."

"This repays that favor," I said, and we clicked off.

"What was that all about?" Zack asked.

I put my phone back in my pocket. "Nothing important."

"It was about the case, wasn't it?"

"Nothing you have to worry about," I said, draining the last of my coffee.

He narrowed his eyes. "It's because I'm a man. You don't trust me because I'm a guy."

"If you want to think that, go right ahead," I said heartlessly and got up. "I have to get home. It's almost supper time, and the Biemers wait for no one."

He followed me to the door. "The Biemers?"

This necessitated a subject-changing explanation of my living circumstances, which Zack seemed to find fascinating.

"It's an honest-to-God boarding house?" he said. "I didn't think they existed anymore."

"They're hard to find," I admitted, chirping open my Jeep. It was parked on State Street, out in front of Café Pretentious. "You'd better get your bike out of the back unless you want to walk home."

He obeyed with poor grace. I gave him a little wave and turned the key in the ignition. My trusty little Jeep turned over, made some coughing noises, and died. Uh oh. I tried again. Cough, cough, sputter, sputter, death. I glanced in my rearview mirror. Zack was standing on the sidewalk with his bicycle, clearly trying not to smirk. I ignored him and tried a third time, with no better result. Swearing, I popped the hood, got out, and looked underneath.

I know some car basics. I can change a flat and change my oil, for example, and I can tell if the battery is disconnected or a cap is loose. Anything more complicated than that, and I'm lost. I could smell gasoline, which wasn't a good sign, but other than that, I couldn't see anything wrong.

Zack came up behind me. "Won't start, eh?"

"No, I just thought I'd drive from under the hood for a change," I said in a deadly even tone. "I don't suppose you know anything about cars, he-man that you claim to be."

"Nope." He gestured at his bike. "Great reason to ride one of these. Not much goes wrong that you can't fix on the spot."

"Great." I slammed the hood down. My hands had that swipe of greasy dirt you always get when you open a car hood. "Now I have to call a tow truck, and then I have to get home, and I'm going to miss supper. And, no, I won't go to supper with you."

"Wasn't going to ask." Zack mounted his bike. "Guess I'll see you later."

I stared after him as he pedaled away, not sure if his parting remarks made me feel better or worse. I called my auto club, and they said a tow truck would arrive within the hour. Nothing to do after that but wait. I stood fuming in the shade of the coffee house. I tried to tell myself that this was a minor inconvenience, that in a week I'd barely remember the incident, but I just got madder and madder about it. Caffeine fix notwithstanding, I was hot, I was hungry and I was tired from crawling around a filthy house and reading blurry microfilms all day.

At last the tow truck arrived. The driver hooked up my Jeep with easy efficiency and asked where I wanted it towed. I gave him the name of my usual mechanic. Dave's place is a little pricey, but he's downtown and easy to get to.

"You want to ride with?" the tow-truck driver asked.

I checked my watch. Supper had just started at the Biemers'. With luck, I could make it before the dishes were cleared. "I'll call a cab," I said, and gave the driver my Jeep key.

The tow truck drove off. I called Dave to tell him my Jeep was on the way, then called a cab company.

"It's rush hour," the dispatcher said. "So it'll probably be half an hour or more before someone gets there."

More anger, mixed with disappointment. There went supper. I'm not sure why I had so much invested in getting home in time for dinner. Probably because the day was turning rotten and Mrs. Biemer's cooking took the term "comfort food" to new heights. I didn't want to grab something at a restaurant or pick through leftovers when I got home. I wanted a home-cooked meal, but I wasn't going to—

A horn beeped, and an ancient brown VW bus pulled into the parking space recently vacated by my Jeep. I stared as Zack leaned across the cab and pushed the passenger door open.

"Hey, lady," he said with a grin. "Need a ride?"

I could have kissed him. Instead, I hopped inside and slammed the door. The bus's interior smelled of hot vinyl and old carpeting. An antique peace medallion hung from the rearview mirror.

"My God, it's all true," I said in awe.

"Yep." Zack put the bus into gear and guided it carefully into traffic. "Where to, ma'am?"

I told him, and Zack set out. It looked weird, seeing him behind the wheel of a vehicle instead of on a bicycle. The muscles on his forearms bunched and moved as he wrenched the wheel around. No power steering. All the windows were open, and hot August air blew gently over us. No AC. I glanced behind me. The rear of the van was piled with closed metal boxes, the kind with padding inside. Photography equipment, probably. Benches lined the sides, and I could make out places where other stuff had once been fastened to the walls. A stove and table, maybe, for people who followed deadheads around the country?

"Thanks for this," I said. "Especially after I was so bitchy at you earlier."

"I'll be gallant and blame it on low blood sugar," he said

airily. "God willing and the creek don't rise, we'll have you home in time for dinner. Most of it, anyway."

True to his word, we pulled into the Biemers' driveway less than fifteen minutes later. I invited Zack inside, and he accepted. Everyone was already at the table, of course—supper was halfway over. I introduced Zack to a chorus of hellos, and Mrs. Biemer jumped up to get an extra place setting. The Biemers don't mind the occasional dinner guest, as long as it's occasional.

Lasagna was on the menu for tonight, and smells of cheesy tomato sauce filled the dining room. Garlic bread lay half-covered under a towel on a cutting board, and crisp green salad mounded a bowl. Zack and I were washing our hands in the kitchen when Mrs. Biemer bustled up behind me with a manila envelope.

"This was in the mail for you," she said. "It looks important, so I thought I'd better give it to you now."

I dried my hands on a dishtowel and accepted the envelope. It was a little stiff, and my name and address were printed in neat block letters on the front. So were the words *Urgent! Open Immediately!* It didn't have a stamp or a postmark. When I pointed this out to Mrs. Biemer, she blinked.

"I didn't notice that," she said. "It was in with the rest of today's mail."

I set the envelope on the counter and examined it, Zack staring over my shoulder. Out in the dining room, flatware clanked against plates as dinner continued.

"Do you think it's dangerous?" Zack asked quietly.

"I doubt it," I said. "It's not thick enough to be a…to be anything nasty." I had been going to say "bomb," but didn't want to use that word with Mrs. Biemer in the room. Finally I picked up a paring knife and slit the envelope on two sides so I could get at the contents without sticking my fingers inside. I have to admit I was more than a little nervous. The FBI never did catch that anthrax guy. On the other hand, I didn't think it'd be a good idea to call the police for something like this. It might just be private information, something I wouldn't *want* the cops to see.

I peeled back one corner. Glossy black and white images looked back at me. Photographs. I set the knife aside and pulled them out with Zack and Mrs. Biemer continuing to hover nearby. Puzzled, I flipped through them.

All of them were of me. Six of them showed me examining the outside of Uncle Lawrence's house. Another three showed me walking up to and entering the Biemers' house. What the hell? I turned to Zack.

"Did you take these?" I demanded.

"Nuh uh," he said. "For one thing, I'd do a much better job. And I certainly wouldn't send them to you anonymously."

"So who took them?" Mrs. Biemer asked. "And why?"

Feeling uneasy, I checked the back of each photo. On the rear of the last one was written, *We know where you live. Mind your own business.*

NINE

THE NEXT HOUR was a flurry of activity. Henrietta Flinch and Carl dela Cort came, took the photos, and left. Ms. Hawk came, made sure I was all right, and left.

Zack vanished moments before the detectives arrived. Was I surprised?

Slava paced the front porch, waving her arms. I had called her right after getting hold of Ms. Hawk and the police. I wasn't entirely sure why I did until she rushed over and her expansive voice filled the porch. Her outrage on my behalf calmed me down, as if she were siphoning away the trickle of unease the package had given me.

"Who would so such a thing?' she boomed. "I will cut his genitals off with a dull knife—*thwack!* Just like KGB."

"Thanks, Slava," I said, unable to hold back a smile. "I might let you."

She rounded on me. "Did you have supper?"

Her words reminded me that I hadn't, and my stomach growled. Slava caught the noise and nodded.

"I thought not. You wait here. I get food from Mrs. Biemer."

I sat in a wicker chair while Slava went into the house and returned bearing a microwaved plate of hot lasagna and a can of cold pop. I slugged down some soda first—caffeine fix— then started in on Mrs. Biemer's delicious lasagna.

Some of the other boarders popped out to see what was going on, but Slava bullied them into going back inside, for which I was grateful. I didn't feel like explaining everything yet again, and I wasn't up to reassuring anyone that there was no danger, partly because my overactive imagination put snipers on nearby rooftops and bombs in my closet.

"So," Slava said as I finished the last bit of lasagna. "Is this a cheesecake emergency? I bring some with me."

"I'm not that upset," I repeated in exasperation. Then I glanced toward the shopping bag at Slava's feet. "What kind of cheesecake?"

Slava, it turned out, had two kinds with her—a slice each of cherry and blueberry from Zingerman's deli. She produced plastic forks, and we dug in. My spirits steadied with every melty bite.

As I was spearing the last bit of graham-cracker crust, my cell rang. I jumped and all but tore it open, expecting to hear Ms. Hawk's voice, or even Zack's. It was Dave down at the garage calling to tell me he was swamped and wouldn't be able to look at my Jeep until late afternoon tomorrow. Was that all right? I told him it was and hung up.

Slava stayed with me, and we holed up in my room watching *The Two Towers* on DVD. Slava isn't a big Orlando Bloom fan, but she always says, "Viggo Mortensen has nice ass, so I watch him run with little dwarf."

She left when the movie ended, and I surprised myself by falling almost instantly asleep. Ms. Hawk called in the morning as I was finishing up a short stack of pancakes in the dining room.

"I talked to Ms. Harris," she said. "She says she has no idea who might have sent those photographs, and I believe her. I also checked with the police. They have finished with the house and it is no longer a crime scene. We can enter it again."

"We?" I said.

"Both of us. Shall we meet there in half an hour?"

Pride tingled in my chest—Ms. Hawk hadn't even asked if I wanted off the case. I wasn't working out today, so I told Ms. Hawk half an hour would be fine. At that moment, the taxi I had called for pulled up—my Jeep still with Dave—and honked.

I spent the ride to the house in a pensive mood about the photos. I didn't think there was any real danger. Yet. If whoever had taken those pictures had wanted me dead, I would be dead. Just as easy to aim a rifle scope as a telephoto lens. Except I didn't know if the sender had sent the pictures in the hope I'd back away from his bluff, or if he was firing a warning shot across my bow, with real bullets to follow.

Their mistake was, I don't appreciate *anything* going across my bow, let alone warning shots. Sure, I'd been uneasy yesterday, but now I wanted even more to know what was going on and what the hell was in that house.

I had the driver make two important detours on the way. First we stopped at the office so I could grab my Glock from the safe. I checked to make sure it was loaded and holstered it in my supply belt. The cabbie didn't show any signs of noticing the addition when I got back to the car.

Second, we stopped at the Sweetwater Café. I ran inside and emerged a moment later with a large foam cup filled to the brim, which I then poured into my insulated canteen. What more can you need in the world?

Ms. Hawk's car was already parked in the mansion's gravel driveway. The vehicle looked oddly new and clean amid the aging squalor around it. I paid the cab driver, included a generous tip for all the stopping, and trotted around back, my supply belt dragging at my waist.

The back door was open at the bottom of the stone steps, and I gingerly crossed the threshold into musty darkness. "Hello?" I called, and realized there was no way Ms. Hawk would hear me with all the boxes of junk to absorb sound. Flashlight out, I wound my way along the now-familiar cardboard pathways to the kitchen stairs.

The kitchen was still in a state of disarray, though I couldn't remember enough about the place's condition to tell if anyone had gone through it again since yesterday. I wandered into the dusty dining room, letters still scattered across the floor, and then to the stuffy study beyond, calling for Ms. Hawk all the while. Still no answer. I was getting nervous. The house was still full of traps and perhaps even an intruder. Ms. Hawk could have fallen victim to either one. What if she were lying on the floor somewhere, broken or bleeding? I tried to call her cell phone, but all I got was a No Signal message.

Rather than try to renegotiate the labyrinth of boxes at the front of the house, I returned to the dining room and went up the shoe staircase, barely remembering to skip every other step. My heart started to pound. Ms. Hawk might be in trouble, and I needed to—

I almost crashed into her at the top of the stairs. Ms. Hawk was wearing khakis and a ball cap again. The hawk pendant glittered at her throat. She held up a battery-operated camping lantern like a hermit seeking the truth.

"There you are," she said. The fluorescent light of the lantern gave her face an eerie cast. "Mr. Archer is already here. We're continuing the survey from yesterday."

"Zack is here?" I blurted.

"Ears burning," Zack said, appearing from the gloom of the hallway.

For some reason, the idea that Zack and Ms. Hawk had been working together when I wasn't around really bugged me. I took a swig of coffee from my canteen to cover my annoyance. "So what are we doing?"

"I was about to check the third floor," Ms. Hawk said. "Mr. Archer here was going to examine two more rooms on this one. Why don't you come up with me, Terry? There are more rooms up there, and they will require more people to search."

"You smell like coffee," Zack said as I passed by him. "Got a sip for me?"

I handed him my canteen. "You realize what a sacrifice this is. Every drop is gold."

"You are a fine and generous soul," he said, clasping his free hand over his heart. "I am not worthy."

"Damn right," I said. Then I noticed I was smiling.

"Did anything else happen last night?" Ms. Hawk asked.

"Just a whole lot of cheesecake and Orlando Bloom with Slava."

Zack swallowed a mouthful of coffee. "Okay, I figured out the cheeseburger thing, and cheesecake goes without saying, but I would never have guessed Orlando Bloom."

"You did say you love a mystery woman," I replied blandly. "Why'd you cut out before the cops showed up? Again."

He shrugged indifferently. "I told you. Cops don't like reporters. And my ex-hippie parents did manage to instill *some* values."

"Never trust The Man?" I said.

"Right up there with 'Cops are pigs.' The police make me nervous, so why hang around?"

"Yes, well," Ms. Hawk said. "I believe we were going upstairs, Terry?"

Ms. Hawk and I made our way through the stacks of junk to the pan staircase at the far end of the hallway while Zack remained behind to check the last couple of rooms. My boss and I climbed carefully up the pot-and-pan staircase with Ms. Hawk holding the camping lantern above her head. I admired her forethought. The lantern cast light in all directions instead of in a single beam and made it easier to see. Metal clanked and clattered as we climbed, and a whiff of rotten meat wafted down to me. Great. No bodies, but the smell of decay was still hanging around.

Halfway up the stairs, I felt for the canteen at my belt. It wasn't there. I had left it with Zack. Dammit! No way was I going to investigate dusty, smelly rooms without my drug of choice at hand.

"I'll catch up," I told Ms. Hawk. "I forgot something."

She waved a hand, and I went back downstairs, avoiding as many pans as I could—the noise grated on me. I entered the narrow, cardboard-lined hall, my footfalls hushed by looming piles of nothing. My eyes had adjusted to the dim light, but I was reaching for my flashlight anyway when I saw something strange. Ahead of me, Zack's flashlight beam was shining on a door at waist height. It took me a moment to make out that Zack was kneeling in front of the door holding the flashlight in his mouth and doing something to the lock. Metal glinted. I stared. A moment later, I heard a scraping click. Zack straightened with a satisfied grunt, opened the door, and vanished into the room beyond.

I continued to stare. What the hell was he doing with picklocks? And where had he learned to use them? I doubted they taught locksmithery at the hippie commune. My first instinct was to rush in and confront him, but I checked myself. Being able to pick locks isn't illegal, and neither is owning a set of picks. Hell, Ms. Hawk is a dab hand at it, and even I can open a simple spring lock without a key. But it's still a little suspicious when someone else turns up with the skill. I also remembered the scratches on the lock to the basement door, the ones Ms. Hawk and I spotted when we first arrived at the *maison d' trash.*

I waited for a count of fifty, then strolled casually down the hallway and into the room. The door, I noticed, was the one with the Beebo's warning to stay out tacked to it. The interior was lit by an unblocked window, just like the bicycle room, and I blinked at the unaccustomed illumination.

A bookshelf took up one wall, and the other three were lined with pigeonhole shelving. The pigeonholes themselves overflowed with paper. Shoeboxes were stacked knee-high all over the floor. Zack stood with his back to me, examining some papers he had pulled from a pigeonhole. What drew my eye, however, was the bed.

It was an old-fashioned iron-framed thing with a thin mattress over sagging metal springs. It was neatly made with a green blanket and flattened pillow in a grayish pillowcase. Next to the bed sat a small nightstand with a reading light and a windup alarm clock. The clock was ticking.

"Wasn't this door locked?" I asked, hoping Zack would jump or scream or shit a brick.

No such luck. He calmly turned around, still holding the

papers. "Guess not," he said in a perfectly natural voice. "Must've just been stuck."

I was all set to string him along, keep my knowledge a secret, but then my mouth said, "Liar."

Zack raised an eyebrow. "Sorry?"

"I saw you pick that lock, and now you're lying about it. What's up with that?"

"If you saw me do it, why didn't you say so?"

"You're evading."

"And you're nosy. Belinda—your client—wants me here, remember?"

"Answer the question, Sunshine," I said. "Why pick the lock and lie about it?"

"Because people always think someone who can pick locks is crooked," he said. "You're thinking it right now."

"Am not," I lied.

"Are so."

"Am n—oh, never mind. Just give me my canteen back." He did so, and I jerked a thumb at the nightstand. "Sounds like someone's been winding that alarm clock. Uncle Lawrence?"

"Could be." Zack went back to examining papers.

I turned away from the bed and pulled a handful of papers of my own from a nearby pigeonhole. It was a series of bank statements from 1969. A fair amount of money had been in Uncle Howard's account back then. I put the statements back and checked the papers from the next hole over. Bank statements from 1970. The hole below it contained a stack of canceled checks, all from the same year. Below that was 1970's utility bills.

"This place seems to be a little more organized than the rest of the house," I mused aloud. Dry dust coated my fingers. "If this whole room is full of records, it might be a good place to look for the uncles' wills."

"Uh huh." Zack was methodically pulling down papers, glancing at them, and putting them back. His face wore a look of heavy concentration. Dust motes danced in the air in the

golden sunlight around him, making it look like he was standing in a cloud of fairy dust. He had rolled his sleeves halfway
up his forearms, displaying fine, corded muscle.

"Terry?" Ms. Hawk peered into the room. "Aren't you coming upstairs?"

I jerked my eyes away from Zack. "Sorry. I came down to
get my canteen and saw Zack in here. It seems a likely place
to search."

"We really should complete the survey first," Ms. Hawk
said, though I saw her eyes roam over the old records with
obvious interest.

"You go ahead," Zack said. "I'll let you know if I come
across anything."

His tone was a little too casual for my taste. Because he
wanted us to leave? In that case, no way was I going to leave
him in here alone.

"We might save ourselves a lot of time and effort if we
search here first," I countered.

"That's all right," Zack said. "You go on."

I shot Ms. Hawk a quick glance, then flicked my eyes at
Zack. Ms. Hawk didn't visibly react, but said, "No, I think
Terry has a point. Let's see what the three of us can find."

"Sure. Fine," Zack said. Was his face a little tight, or was
I being overly suspicious? I couldn't tell.

The three of us each took a wall of pigeonholes and set to
work. Everything was definitely well-organized. Each column
held records for a certain year, and each row was a different
type of record. Statements and bills on the upper rows, letters
in the middle rows, and miscellaneous stuff toward the bottom. It was like a giant spreadsheet, really. I sifted through
several sets of records, often having to shake dust off the papers. One thing I noticed was that the records before 1967 were
all in Victor Peale's name. By 1968, everything was in
the name of either Lawrence or Howard Peale. I pointed this
out to Zack and Ms. Hawk.

"So Victor must have died in 1967," I finished. "He left

several million to his two sons, but I'm not finding stock certificates or anything like that. Sold off to pay debts, I'm guessing."

Ms. Hawk was down at the far end of the pigeonholes. The last two columns were completely empty, and she was examining the last sets of papers. "These bank statements are for just this year," she said. "They had a few dollars, nothing more, until just a few weeks ago. Look—a deposit for nine thousand, nine hundred dollars."

"What?" Zack looked up. He had shifted from pigeonholes to shoeboxes. "Where did the uncles come up with ninety-nine hundred bucks?"

"The bank is required to report any cash transaction of ten thousand dollars or more to the IRS," Ms. Hawk said. "I suppose they received ten thousand in cash and deposited all but the last hundred to avoid attention."

"That must be how they paid their property taxes at the last minute," I mused. "Are there withdrawals?"

Ms. Hawk shuffled through the papers. "Several, including one for almost seven thousand dollars. Property-tax payment, I'm sure."

Zack gasped. "Oh. Oh, God."

"What's wrong?" I demanded.

There was some frantic shuffling of papers over at Zack's shoebox. "I think I found the uncles' wills. Look." He held up two pieces of paper. "'I, Howard Peale, being of sound mind and body, yada yada yada.'"

"Does it really say 'yada, yada, yada'?" I asked. "Doesn't seem too sound of mind if he did."

"Har har." Zack read quickly. "Looks like Howard left everything to Lawrence. Let's look at the other one...uh huh. Yep."

"What?" Ms. Hawk said.

"Lawrence left everything to Howard."

I blew out a heavy breath. "Belinda's going to love that. People who die intestate are a real pain in the patootie."

"Patootie?" Zack echoed. "What kind of word is that?"

"One that's more genteel than the one you were thinking," I replied primly. "I'm in a ladylike mood for once. What else is in that shoebox?"

Zack rustled through it, sitting cross-legged on the floor with more shoeboxes piled around him. "The uncles' birth certificates, a death certificate for Victor Peale—Terry was right, he did die in 1967—and…huh. A divorce decree."

"For whom?" Ms. Hawk said.

"Darlene and Victor Peale. It's dated 1949, just like that gossip column."

"Not easy to get a divorce back then," I said. "Does it say anything about kids?"

More rustling. "Nope. That's it. But there's another box underneath this one. Let's see if…ah! A transcript of a hearing. Whoa. It's a carbon copy of a document done on a typewriter. Haven't seen *that* in a while."

"Tell us what it says, Mr. Archer," said Ms. Hawk.

Zack's eyes tracked quickly across the pages. "Darlene Peale is suing for divorce. Says her husband Victor Peale keeps a strange house. Never lets her throw anything away. Piles of junk everywhere. Mr. Peale never goes out, lives like a hermit, bad climate for teenage sons Howard and Lawrence and ten-year-old daughter Nell."

"Nell must be Belinda's mother," I said. "That gossip column mentioned her."

"Sounds about right. A social worker testified that the house was dark and dreary, that Nell was pale and sickly, that the boys were overly shy and anti-social." Zack furrowed his forehead. "Now that's interesting. The judge granted the divorce and gave custody of Nell to her mother Darlene. But both Howard and Lawrence begged the judge to let them stay with their father. The judge agreed to it because, and I'm quoting, 'These young men are old enough to know their own minds.'"

"Which is why they stayed with the house and why Belinda and her mother were so far away from it." I sank thoughtfully onto the squeaky bed. "So let me reconstruct a few events. Victor Peale marries a woman named Darlene in Detroit. Their house is broken into several times by their Chicago relatives. The two branches are stealing some kind of paper treasure back and forth, maybe. The house in Detroit burns to the ground and everyone assumes the papers are destroyed, but they actually aren't. Victor, Darlene, their two teenage boys and their young daughter all move to Ann Arbor, where Victor has this house built. Victor becomes a recluse, either because of trauma from the fire or because he's afraid that word of the papers will get out or a combination of both. Eventually Darlene gets fed up with it and divorces Victor. She takes their daughter Nell with her, but their sons—and the papers—stay with Victor. Nell grows up away from her father, marries, and eventually has a daughter named Belinda. Victor dies in 1967, leaving a tidy fortune to Lawrence and Howard. The papers, meanwhile, are still somewhere in the house. Lawrence runs into Zack, here, and offers to show him something, starting with pressed leaves but maybe, eventually, the papers. Before he can do it, however, Uncle Howard dies in bed, and people start breaking into the house again. One of them trips a trap and is suffocated in a pile of magazines. It's possible everyone involved is looking for the papers. Did I miss anything?"

"That about sums it up," Zack said. "Except for the fact that if I wanted to hide some valuable papers in this house, I know where I'd do it."

"Yes," Ms. Hawk said, and her gaze went to the enormous number of them neatly shelved in pigeonholes. My heart sank, and I did a quick count. There were two hundred columns and twenty rows. That made four thousand pigeonholes. Each hole looked to be about four inches wide, four inches tall, and twelve inches deep. I pulled out my cell phone and called up the calculator function. Each hole had a hundred and ninety-two cubic inches. Multiply that by four thousand holes, divide by one hundred forty-four, and you had something like five thousand three hundred cubic feet of paper to search. And that didn't include the shoeboxes.

"So what's the bad news?" Zack asked, trying to peer over my shoulder.

"We'll be older than the uncles before we find anything," I said. "There has to be a way to narrow it down. If we knew what we were looking for, that would help a little. I mean, this entire house is organized—in its own weird way—and the uncles wouldn't stash a treasure someplace where they couldn't find it themselves, right? So it must be someplace findable. We just have to figure out where that would be."

"And how do we do that?" Zack asked. "Short of resurrecting Uncle Howard and asking him?"

I gestured at the ticking clock. "Someone's been winding that thing. I'm willing to bet Uncle Lawrence is still alive. He may even be the intruder we chased. He would know everything."

"Assuming we can even find him," Zack grumbled. "And why would he try to hurt you with that avalanche of pans? And why didn't he report his brother's death? And did he kill the magazine guy?"

"All questions to ask when we catch up with him," Ms. Hawk said. "Meanwhile, we could go through the bookcase over there. All the other books in the house are in the parlor, so why are these up here? The answer might be a clue."

I readily agreed and crossed the creaky wooden floor to the bookcase, carefully stepping around piles of shoeboxes. The room didn't have anything personal in it. No pictures or posters, no decorations. I didn't even see any clothes. Did Uncle Lawrence just root around in the hallways to forage for something to wear?

The three of us spread out in front of the wide bookshelf, me on the left, Ms. Hawk in the middle, and Zack on the right. I ran my finger across several bindings.

"These books aren't dusty," I said. "Someone reads them regularly."

"A History of the American People," Zack read aloud, his head cocked sideways as he looked at titles. *"Constitutional History. Great Issues in American History, Volume I* and *Volume II. How the Constitution Was Created. American History for Dummies. American History to 1877.* Anyone seeing a theme here?"

I pulled down a volume at random and flipped it open. The pages fell open to a chapter about the establishment and ratification of the United States Constitution. I riffled the pages to see if anything fell out. Nothing did. The flyleaf was inscribed with *Property of Lawrence Peale* written with a fountain pen. I put the book back and took down *Your American Heritage.* It also fell open to a section about the Constitution. So did *American History: A Survey* and *Great Historical Events of America.* In the latter I found an underlined passage:

In 1789, George Washington ordered fourteen copies of the Bill of Rights printed up. He signed them and wrote "1789 Proposed amendments to the Constitution of the United States" on the back of each one, then sent thirteen copies by thirteen horses to each of the colonies so their governors and assemblies could discuss them for ratification. The fourteenth copy he kept with him in Philadelphia.

Weird. I called Zack and Ms. Hawk over to have a look and pointed out that all the books I'd looked at were creased at similar areas.

"There's even a single volume of the *World Book Encyclopedia,*" I said, pointing. "It covers the letter *C.*"

"Another obsession?" Zack said. "The uncles love junk and Constitutional history?"

"The Constitution and the Bill of Rights are written on paper," I observed. "You don't suppose…"

"Right," Zack scoffed. "They have the originals somewhere here in this house and a fake is on display in Washington, DC?"

"The Peales came from Philadelphia," I pointed out. "That's where all this stuff came down. The Peale family papers might not be the Constitution itself, but they might be related to it somehow. You yourself told us about that copy of the Declaration of Independence that turned up."

"What do you two make of this?" Ms. Hawk asked. She was holding a spiral-bound notebook. The wires were bent, the blue cover was battered and half torn off. A pencil had been slipped among the wires. She opened the notebook onto a list of figures. I ran my eyes down it. It looked like a schedule. There were listings for arrivals, departures and number of "parcels" delivered. I took the notebook from Ms. Hawk and leafed through it. The notebook listed two locations— a warehouse in Chicago, and a warehouse in Detroit. At the top of the first page was a set of map coordinates: 41E59' N, 83E08' W. Someone had circled them in red.

"What are these coordinates for?" I wondered aloud.

"I'd need a map or computer to pinpoint them," Ms. Hawk said, "but at first glance, they appear to point toward a spot near the southeastern coast of Michigan, out where the Detroit River becomes Lake Erie."

I stole an admiring glance at Ms. Hawk. It would have taken me several minutes to figure that out, and that's assuming I had a map in front of me.

"An island, then?" Zack said. "Or a rendezvous point for a ship?"

"Or both," I said. I leafed through the notebook some more. "These records start last February and end last May."

"Exactly when Ms. Harris stopped hearing from her uncles," Ms. Hawk said. "I wonder if Howard Peale died in his bed in May."

We searched the rest of the bookshelf but found nothing else of interest. By now it was past lunchtime and my thermos was empty, so we decided to call it a day for now.

Ms. Hawk took the notebook back from me, then picked up the dusty shoebox containing the wills, divorce decrees, and other documents. "I think we should meet with Ms. Harris to discuss these matters. Perhaps she can tell us more."

Outside, I inhaled the fresh, hot air with appreciation. A gentle breeze stirred the trees and birds sang. It was always a relief to leave the uncles' cramped, dark house. Zack pedaled away on his bicycle, and Ms. Hawk offered me a lift home so I could clean up and grab something to eat. On the way home, I called Belinda on my cell and asked if she could meet us later at the office. She was only too glad to agree.

Ms. Hawk dropped me off, waved, and backed out of the driveway. Not for the first time, I wondered where Ms. Hawk lived. I had never been to her house—apartment? Condo? Hell, I didn't even know if she lived in Ann Arbor. All the paperwork I had ever seen had the office's address on it, and her phone number went straight to her cell. No mention of a home address anywhere. For all I knew, she commuted from Zimbabwe.

I went in, and for the third time in as many days, I peeled off sweaty, dusty clothes and took a shower in the afternoon. I'd have to do laundry pretty soon—I was running out of adventure clothes. A gal only has so many sports bras and khaki slacks.

As I was heading out the door, a sandwich in my hand, my cell chirped. It was Dave, calling to tell me my Jeep was done.

"You had some loose wires around the spark plugs," he told me. "We just reconnected 'em and the Jeep was fine. Twenty bucks, and you can pick it up in five minutes."

Wow. How often do you get a call from your mechanic like that? As it happened, Mark, the psychology student, drove up at that moment, and he offered to zip me over to Dave's. Dave's garage wasn't far from Ms. Hawk's office, so I could make it there in time for the meeting with Belinda if I hurried.

At the garage, I handed Dave a twenty, thanked him, collected my keys, and jumped into my trusty little Jeep. I hadn't realized how unsettled I was feeling until I was behind the wheel of my own familiar car again. I was just putting the key into the ignition when I saw the box on the passenger seat. It was a metal box, painted a dull blue. What the hell was it?

Had one of the mechanics left some weird tool in my Jeep? I put out a finger and poked it.

The lid popped open and a bright blue clown sprang up. I jumped back in my seat, startled. Pinned to one of the clown's hands was a small white card. It read *BOOM!*

TEN

I BOLTED OUT of my Jeep, ran back into Dave's office, and slammed the door. My heart was pounding a mile a minute, and I expected any moment to hear a thumping *kaboom* from the parking lot. Dave, standing at the grimy computer behind the battered counter, blinked at me in surprise. The pop machine hummed quietly in the corner, and NASCAR race cars whizzed around a track on the TV. Through a giant plate-glass window, I could see Dave's employees working on half a dozen cars. Parts were scattered about like bits of meat in a Civil War operating room, and I wondered what would happen if the plate glass shattered in an explosion.

"Something wrong with the Jeep?" Dave asked. He's in his early fifties, silver hair receding at the temples and thinning on top. Like every other mechanic I've ever met, his hands are scarred and permanently stained with grease.

I shook my head, pulled out my cell, and punched 911. "I'm at Dave's Garage in downtown Ann Arbor," I told the operator. "And I think someone's planted a bomb in my car."

That brought Dave around the counter. He dashed for the front door, his eyes wide and white. I grabbed his elbow and jerked him to a stop. "Don't go near it," I hissed. "Just keep an eye on it and stop anyone who might get close."

Dave nodded and stationed himself by the door.

Next I called Ms. Hawk, who agreed that we should postpone the meeting with Belinda. I was just hanging up when sirens screamed around the corner. Two police cars and a white van pulled into Dave's tiny parking lot. The car shared by Carl dela Cort and Henrietta Flinch parked itself at the curb. A moment later, both detectives dashed inside, their faces tight and drawn. Two uniformed officers followed.

"What's this all about?" Henrietta asked.

By now I was feeling a little calmer. I had fed a dollar into the pop machine and slugged down most of a Diet Mountain Dew, so the caffeine was steadying my nerves. Valium is for wimps.

"Yesterday afternoon my car wouldn't start," I said. "I had it towed here for repairs. Dave said the spark plug wires were loose, and he put them back in. When I came to pick it up, I found a jack-in-the-box on the front seat. I touched it, and it popped open. The clown was holding a note that said BOOM. I jumped out of the car and called you guys."

"Jesus," Dave said.

I downed another gulp of Dew. "In light of the pictures, I figured the threat might be real."

"Someone has it in for you, sweets," Carl said. His notebook was out and he was scribbling furiously. "You think there really could be a bomb in your car or was this just a warning?"

I cocked my head. Carl's earlier chauvinistic attitude seemed to have lessened quite a bit. "Dunno. I don't want to turn the key and find out the hard way."

Henrietta asked me a couple more questions while Carl talked to Dave, but no new information turned up. Dave said he had no idea where the jack-in-the-box came from, and he didn't remember seeing it in my Jeep when he parked it in the lot, which had to mean someone had put it there this afternoon. My Jeep hadn't been locked, so anyone could have walked up.

One of the uniforms spoke into his microphone. Someone crackled an acknowledgment, and outside two men in bulky off-white bomb suits got out of the van. They trundled toward my Jeep. The officers gently but firmly ushered us out of the garage to a safe distance away.

A crowd was gathering around the perimeter tape the cops had set up, and a news van had already arrived. Cars slowed as they passed on the sun-drenched street. A bus rolled by, spewing the sharp smell of diesel exhaust. Someone touched my arm, and I found Slava standing next to me. She was wearing a red blouse and a voluminous pair of white slacks. Her curly black hair had been forced into a long, chunky braid that hung down her back.

"What are you doing here?" I asked, startled.

"I see big crowd gather and come to gawk," she said without a trace of shame. "Then I see you and know you must be cause. What is going on?"

I gave her a ten-second explanation in low tones that went no farther than the two of us. Slava's face hardened and she put an arm around my shoulders. She smelled faintly of tobacco smoke.

"Sons of bitches," she muttered. "Bad as KGB. Give me five minutes alone with them, they never bother you again. My mother always say, 'You can't run if legs are broken.'"

That got a smile from me, and I felt a little less uneasy.

The guys in white continued to work on my car. And then Ms. Hawk found us in the crowd. She wore a severely tailored navy suit with a small matching bag. The silver hawk pendant gleamed at her throat. Her serene, competent presence granted me even more relief than Slava had. It was good to have people looking out for you.

"I ran over from the office," Ms. Hawk said calmly. "You're having an interesting series of days."

Inside the perimeter, the bomb guys had opened the hood of my Jeep. They'd already checked underneath and gone through the inside. I held my breath. I didn't *really* think there was a bomb in there, but—

One of the bomb guys pulled off his headgear and waved an okay at the officers. A ripple went through the crowd and my knees quivered with relief. Some of the crowd drifted away, but most of the people stayed, clearly hoping for more of a show.

A TV reporter with a microphone was moving through the crowd, asking if anyone knew whose Jeep was involved. Ms.

Hawk and I exchanged looks, and as one we slipped away and ducked into the garage's office. Slava followed. Henrietta and Carl were both there, talking to one of the bomb guys.

"Your Jeep?" the bomb guy asked. At my nod, he said, "It's clean. We didn't find any kind of explosive."

"Makes for a boring day," I managed.

"Best kind, in my line of work," he said, and gave me my key back. I didn't even remember giving it to the cops.

"Are you going to be all right?" Henrietta asked solicitously.

"I think so," I said. "The more I think about it, the more this feels like an empty threat. If whoever's behind all this really wanted me dead, all it would take is a high-powered rifle from a distance."

"Don't laugh, chicky-boo," Carl said. "Warnings escalate. I see it all the time. You just watch yourself." Then, as if he had realized he was expressing concern, he added, "Because I don't want to be stuck hosing your blood off the sidewalk." Then he strode quickly out the door.

I turned to Henrietta. "What was that all about? He's been acting almost human lately."

"This whole thing touched a nerve with him," Henrietta said quietly. "Carl's son is gay, and—"

"He has a *son?*" I interrupted. "That implies a wife. And actual physical contact with her."

Slava lit a cigarette. "They say there is someone for everyone," she said.

"And he's gay?" I continued. "I'll bet *that* coming out went over well."

"They were on the outs for a while," Henrietta said. "But then Jeff received a bomb threat, one addressed to 'The Fag,' though his bomb turned out to be real. Jeff didn't die, but he spent six weeks in the hospital, and he still walks with a limp. Carl hates bomb threats."

"As if I needed more sobering thoughts today," I muttered.

"Do you need anything else, Detective?" Ms. Hawk asked.

"Terry needs to stop down at the station sometime this evening or early tomorrow and sign a statement," she said. "We've taken the jack-in-the-box as evidence. Do you want a receipt for it?"

"God, no," I said.

"Then that's pretty much it for now."

The door opened and a dark-haired, square-jawed, blow-dried reporter strode in. A cameraman followed. "Can anyone tell me whose Jeep that is out there?" he boomed. "It's yours, right ma'am?" This last was addressed to me.

I froze like a deer in headlights. The stress of the entire incident combined with the unexpected question to lock down my higher brain functions. The reporter took my lack of response for a "yes" and started forward, holding his microphone out like a royal scepter. I blanched. A Hawk Enterprises employee appearing on television news—bad, bad, bad. Too many old enemies floating around out there, too many disgruntled men. I shot Ms. Hawk a desperate glance, but if she stepped forward, the camera would only focus on her, which would be just as bad.

"Is my Jeep," Slava said, leaping in front of me. Her expression was wild eyed and frantic. "It was horrible! Just awful! Terrible men break into helpless woman's car to plant bomb. Just like KGB. I tell *everything* to handsome reporter. You turn on camera and listen good."

Ms. Hawk and I were already out the door. We both leaped into my Jeep and I put the key into the ignition. There was a moment when the two of us traded looks. Then I held my breath and turned the key. The Jeep purred to life as if nothing at all had ever happened to it. The door to Dave's office opened and the dark-haired, square-jawed, blow-dried reporter sprinted out, the cameraman hot on his heels. Slava stood grinning in the doorway.

The reporter shouted something, but I was already peeling out of the parking lot. I was giggling and Ms. Hawk shook her head with a small, restrained laugh. Our laughter increased until I was wiping my eyes, barely keeping control of the Jeep and Ms. Hawk was laughing like a little girl. Release of stress, I suppose, though it felt odd to be sharing a laugh with someone like Ms. Hawk. It was like seeing a cat with a fit of the giggles.

Ms. Hawk's cell phone rang, and she answered, a wide smile still on her face. "Diana Hawk." Her face brightened. "Hello, darling. You got my message, then? Yes, a few things have come up and I'll be a little late tonight. How's eight-thirty instead? Good. See you then."

She clicked off.

"I didn't know you had a boyfriend," I said, greatly daring.

"Mmm."

"What's his name?"

She arched an eyebrow and fingered the hawk pendant at her throat. "All the men in my life are named 'Darling' until I find the one who is willing to become Mr. Hawk."

"You mean you wouldn't change your name to—"

"Certainly not."

Funny thing is, I couldn't tell if she was kidding. I turned my full attention to the street, realizing just how little I knew about Diana Hawk. I didn't even know how or why she had started Hawk Enterprises. Sure, I'd done some checking around. The paper trail on Hawk Enterprises began about five years ago, but we have files going back at least six. I've never asked Ms. Hawk, and she's never volunteered. Maybe one day.

As we continued down the street, Ms. Hawk called Belinda to tell her we were on our way and to apologize for our tardiness, though she told me in an aside that she had left a note for Belinda on the office door, along with a key so she could get inside with the air conditioning. Our client was waiting for us on the window seat, paperback book in her hand, purse at her feet. She wore a different sun dress, a blue one with white buttons this time, but still Neiman Marcus-y, and she carried a different handbag—Prada, if I wasn't mistaken.

Ms. Hawk sailed in and escorted Belinda into the conference room with more apologies but no explanations. Belinda accepted this with quiet equanimity as we settled around the table. The battered notebook and the shoebox with the documents sat to one side, and Belinda eyed them with curiosity, though she made no move to touch them.

"We have a great deal to discuss," Ms. Hawk said. Her firm demeanor and her navy suit made it clear she was in charge here, no matter how many checks Belinda might write. "Terry, why don't you tell Ms. Harris what you've learned so far?"

I outlined what Zack and I had learned about the paper treasure, the Peale family history, and the Chicago Peales. I left out the pictures and the bomb threat. Hawk Enterprises doesn't worry its clients unless absolutely necessary.

"Did you know about the treasure?" Ms. Hawk said.

"I'd heard of it from my mother," Belinda said, her eyes a little wide, "but I'd dismissed it as a legend. It's sounds so improbable, you understand—a bunch of papers or a diary worth a fortune. Do you think it's real?"

"Someone does," I said.

Belinda jerked her head at the shoebox. "Is it in there?"

"No," Ms. Hawk said, drawing the box to her. Even this simple movement crackled with energy. "We found your uncles' wills and various other papers you might need, including your grandmother's divorce records."

"Really?" She clapped her hands in delight. "That's wonderful! How on earth did you find them so fast?"

"Actually Zack found them," I said. "He came across a room filled with papers and found them."

"Then I'm certainly glad I asked you to include him," Belinda said with a twinkly smile. "Have you read them? I don't know if I should open that box, you understand. Mold."

"Of course." Ms. Hawk tapped the box lid. "Your uncles appear to have left their estates to each other."

"Oh, dear." Belinda sighed. "This will make things so much more complicated. Well, family's family, and I'll do what I can."

"Do you think the house would go to you?" I asked.

"Probably," Belinda said. "I'm their closest living relative, as far as I know. The house is probably a total loss, you understand, but I've done some checking and the property is worth quite a lot."

"We also found this," Ms. Hawk said, and slid the notebook over to Belinda. "Does it mean anything to you?"

Belinda flipped the notebook open and leafed through it. "Well, it's Uncle Lawrence's handwriting. The last entry is dated around the time of his last letter. Other than that, I have no idea. What *does* it mean?"

"We were hoping you could tell us," Ms. Hawk said. "Terry learned that the Chicago branch of the Peale family is known for smuggling, though the police have never managed to prove it. Lately, rumor has it the street supply of drugs the Chicago Peales usually spread about has dried up and that the family is involved in something new. I'm wondering if this notebook might have something to do with that. Do you now know anything that might be helpful?"

"The Chicago Peales are criminals?" Belinda said, clearly taken aback. "My lord! Where did you hear this?"

"We have contacts in Chicago," I said. "You really didn't know about this?"

"I had no idea." Belinda fanned herself with one hand. "I don't know anything about them, really. Drug smugglers! That's terrible!"

"I'm sorry to be the bearer of bad news," Ms. Hawk interjected.

"It's not your fault. I'm just a little shocked, you understand."

"Would you like some tea?" I said. "Coffee? A soda?"

"No, no. Thank you." Belinda drew herself up in her chair. "We might share blood, but they aren't me. May I keep that notebook? I can look at it some more and see if anything comes to me."

"It came from your uncles' house," Ms. Hawk said, "so you

are certainly entitled to keep anything you wish. Though may I ask that we keep the original and give you a photocopy?"

"Please," Belinda said.

I felt like I was at a tea party, everyone was so excruciatingly polite. Southern manners meet Diana Hawk. Ms. Hawk gave me the notebook and I popped out to the entry area, where we keep the copy machine. When I returned, Ms. Hawk was giving Belinda a more detailed description of the house's interior.

"Those poor men," Belinda said, shaking her head. "What's the next step in your investigation?"

"We need to look into the warehouse mentioned in the notebook," Ms. Hawk said.

"What will you be looking for?"

"Anything that might tell us what's going on with the Chicago Peales," Ms. Hawk replied. "Back in the days of Prohibition, Detroit was a major entry point for illegal liquor coming in from Canada and even overseas. Bootleggers, which no doubt included your family, ran alcohol down Michigan Avenue from Detroit to Chicago. Nowadays they use I-94, and the illegal materials are drugs, but the general principle is the same. No doubt the Chicago Peales have been using this warehouse as an entry point for quite some time, possibly even for generations. They've stopped smuggling drugs, but I doubt they've stopped smuggling altogether. We need to learn what they're up to."

"How does this relate to my uncles and the treasure?" Belinda asked.

"I don't know," Ms. Hawk admitted. "That's why we need to investigate."

A few more pleasantries were exchanged, and we ushered Belinda to the door. Once she was gone, I said, "When do you want to leave for the warehouse?"

"Just after dark," Ms. Hawk said. "I would prefer not to be observed."

Ms. Hawk left the office. I passed the time at my desk,

looking up directions to the warehouse on MapQuest, catching up on filing, answering e-mail, and performing other sundry tasks. After a while I realized I was engaged in busy work, putting off something I knew needed doing. The sun headed for the horizon, and I tapped a pencil against a message pad, chewing the inside of my cheek. My dad's voice popped into my head: *The longer you put it off, the harder it gets.*

I sighed. Words of wisdom from a surprising source. Well, my dad wasn't all bad. No one is. Yeah, Dad liked to drink and slap and think up some weird-ass punishments for stupid little shit, and, yeah, he liked to pretend he had more money than he did, but he paid all my college bills and didn't seem to mind that I changed majors at least once a semester. I dropped out of college and married Noel partly to piss Dad off, not realizing that I had run away from my father only to marry someone even worse.

Anyway, Dad was right—the longer I put it off, the harder it would get. So I picked up the phone and dialed the home number of Wendy Schultz, a woman I know who works in the Washtenaw County sheriff's department.

"Wendy," I said after hearing about her kids, her dogs, and the latest complaints about her neighbors, "when you get in to work tomorrow, could you run a background check on someone for me? It's worth lunch."

"Oh, sure, hon," Wendy said. Gum cracked in my ear, and I imagined Wendy sitting on the couch with her feet up, her wild red hair poofing out in all directions. "What's the name?"

"Zackary Archer."

"You better spell that, hon," she said, and her gum cracked again. "And give me any aliases he might have."

I spelled Zack's name for her. "I don't know if he has any aliases," I said. "But let me know anything you might find."

I hung up and dashed home, feeling oddly guilty. I wasn't snooping, I told myself. I needed to learn more about Zack and his motivations. The problem was I *liked* Zack. He was funny and smart and damned sexy. I didn't *want* to learn anything bad about him. But I also knew it was stupid to ignore various suspicions.

Back at the Biemers', I grabbed a snack to make up for missed supper, breezed past the other residents—the Biemers had long since retired to their basement apartment—and headed to my room, where I put up my hair and pulled on my black Catwoman outfit. All the better for skulking in, my dear. I exited out my sliding door and made my way through the back yard to my Jeep. Easier to sneak out than explain my outfit to the other boarders. It was already dark out, and crickets chirped all around me. Warm air slid sultry around me, and I felt like a creature of the night, gliding around the oak tree and across the grass to the driveway. I got into my Jeep and drove down to the office. Ms. Hawk, also dressed in dark clothing, was waiting in the foyer. We made a hell of a pair, slinking back out to the parking lot like two black cats on the prowl.

We decided to drive separately to the warehouse because sometimes it's best to have two getaway vehicles. I was armed to the teeth—pistol, pepper spray, illegal stun gun, and my own two hands. My cell phone was plugged into my ear so Ms. Hawk and I could talk to each other without being over-heard. I followed my GPS directions carefully—even with detailed instructions, it gets tricky driving around Detroit, especially at night.

Downtown Detroit's national reputation as a crime-ridden city is exaggerated. Slightly. A little. I kept my windows up, the doors locked, and my senses alert. The casino district is well lit and quite clean—the casinos don't want potential gam-blers to be frightened away by anything unseemly—but the areas around it are a little nerve-wracking. Streets are stud-ded with half-wrecked buildings of crumbling brick, some boarded up, others not. Street lamps are often broken, leav-ing large sections of town in a blanket of dark pierced only by headlights of passing cars.

Eventually I reached a section of warehouses down by the

river in what had to be some of the most depressing areas to work ever. I checked the directions again and located the building. It looked perfectly anonymous, surrounded by a litter of near-identical brothers and sisters. I found a side street where I could park my Jeep, took a quick look around, locked my steering wheel with a big red bar that said, "Sorry pal—you ain't driving this Jeep anywhere," and got out. Ms. Hawk parked a little ways up the street and got out herself. She looked like a shadow pouring itself into a pool of ink. I switched on my cell phone's walkie-talkie function and set it to voice activation.

"Can you hear me?" I murmured.

By her car, Ms. Hawk put a hand to her ear and nodded. *"I hear you, Terry. Let's get into that alley, shall we?"*

The area was not well lit, which worked to our advantage. We slipped into a wide alley that ran between two warehouses. Cracked concrete pushed against the soles of my shoes, and ahead of me I smelled dirty water. The Detroit River is a ribbon that connects Lake Huron to Lake Erie and is more of a channel than a river, a narrow place where Michigan's thumb almost touches Canada.

The warm night air was humid enough to drink. Water lapped against a dock in the distance, and through the mouth of the alley I saw a large boat or small ship drifting slowly down the river, its running lights ablaze. For a moment I was back in Russia, hunting down little Andy and rescuing his fellow slaves, though it had been way colder in Moscow.

Bright lights illuminated the side of the warehouse that faced the river. A set of huge loading doors took up most of that wall. Near the corner stood a normal-sized door, though it still looked formidably thick and heavy, and it was brightly lit. A car *whooshed* by in the street behind me, and I glanced around nervously.

"Do you see anyone watching?" Ms. Hawk asked, her voice echoing in my earpiece.

"No," I said. "Which doesn't mean there isn't anyone."

"Well, this is why we get paid. Keep an eye out." With that, Ms. Hawk drew on a pair of black latex gloves and strode boldly to the small door, a bag slung over her shoulder. I held my breath. God, she had nerve. The door was locked, of course, with both a deadbolt and a spring lock. Ms. Hawk knelt to examine the locks, then opened a small case from her belt and extracted a pair of tools. The spring lock barely slowed her down. The deadbolt took a little more work, but Ms. Hawk worked patiently at it. I tried to watch in all directions at once, feeling exposed and vulnerable even though I was still in the alley.

One minute went by. Then two. Ms. Hawk's expression didn't change. She looked like she had every right to be poking at the door with picklocks and who would dare question her? I, on the other hand, was starting to sweat. Every shadow held a posse of gang members with guns, or a collection of cops with guns, or—

I heard a *click,* and Ms. Hawk pushed the door open with a gloved hand. I had already pulled my own gloves on, and I hurried into the warehouse after her. Ms. Hawk quickly shut the door and threw the deadbolt. Next to the door, a keypad flashed insistently. A digital countdown informed us we had less than a minute to enter the proper code. Without a word, I pulled a small electric screwdriver from my belt and had the cover off the alarm in seven seconds. Ms. Hawk was already attaching a lead to the netbook she had pulled from her shoulder bag, and she connected it the moment the cover came away. She tapped at the screen while I held my breath.

"It's not a complicated alarm," Ms. Hawk murmured. "We should be able to—there."

The countdown flicked from twenty-eight seconds to two hours. I had no idea where she'd learned that trick, but I was grateful she had.

"That should be enough time." Ms. Hawk slid the netbook back into her bag. "And much easier to change the timer than hack the access code."

As one, we turned to face the warehouse. Only a few scattered lights were on, leaving most of the echoing space in shadow. Both of us took out flashlights and shined them around. The place wasn't that big, as warehouses go. Maybe half a dozen semis could park inside. A catwalk made a lattice overhead, and one section had been walled off for office space.

"I don't suppose," I muttered, "that we'll find any crates conveniently marked *Contraband* or *Smuggler stuff*."

"Doubtful. Let's spread out."

There were indeed a few wooden crates scattered around the floor, but the ones I could open were empty. Every sound echoed around me, and I could hear Ms. Hawk rustling around in another section. My senses were on high alert. My own breathing rasped in my ears and my hands sweated inside my latex gloves. Something clattered to the floor and I jumped, my hands snapping into fighting stance.

"That was just me," Ms. Hawk's voice said in my earpiece.

I got my heart started again, then moved around a clump of crates and barked my shins painfully against something that made a metallic hissing sound against the floor. I heard Ms. Hawk's quick intake of breath in my ear.

"And that was just me," I said, shining my flashlight over the object. Several objects, actually. Wire gleamed in my beam. I stared for a long moment, then said, "Ms. Hawk, you might want to come and see this."

Crisp footsteps approached behind me, and I played my flashlight over the wire kennels scattered about the concrete floor. Each was big enough to house a German shepherd, or maybe a small St. Bernard, and each one sported a set of plastic dog dishes.

"The Peales are smuggling dogs?" I said. "That's...unexpected."

"And I can't imagine it's anything as profitable as drugs," Ms. Hawk said, playing her own flashlight around. I counted over a dozen kennels. They looked to be the sort people put their dogs in before going to work. "Let's see what else we can find."

We split up again, and a few minutes later, Ms. Hawk called me over to the office area. She already had the lock open and had turned the lights on. The large room beyond was almost bare. A card table and folding chairs sat in one corner. Two dirty ashtrays lay on top of it. A door opened onto a dirty bathroom with a moldy shower stall. Near the table were piled several cardboard boxes. I rummaged through them.

"Dry cereal, canned spaghetti, beef stew, beans," I said. "Food for thought?"

Ms. Hawk was standing in the middle of the room, toying with her hawk pendant. "Where do they keep their records?" she muttered. "There has to be *something.*"

A black cord caught my eye, and I picked it up. It was the power brick to a laptop computer. "It looks like they don't leave them here."

"Eminently sensible of them," she said. "We should leave, Terry. I don't think we're going to find anything helpful."

I agreed. We still had half an hour on the alarm system, and Ms. Hawk didn't bother resetting it on our way out. If the alarm went off and anyone came to investigate, they'd find nothing but a locked, empty warehouse.

Outside, I stood guard again while Ms. Hawk relocked the door. We were heading for the alley when Ms. Hawk abruptly dove ahead of me into the darkness. Someone yelped and I heard a *thud,* but my body was already moving. I rushed into the alley, pistol in one hand, flashlight in the other. My heart pounded the rhythm of adrenaline. I crossed my wrists so my pistol hand was steadied on my flashlight hand, allowing me to sweep the alley with light wherever my pistol pointed. The beam landed squarely on Ms. Hawk's lithe form. She had someone in a half nelson on the alley ground. Her victim was struggling to break free. I aimed my pistol upward—I didn't want to hit Ms. Hawk—and scooted around them until I could get to the person she was fighting with. Shadows and the bobbing light of my flashlight made it hard to see.

"Freeze, asshole!" I snarled, pressing the pistol against his temple.

He froze. Ms. Hawk disengaged and backed away, drawing her own pistol in the process.

"Good work, Terry," she said, and my heart swelled with pride.

"Lie face-down on the ground," I barked at her victim. "Move!"

"Yuck," he said.

"What?" I replied, caught off-guard. It wasn't the response I'd been expecting.

"I'm not lying down. I think someone peed here."

The tension drained out of me. I holstered my pistol and shined my light more carefully. It illuminated the face of Zack Archer.

"What the hell are you doing here?" I demanded.

"Same thing you are," Zack said. "Sniffing around the warehouse from Uncle Lawrence's notebook. You mind getting that light out of my eyes? I can't see the delightful animal snarl on your face."

I shut the flashlight off. Zack stood blinking in the dim light of the alley for a moment, then leaned casually against one wall. "So what did you find out?"

"Why should we tell you?" I said.

"To save me the trouble of breaking in and finding out for myself. Duh."

"How are you with alarm systems?" I asked a little nastily. "As good as you are at picking locks?"

"Just as good as Ms. Hawk here," Zack shot back.

"Mr. Archer can pick locks?" Ms. Hawk said.

Oops. Hadn't I mentioned that to her? I tried to remember, but so much had happened since I caught Zack with his little tools.

"It's a hobby," Zack said with an amiable smile. "Maybe we can trade tips sometime."

"Can you circumvent a burglar alarm, too?" I asked.

"Meh." Zack shrugged. "The police almost never answer those, you know. Too many false alarms. If one goes off, you have a couple-three hours before the cops show."

"And how would you know that?"

"I read the newspapers," Zack said nonchalantly. "There was an article about it not that long ago."

"I don't know that this is the best place to discuss it," Ms. Hawk said.

"Yeah, this place isn't all that fun," Zack said. "Want to get something to eat? All three of us, of course."

I looked at those green eyes and really wanted to. But my brain told me it would be a bad idea until I heard back from Wendy.

"No," I said, turning to head for the car.

"Then at least tell me what you found out," Zack said reasonably. "I'll tell you what I found."

"We didn't find much of anything," Ms. Hawk said as we reached my Jeep. "A laptop cord, some dog kennels and some canned goods."

"Dog food?" Zack asked.

"Spaghetti-Os," I told him. "Looks like the smugglers had some snacks laid by."

"Which means they stay for long periods of time," Zack pointed out.

Something itched at the back of my mind when he said that. I tried to put my finger on it, but whatever it was danced away from me.

Ms. Hawk nodded. "Perhaps they do. Now would you be so kind, Mr. Archer, as to tell us your findings?"

Zack leaned against the hood of my Jeep. "I found a lookout post on the warehouse roof."

"Go on," I said.

"I climbed to the top to see if there was an easier way in,

and I found a pile of old clothes wrapped around a ratty sleeping bag. Judging by the condition of the clothes, no one's been up there in quite a while."

"How can you tell that?" Ms. Hawk asked.

"There was a bird's nest in them. I also found these." He held up a pair of binoculars that looked old enough to have stormed the beach at Normandy. "Someone's been watching this place, though not for a while now."

I thought of the notebook and its records of all the comings and goings. "Uncle Lawrence?"

"Sounds likely."

We split up and climbed into our respective vehicles. Zack rattled off in his VW bus. I drove back to Ann Arbor in a puzzled fog of whys. As in, why had Uncle Lawrence been watching the warehouse? Why were the Peales smuggling dogs? Why did Zack's comment about the smugglers needing the food because they stayed for long periods bug me?

I thought about it as I pulled into the Biemers' driveway and I thought about it as I undressed and I thought about it as I climbed into bed, but nothing came to me. Eventually I fell asleep and dreamed that Ms. Hawk was calling to me in the Peale mansion, but I couldn't get through all the junk to find her. I finally reached her, but she was Zack instead, and he fell into a deep pit before I could touch him.

In the morning, Ms. Hawk called to say she was working on something else. Would I be willing to go back to the mansion and look around some more to see if anything else turned up? I told her I would be happy to and was just clicking off when the phone chirped again. It was Wendy Schultz.

"I've got the goods on Zack Archer, hon," she said. "You sitting down?"

I sank to my bed. "Go," I said.

"Mr. Archer has quite the interesting history. Three arrests for B-and-E and burglary." Gum cracked in my ear and I heard Wendy's chair squeak. She had to be sitting in front of her computer terminal at work. "The first two times he was released for lack of evidence. The third time was the charm. He was sentenced to two years, and he served ten months. His mug shots are pretty cute. A real looker, hon."

"I know," I said faintly. "Where did all this happen?"

"Detroit once, Ann Arbor once, and Grosse Isle once. That last one is where he got sentenced. He stole some valuable artwork from a private collection."

Treasure, I thought.

"Lots of notes on him in here, too," Wendy continued. "He was suspected—but never arrested—for several other break-ins. Museums, galleries, private homes."

"When did he serve his sentence?" I asked.

The gum cracked again. "Six years ago, hon. There's nothing about him after that, actually. Either he went straight or he got a lot more careful."

I grimaced. Zack *did* say he had gotten into trouble for breaking into someone's house when he was young and stupid, but he had said it was on a dare, not that he made a career out of it. "Is there anything else?" I asked, dreading to hear an answer.

"Last known addresses are all in Detroit or Ann Arbor. Do you want those?"

"Not really."

"Mother's name Eileen Archer, once a resident of Ypsilanti, now deceased." *Crack, crack.* "Father's name is…oh. That's odd."

"What?" I asked. "What is it?"

"Apparently this guy has his mother's last name and not his father's. A little strange but not unheard of these days."

I grabbed the phone with both hands. "What's his father's name?"

"Says here it's Arthur Peale."

ELEVEN

CLOUDS DRIFTED OVERHEAD, partially obscuring the sun and cutting back on the heat. I leaned on my yellow Jeep and stared at the mouldering mansion, trying to think. Zack had said his father's real name was Arthur, but he hadn't said anything about being a Peale. Was he a Chicago Peale or a Detroit Peale? Belinda hadn't mentioned any other relatives and unless she was a fantastic actress, Zack had been a total stranger to her. A Chicago Peale, then. Was he in on the smuggling? No, that didn't make sense. He wouldn't have had to sneak into the warehouse if he was.

So what the hell was his angle? I took a long pull of coffee from my canteen. It was possible everything he had done from the beginning had been a ploy to get his hands on the Peale family papers. I didn't want it to be. I slapped the hood of the Jeep in frustration, and the metal stung my palm. Dammit, I *liked* Zack. Against all probability, I did. He was funny and handsome and...reliable.

I chewed over that thought for a long moment. Zack was reliable. It was strange, but there it was. He always turned up when he said he would, he was ready and willing to help even when there was nothing in it for him. Hell, he even turned up when I *didn't* want him to. Unlike most of the other men in my life, who came around when it suited them and left equally quickly. Noel had been like that.

And now Zack had to go and do this to me.

Strictly speaking, he hadn't done anything illegal on this case—unless he had been the one to pick the back door open.

Strictly speaking, he hadn't even lied. He had just withheld information. I had withheld information from him, come to that.

Was I telling the truth to myself or making excuses for him?

The house's blank windows stared mutely at me, as if it were begging to be put out of its misery. I sympathized. I was getting tired of this case, tired of threats, tired of dusty lies. And I didn't want to go inside again, even on Ms. Hawk's orders.

Shit.

I spent several minutes wandering the perimeter of the house. A squirrel cheebled at me again, but I ignored him. The dry, dead grass crackled beneath my boots, and I sipped coffee from my canteen. Zack was a shit. A not-quite-lying bastard. On the other hand, so what? People lied to me all the time. Noel certainly had.

Unbidden, more memories of Noel slid into my mind. I met him at a frat kegger when I was a freshman at Michigan State. He was a junior. We got married within a year, and both of us dropped out of school, which pissed off my parents something fierce. Noel got a job selling educational software and training teachers how to use it. He traveled a lot, and when he was home, his main form of recreation involved various illegal substances. I didn't use, but I watched. I felt alive when I was with Noel, like I was living on the edge. After life with an overly strict father, Noel was exactly what I needed. Or so I thought.

One day while Noel was on a sales trip, three gorillas barged into our house and demanded money in the order of twenty thousand dollars. I was terrified.

"Tell your husband that if he doesn't pay up by the end of the week," one gorilla said, "we'll break your left arm and your right leg." He stiff-armed me, and I fell against the coffee table. One corner dug painfully into my side. "Go to the cops, and we'll kill you."

They left, and I called Noel in a panic, demanding to know

who these guys were. Noel admitted that he had borrowed money from them to buy drugs.

"But don't worry about it," he drawled. "They're all talk. Besides, I'll get the money soon."

I clutched the phone against my ear. "How? We've got maybe two thousand in the savings. They're asking for twenty."

"I've been skimming money off the top of my sales," he said proudly. "I overcharge the school districts and keep the difference. Don't worry about a thing, sweets."

I worried. Two days passed, and I couldn't reach him on his cell phone. I called his work number to see if he had checked in. They told me Noel had been fired, and the company was filing charges of fraud and embezzlement. That same day, the three gorillas came back and told me Noel had three days to fork over the cash or I'd pay the price. They didn't seem to care that I hadn't heard from Noel, or that he had lost his job.

Then my friend Stace took me out to lunch. I had intended to keep the story to myself, but ended up making a terrified, tearful confession to her.

"I don't know what to do," I sobbed over a tray of McDonald's French fries. "I'm completely alone."

"Try this," Stace said, and handed me a card.

I glanced at it. "Hawk Enterprises?"

"They solve problems for women," she said. "And you sound right up their alley."

I remember being nervous as I walked into the offices of Hawk Enterprises and I remember being awed as I shook the hand of Diana Hawk. She wore a snappy blazer in green silk and the silver hawk pendant. She exuded quiet power, and I half expected an electric shock when I accepted her hand. I told her the entire story from start to finish, and when I was done, she nodded thoughtfully.

"I think we can help you," she said, and I felt a relief so profound, I nearly fainted. "The fee will be two thousand dollars and two favors."

I don't know how she did it, but in less than two days Ms. Hawk tracked down Noel. He had hanged himself in a public park down in Cincinnati, no ID, no note, nothing to tell the cops who he was. Ms. Hawk drove me down there to identify him. The morgue was cold and Noel's naked body was pasty gray in the drawer. A ligature mark made a purple ring around his neck. I stared down at him, surprised that I felt more anger than sorrow. The lying bastard had copped out and dumped everything on me.

Ms. Hawk took me home, and we discovered the gorillas waiting for me in the kitchen. They had baseball bats. I cowered against the stove, but Ms. Hawk went into a whirlwind of action. She snap-kicked one guy in the groin and back-punched a second. The third, however, was moving in behind her, gun drawn. I didn't even think. I grabbed the heavy butcher-block knife holder from the cupboard and smashed him down with it.

I remember staring down at the three gorillas lying on the linoleum. Two women had taken out three men. An incredible sense of power thrilled through me. All my life, I had thought men—my dad, my husband, the collection gorillas— were stronger than me. But they weren't. I could be just as strong as they were.

Ms. Hawk, meanwhile, got word to the local drug lord that Noel was dead and there was no point in trying to collect from his widow. I never heard from them again. A few weeks later, I was moving from Toledo to Ann Arbor as Hawk Enterprises's newest employee.

Which didn't change the fact that a lying bastard had gotten me there.

I grimaced. Like Noel, Zack was supposed to care about me. Like Noel, he had lied, for all that they were lies by omission. I didn't want to become involved with another Noel.

Ahead of me, at the end of the gravel driveway, stood an old-fashioned carriage house. I'd seen it before but not paid it close attention. It had once been white, though now it was mostly gray with flecks of white paint. A set of double doors sagged against the ground. These days the place was most likely used as a garage.

I stared at the little building. The uncles had to have some sort of vehicle. A lot of the stuff in the house wasn't easily portable—the pianos in the music room, for example. And come to think of it, Zack had mentioned riding in a truck with Uncle Lawrence.

The double doors were padlocked, and the normal-sized door to one side had a deadbolt. Where were Ms. Hawk or Zack when you needed them? Deadbolts and padlocks are beyond my meager B-and-E skills. I did note that the padlock was fairly new and the shackle was shiny from use. Someone went in and out on a regular basis.

The window in the little door was boarded over with a sheet of plywood. I trotted over to the toolbox I keep in my Jeep, extracted a hammer, and returned to the carriage house. The plywood came away with a great screeching of nails. A few more judicious yanks, and the window was exposed. It had no glass in it, so I reached inside and undid the deadbolt. I caught a whiff of stale, oily air. The door creaked when it opened. No light switch, so I was forced to rely on my flashlight.

Inside I found the same old, same old—boxes, crates, two engine blocks, stacks of tires, a pile of rims, a jumble of tools. No vehicle, but there was just enough space to park one. I found some damp spots on the earthen floor. Radiator fluid and oil.

I also found a small plastic container with a screwtop lid. The sides were sticky. I removed the top and smelled something similar to rubber cement. It was a bottle of waterproofing material, the kind you spread over the seams of a nylon tent so it won't leak. Stuck to the side was a piece of nylon netting. I pulled it off and took it outside to examine it in better light. It was brownish green, and there seemed to be dried plant material caught in it. Uncle Lawrence was a camper?

Seemed an odd hobby for a recluse who took care of a bed-ridden brother.

"So how goes investigation?"

I jumped and spun. Slava stood silhouetted in the doorway. I shut off my internal combat computer and got my heart started again.

"Don't you have a job?" I asked.

"Of course. Today I teach grad students rudiments of Ukrainian history, then show little freshmen how to conjugate Romanian verbs. Afterward, I stop by your office, but place is empty, so I drive here to find you. I make good detective, yes?"

"If you're fishing for a job as a field agent, you're talking to the wrong person."

Slava lit a cigarette and blew out a long feather of smoke. "One day you beg me to join Hawk Enterprises. It happen soon. My mother always say, 'What will happen, will happen.'"

"Wise woman," I said dryly.

"So what does strange hoarding man keep in garage?" she asked. "Treasure?"

"No." I sighed. "And I'm starting to get frustrated. Not only do I not know what I'm looking for, I don't know *where* I should be looking for it." I scuffed the dirt floor with one boot. "This whole house is organized, in its own weird way. So the treasure or papers or whatever the hell it is has to be hidden somewhere logical."

Slava tilted her head. "This makes no sense. If you want to hide something, you don't put it somewhere logical. My mother never kept real jewelry in her jewel box. She hid her jewels in outhouse. She always say, 'No one looks for pearls in shit.' And she was right. Look for something out of place, and you will find treasure."

"Oh, great," I groaned. "That narrows it down."

"You ask, I tell you what I think. Is why you love me."

That got a laugh. Impulsively I stepped forward and kissed her cheek. "I do love you. Now get out of here—I have work."

"I go, I go." She exhaled smoke like a contented dragon. "Just remember me when the great Diana Hawk posts new position." And she left.

I stood there for a moment, pondering what she had said. Look for something out of place. Trouble was, the whole house was full of stuff that was out of place. I mean, Lawrence dumped bags of cement in the dining room, for God's sake. Still, Slava's words scritched at the back of my mind. Something was there. Something I had seen fit what Slava was talking about. But the idea refused to coalesce.

I'd have to figure it out later. Right now, I needed to follow up on the truck, and the easiest way to do that lay right in front of me. Or rather, to my left and my right. Neighbors.

The uncles' mansion lay at the end of a street in an otherwise pleasant, shady neighborhood. I crunched down the driveway toward the other houses and started ringing doorbells.

An hour later, I had made a complete circuit of all the homes whose residents might be able to see comings and goings, and I had an earful of complaints. The house was ugly. It was falling apart. The yard was an overgrown eyesore. The crazy old men who lived there were bringing down property values all over the neighborhood.

And they owned a truck. Dark red, rusty, with a camper top. I got this from two different sources—a teenager plugged into her iPod in one house and a stay-at-home dad with a baby over his shoulder in the other. The teenager even told me she'd seen someone unloading stuff from the back and hauling it into the house, though not since early last spring.

I thought some more, then hammered the plywood back over the garage window, climbed into my Jeep, hopped on I-94, and drove down to the Detroit River.

The dock-and-warehouse area was a completely different

place during the day. Semi trucks, vans and cars grumbled over the concrete roads. Enormous ships lumbered down the river, and enormous cranes unloaded storage containers like giant children unstacking blocks. I drove cautiously past the Peale warehouse but saw no sign of activity. No ships, no boats, no trucks. Good. The warehouses on either side, however, boasted both trucks and workers. I parked, crossed the street, and headed for the warehouse on the left, since I'd gone right the last time.

I spent the next four hours telling dock workers and truck drivers I was a private investigator. Had any of them seen a rusty red truck with a camper top around? A series of no's, three leers, and one proposition were all I got for my pains until I came across a crane operator climbing down from the cab. He wore a hardhat, denim work shirt and jeans, and he looked a little older than my father, though he was in great shape.

"I seen a truck, yeah," he said. "Why?"

I got excited but tried to hide it. "When was that?"

"Two days ago, maybe three," he said. "I seen that truck parked around here lots. I remember because I used to own one just like it. Chevy. Best trucks ever built."

I made a mental note of the make. "Did you see who was driving it?"

"Nah. It was just parked a ways up the street."

So Uncle Lawrence had been alive two days ago, and was probably alive yet. I gave the guy my card. "Call me if you see the truck again, would you?"

I braced myself for another leer or a smarmy comment, but the guy just nodded, put my card in his pocket, and walked away. A few gentlemen still left in the world, anyway.

If Uncle Lawrence was still alive, I needed to find him. Where the hell was he hiding? It was possible he had squirreled himself away in the house, but I had my doubts. Lots of people were going in and out of the place these days, and

Uncle Lawrence didn't seem the type to stomach all the invasions. His truck was also gone, meaning he had driven it somewhere. But where?

I thought about the house, the paper blizzard in the dining room, the leaf collection, the cardboard forest, the pan avalanche, the magazine deadfalls. There had to be something in all that to tell me where he was. I had the feeling I was missing the forest for the—

—trees.

An idea took root and grew. I went back to my Jeep and climbed inside to turn it over in my head. The more I thought about it, the better it looked. But I would need some help.

At just that moment my cell chirped at me. It was Zack. I almost hung up on him, but it occurred to me that I could get his help *and* keep an eye on him at the same time.

"Where the heck are you?" he asked.

"On my cell phone," I replied. "Where are *you?*"

"Your place," he said. "It's almost supper time, and I stopped by the Biemers'. They said you weren't there."

I glanced at my watch. Holy shit—I'd worked my way through lunch and out the other side. Dammit! No way I'd make it home for dinner now.

"So I figured...you know...you might want to get some supper," Zack said. "Um...with me?"

He sounded so uncertain and boyish. It was so...*normal.* Hard to believe he was a convicted felon with a penchant for other people's property and a card-carrying member of the Peale family to boot.

"Sure," I said.

"Okay, I under—what? Really?"

"Make it a picnic supper," I said. "Bring everything—fried chicken, potato salad, the works. I have a couple errands to run first, so you'll have time to get it together."

"Cool! Where do we meet?"

I told him.

It's a well-known fact that parking in Ann Arbor is a horrible mess. Students suck up most of it. The rest is wiped out by businesspeople, yuppies, visitors and patients at the University hospital. It's a lesser-known fact that most of us natives know the secret spots where you can park for free. The parking meter readers always miss this street. That business doesn't tow. The side street over there allows parking at the curb. It was in the latter place where I parked my Jeep. Feeling smug, I trotted downhill past the children's hospital toward a wrought-iron fence, beyond which lay enormous trees. I carried a dusty looseleaf notebook under my arm and my Batgirl belt dragged at my hips. Zack stood at a gate in the fence, and damned if he wasn't holding an actual picnic basket. He was wearing a red polo shirt and a red baseball cap.

"Hey, Red Riding Hood," I said. "You got something for Grandma?"

He tipped his cap with a grin. "I was wondering if you'd notice."

"That basket looks brand new," I said. "Did you buy it just now?"

"Right after you called." He drew my hand into his arm. His skin was warm and smooth, and I could feel its corded muscle. "Let's find a place to sit and you can tell me what this is all about."

We strolled through the gate into Nichols Arboretum. Ahead of us stretched several acres of hilly green lawn surrounded by thick stands of enormous trees, all drenched in August sunlight. Birds sang in the trees, and a creek burbled past us. Stone benches were scattered here and there in both sun and shade. Trails snaked into the woods and, I knew, eventually led down into a deep valley with the Huron River at the bottom. It was a perfect day for a stroll, and for a few minutes I let myself forget that I couldn't trust Zack.

"What's in the notebook?" Zack asked as I nudged him toward a section of shade.

"Supper first," I told him. "I'm starving."

We were just sitting down when my cell chirped. It was Ms. Hawk.

"I've just heard from the office of the medical examiner," she said. "Dr. Wilewski has identified the man crushed under the magazine deadfall, though she had to consult immigration to do it."

"Really?" I said as Zack spread out a red-checked picnic blanket. He had really gone all the way. "How so?"

"Dr. Wilewski realized the man's dental work contained steel, which is only used in Eastern Europe and Russia. Its use has been discontinued, many people of this…gentleman's generation still have steel teeth."

"Interesting." I was keeping my remarks non-committal, not sure how much Zack should overhear. He was setting out china plates, cloth napkins, and wine glasses, all the while pretending not to listen in.

"I shall assume you cannot talk freely," Ms. Hawk said.

"Good idea."

Zack produced a Zingerman's Deli container with a cold chicken in it. I was impressed. Zingerman's ain't cheap.

"According to Dr. Wilewski," Ms. Hawk continued, "the man's name was Ilya Konanykhine, late of Georgia—the one-time Soviet republic, not the state—and he was here on a temporary visa. The police are currently checking into who he is and what he might have been doing in the Peale mansion."

It occurred to me that Ms. Hawk must have a pretty good contact in the medical examiner's office, since Dr. Wilewski had been less than forthcoming about these matters before. In any case, the information created more questions than it answered. What the hell was someone from Georgia doing in Uncle Lawrence's house? Did it have something to do with the treasure? If it didn't, what *did* it have to do with? And how did a dog-smuggling ring fit into all this?

I couldn't voice any of the questions, however. Zack had finished with the place settings and the chicken and he was now laying out an endive salad, rolls and butter. It all smelled fantastic.

"Are you with Mr. Archer?" Ms. Hawk asked.

"Yeah. I've done some checking and learned a few things."

"About Mr. Archer?"

"Yes."

"Then call me when you can." And she clicked off.

"That the boss?" Zack asked.

"Yep." I sat cross-legged on the red-checked cloth. We were back a ways from the main path, and other people strolled down it, chatting and laughing. Zack produced a bottle of wine and a corkscrew. I'm a complete Philistine when it comes to the grape, but I was willing to go along with it.

"Gewurztraminer," Zack said, half filling my glass. "Lightly chilled."

"Thank you," I said, and took a sip. It was sweet, perfect for an uneducated palate like mine. We were sitting side-by-side on the blanket, the food spread before us, warm summer air flowing over us. The breeze stirred Zack's gold hair, and I found myself wanting to brush it back into place. I also wanted to know if he was playing me. Caught between conflicting emotions, I did nothing. Zack didn't say anything either, but I could see him giving me sidelong glances with those green eyes. Silence landed between us like a heavy rock, refusing to budge. My knee was touching his, just barely.

Zack broke first. "I have a confession to make," he said. "I lied to you."

That surprised me, and my eyebrows went up. Maybe this would be easier than I thought. "Really?"

"Yeah." He cleared his throat. "Remember when we first came out of the uncles' house and you poured water over your head?"

"You said I looked awful," I said.

"I was lying. You were beautiful. And you're strong and you're tough and you don't give a shit what anyone thinks— except maybe Ms. Hawk."

Definitely not what I'd expected. I felt a flush come in for a landing. "Don't forget that I saved your life once or twice," I said, to cover.

"That, too."

"So why do you lie to me?" I snapped.

"I just told you I—"

"Not about that," I interrupted, waving a hand. "About who you really are, Zackary Peale."

The shocked look that slammed across his face was almost worth everything else.

"Did you think I wouldn't find out?" I went on relentlessly. I set the wine glass down, picked up a plate, and plopped a piece of chicken on it, followed by some salad and a roll. If I was going to have it out with Zack and maybe never see him again, I was at least going to get a free meal out of it. "Did you think that you could go on lying to me? Play me for an idiot?"

"I...oh, shit."

"Yeah," I said with my mouth full. The chicken was melt-in-your-mouth delicious, but I barely noticed. "Oh, shit."

"You think I'm some kind of crook or a con artist," he said, his own plate untouched and empty before him.

"Haven't seen a lot of evidence to the contrary."

He looked away. His knee was still touching mine, and I pulled away. I tried the salad. Crisp, cool, and perfectly seasoned. It could have been seaweed, for all I cared.

"I'll tell you the truth," Zack said at last. "But I don't know if you'll believe me."

"Hey, I'm open minded," I said, forking up more salad. "Some of my best friends are lying, thieving crooks. That was sarcasm, in case you were wondering."

"Sure. Okay." He took a deep breath. "Everything I told you about my parents—the commune, the Grateful Dead, the breakup—all of that was true. But it's also true that Arthur Peale was my father, and he's one of the Chicago Peales."

I swallowed the salad and realized with a jolt of nervousness that I had left my pistol in the Jeep. It's generally a bad idea to carry a gun in a public place. People call the cops. I wondered if this time leaving it behind had been a mistake.

Oh, calm down, I thought. *Zack isn't going to attack you. And you could break him in half if he did.*

"Go on," I told him.

"Dad was a black sheep," Zack said. Was that a note of pride in his voice? "Or maybe you could say he was the only *white* one. Grandpa Peale—whom I've never met, by the way—ran the family with an iron fist and everyone had to help out in the family smuggling business. Dad finally couldn't stand it and ran away. He hid in the commune, and that's where he hooked up with Mom. They never legally married, so I ended up with her last name instead of Dad's. The rest you know."

"How often do you talk to your relatives in Chicago?"

"Never," Zack said emphatically. "I don't even know if they're aware of my existence. Dad told me stories. Scary ones. They're ruthless and cruel, and all they care about is their criminal empire. They don't deserve the Peale family papers."

"So you *did* know about the treasure," Terry said.

He grimaced. "Yeah."

"Why didn't you *tell* me that?" I snarled. "Because you were hoping to find and keep it for yourself?"

"Well, duh. I mean, I didn't know who the hell *you* were, did I? I'd tracked down Uncle Lawrence, told him who I was, and made friends with him. He thought the way my dad ran away to join the hippies was hilarious, and he was going to show me something important. I was pretty sure it was the treasure, but he only showed me that stupid leaf collection. Then I got the assignment in Alaska and had to take it. When I got back, I found you and Ms. Hawk in his house and then we found that dead guy and I didn't know *what* to think. For all I knew, Belinda had hired you to kill Uncle Lawrence and find the papers for her. Hawk Enterprises isn't listed with the Better Business Bureau, it's not in the phonebook, and it's not listed with the state as an outfit of private investigators. I thought you were some kind of mafia hit squad, and no way in hell was I going to let you search that house without me being there."

"Touché," I said, raising my wine glass.

"Yeah. Maybe being suspicious runs in my family." He picked up his plate and began to fill it. "By the time I realized you were on the up-and-up, it was too late. Be honest, Terry. If I had told you all this yesterday, would you have trusted me?"

"Probably not," I had to admit.

He nodded. "So I kept my mouth shut and hoped."

"What about your police record?"

"Oh, God." He closed his eyes. "You found out about that, too?"

I realized I was tearing my roll into tiny pieces and made myself stop. "The birdies sing to me. Let's hear it."

"Christ. All right." He slugged down some more wine, then took a bite of chicken. "After my parents split up, I didn't do so well. They'd taught me to distrust everything to do with the government, including public schools. 'Conformity factories,' they called them. I rebelled against my teachers and didn't relate so good to the other kids."

"When you grow up naked in a tomato patch, there isn't much to talk about with the mall and chili-fries crowd," I supplied.

"Something like that. Anyway, Mom was always gone, either at work or at the night classes she took. We barely scraped along and I got tired of not having the stuff I saw the other kids had. So I took to shoplifting. What better way to stick it to big business, right?"

"And you got caught."

"Couple times," he admitted. "But by then I'd learned a thing or three. I know I'm not bad-looking, and that always makes it easier to talk your way out of trouble." He made a puppy-dog face that I had to admit was adorable. "'Please, mister, don't arrest me. I did it on a dare. I promise I'll leave and never come back. Please?' It always worked, which didn't exactly discourage me."

"So then what?" I said.

"Mom eventually got a job working for one of those house-cleaning companies, and during the summers she got me hired in, too. I saw all these gorgeous houses while Mom struggled to pay the rent on our crappy-ass apartment. I wasn't stupid enough to steal while we were cleaning, but I was able to learn where spare keys were kept and what the burglar-alarm codes were and who had a dog. It was so easy to sneak back in later and take what I wanted."

"How did you learn lock picking, then?"

"Luck. I was burgling a house and ran into another guy who had already gotten in. I persuaded him to teach me what he knew. Norm—that was his name—taught me lock picking, how to case a house, where the good fences were, and even a little photography."

"Photography?"

"A valuable aid to casing a place," he said. "Carrying a camera around your neck also gives you a good excuse to be in any number of places. Norm taught me that." His face took on a strange cast, as if reliving both pleasant and unpleasant memories. "He taught me a lot. In some ways, he was more of a dad than my real dad. By the time I hit twenty, I was making a decent living on burglary, con games, and theft. I got into houses, museums, galleries. You name it, I've probably stolen it. I got arrested twice but the charges never stuck. The third time, I was sentenced to two years. I was a model prisoner and served only ten months before they paroled me." He shuddered and put his plate down. "Prison was horrible. The idea of going back—" He shuddered again and for a moment I wondered if he was going cry. "Anyway, I went straight after that. Or I tried to."

"Tried?"

"You ever hunt for work with a felony conviction hanging over your head?" he countered. "You beg to clean toilets at minimum wage. So I pulled one more job. I broke into a store and stole some equipment to set myself up as a freelance photographer. I'm pretty good at it. Always was. I sent the store an anonymous money order for the stuff I stole, once I was able. That was three years ago. Now I'm here, sitting in a park with a mistrustful woman I'm completely falling for, wondering if she's ever going to trust me or even speak with me again."

"Why do you want the papers?" I said, ignoring his last sentence. "So you can sell them? Make a tidy profit?"

"Believe it or not, I want to donate them to a museum as a gesture."

"What kind of gesture?" I asked, the image of a middle finger rising in my mind.

"The kind that makes up for all the stuff I'd stolen over the years."

"So what *are* they, anyway?"

He leaned closer, and I could smell his skin. His lips almost touched my ear. I could feel their heat, and I shivered. "If I tell you what I know," he whispered, "will you kiss me?"

No. "Maybe," I murmured back. My nipples were tingling at his almost-touch.

"How about if I sweeten the deal?" He reached into the picnic basket behind him. I expected him to produce a cake or something for dessert, but instead of a pastry box, Zack pulled out a small brown sack. He opened it, and the rich scent instantly told me what lay inside.

"Cocoa-covered espresso beans," I breathed. "You play dirty."

"You don't know the half of it," he said, and gave me a warm, slow smile that stopped the entire world. He held up a single bean and leaned toward me. I did some leaning of my own and took it delicately from him with my lips. My tongue flicked the tips of his fingers and a tiny shudder went through him. He was breathing a little hard. I crunched the bean, and the combination flavors of cocoa and coffee exploded in my mouth.

Zack leaned yet closer. Kissing him would be the most natural thing in the world. My heart was jumping around in my chest like a frantic baby bird. I was aware of every sensation—of the warm August air, of the birds singing overhead, of the blanket beneath me, of the smells of leaves and grass and chicken and chocolate. Our faces came closer. He was so beautiful, a golden-haired God of thieves. I pulled back.

"What's the treasure, then?" I asked.

"Treasure?" Zack swallowed hard, clearly trying to regain his composure. "Uh…right. It's…it's a bunch of old papers."

"Not exactly news," I said, plucking another bean from the sack. Caffeine in its raw, natural form. Can't go wrong with that. It was also the perfect distraction. Zack was right next to me, and I wanted to pull his arms around me, feel his solidness and warmth.

"You need some background to understand," he said. "Look, the Peale family got started in Philadelphia back in the seventeen hundreds. Roger Peale, my great-something-grandfather, was working in a print shop as an apprentice."

I snapped my fingers. "Victor Peale was in publishing before the Detroit house burned down. A generational family business, then."

"Yeah. Roger lived in Philly right when everything was moving and shaking in the colonies. According to family legend, Roger didn't actually want to be a printer. He wanted to study history. But his family wasn't rich enough for that to work out for him. He *did* realize that the events going on around him would be important. Roger attended speeches and meetings whenever he could and kept a very detailed diary of everything. The diary would be immensely valuable to an historian."

"But it wouldn't be worth a gazillion dollars," I said.

Zack shook his head. "Probably not. But Dad said that Roger had kept other papers, ones far more valuable. He wasn't all that interested in talking about it. In retrospect, I think he was trying to forget about his family altogether."

I leveled him a hard look. "So you *don't* know exactly what the treasure is. And for that you wanted a kiss."

"Still do."

"Right." I popped another espresso bean into my mouth and put my dishes back into the basket. "You can earn that kiss by helping me track down Uncle Lawrence."

"You know where he is?" Zack asked, perking up.

"In a way." I picked up the dusty black notebook. "While you were gathering picnic paraphernalia, I went back to the house and checked the leaf collection. Uncle Lawrence may have been a packrat gone haywire, but he was anal-level organized, and my suspicions were correct—the final notebook was an index."

I opened the book and showed Zack a series of lists— leaves, Latin names, volume numbers, and page numbers— all in neat columns.

"Okay, so what?" Zack asked.

"Patience, young grasshopper. Earlier today I confirmed that Uncle Lawrence owns a truck, though it's not at the house. That means he took it somewhere else. I also found some waterproofing goop for tents and some camouflage netting in the garage."

"So he's camping somewhere," Zack said. "And he's camouflaged his tent. Good to know, Terry, but not helpful in tracking him down. We can check the local campgrounds, sure, but he could be hiding on any unused bit of land."

"Now, now," I said. "You're forgetting about the leaf collection he showed you. I took the notebook down to the botany department at the University, did a little asking around, and came up with this." From the notebook I slid a folded sheet of paper and handed it to Zack, who unfolded it. "It's a map of the Arboretum, with all the species of all the big trees marked on it. This place is more than an arboretum—it's a research center for the University, and they have it all mapped out. The map confirms what I suspected."

Zack furrowed his brow. "That all the leaves in Uncle Lawrence's collection came from the Arboretum."

"Ten points," I said, and impulsively kissed him. On the cheek. While he was recovering from that, I added, "I'm willing to bet Uncle Lawrence is camping in the Arb. It's a familiar place, and he obviously likes it here. Camping in the Arb is against the law, but if he's hidden his tent carefully enough, no one would notice. So let's go find him."

We finished putting supper away (except for the espresso beans), stashed the basket and notebook in a clump of bushes so we wouldn't have to carry them, and headed deeper into the Arboretum. The wood-chip trail we chose wound steadily downward, and the ridge rose steadily higher beside us. I was in a good mood. All my instincts hummed, telling me I was right, that Uncle Lawrence was here somewhere. The only problem was that the Arboretum is almost a hundred and twenty-five acres plus various pieces of surrounding land that most people *think* are the Arboretum but aren't. The place is chock-full of steep hills, hidden groves, and unexpected depressions. A decent search could take a whole team several days, and we had only the two of us.

I said as much to Zack, who tapped his chin with one finger as we walked downhill. "There has to be a way to narrow it down," he said. "Where would he *not* be?"

"The open areas, of course," I said, pulling out the map. "And any place with lots of foot traffic."

We finally settled on half a dozen places to check, all of them in the valley, and spent a fairly pleasant hour hiking around to check them out. At first it seemed a beautiful day for it. The green trees kept the sun off us, and our feet tossed up the pleasant smell of earth and wood chips from the trails. But every so often, we had to leave the trail and push through undergrowth to check out groves and thickets, and the hiking turned into hot, sweaty work. I was glad for the water bottle in my belt. Sweat darkened Zack's red polo shirt, and he often removed his cap to swipe at his forehead, revealing blond hair gone dark and curly.

By the time the sun touched the top of the hills cupping the valley, we had found nothing encouraging. I began to feel discouraged. I was probably wrong about Uncle Lawrence's hiding place, which meant looking like an idiot in front of Zack. He never made a smart remark, however, even after he had pushed through something thorny to check a hidden clearing. Purple shadows were slipping out from under the trees and birds sang bedtime songs. We would have to leave soon—the Arb closes at dusk. My disappointment grew. I had been so *sure*.

"I think we need to give it up for now," I said reluctantly. We were skirting the edge of a hilly area that becomes a popular sled hill in winter. "The bike patrol will be coming through here pretty soon to throw everyone out."

"Yeah, you're probably right," Zack said. "We can try again tomorr—" He paused and stared into the woods. "Wait a minute. What's that?"

I jerked my head around, heart pounding. "What? Where?"

He grinned. "Psych."

"You shit!" I punched his shoulder and he fell back in mock pain. "You complete creep!"

And then, without knowing quite why, I lunged for him. A surprised look flashed across his face as he tumbled backward into the bushes with me on top of him. I felt hard muscle move beneath warm skin.

"Hey!" he protested. "Get off!"

I sat on his chest, my knees on his outflung biceps. Zack outweighed me, but he didn't have the leverage to move. I leaned down until my lips almost brushed his. Zack looked up at me, a question in his eyes.

"Apologize," I said.

The question vanished. "Never!"

Zack twisted like a cat and I lost my hold. He rolled over on top of me, but I managed to get my knees up. I gathered my strength and straightened my legs hard. Zack flew backward a good three feet. I shot upright and fled into the brush, laughing over my shoulder at him. Zack crashed after me. Leaves caught in my hair. I felt like Daphne fleeing Apollo, and I wondered if part of her had wanted the God to catch up, wondered what would happen if he did.

The tent popped up in front of me like a forest spirit. I skidded to a halt, and Zack nearly plowed into me. It was a small cabin tent covered in rough camouflage netting with leaves and twigs stuck all over it. We both stared at it, then glanced at each other. There was no way anyone in there wouldn't have heard us coming. The gloom in the thicket was deepening by the moment.

I motioned for Zack to stay where he was and sidled up to the tent. "Hello?" I said. "Is anyone in there?" No response. I tapped the top of the tent, setting it to shaking. "Uncle Lawrence?"

Still no response. Moving quickly, I grabbed the tabs and zipped the tent open. A breath of damp, moldy air puffed over me. The interior was dark, but I could make out a pile of blankets—unoccupied—and a few other non-Lawrence-shaped objects.

"If this is his tent," I said, straightening, "he's not here."

"No kidding," Zack said. "It might not be—"

A twig snapped. I spun and looked straight at a gray-haired man. He wore dirty farmer jeans over an equally dirty t-shirt. His red baseball cap was almost exactly like Zack's except for the dirt. The man's eyes were wide. He stared at me like a startled deer, then turned and ran. The moment he turned his back, I recognized him as the man I had chased through the mansion.

"Lawrence!" Zack shouted, confirming his identity. "Wait! It's me!"

We both gave chase but were at a disadvantage. It was almost dark and Uncle Lawrence knew the terrain. Branches and twigs whipped across my face and roots snagged at my feet. I heard Zack breathing hard behind me.

"Wait!" I called. "I just want to talk!"

The trees ended and we burst into an open area of mowed lawn. The light was better out here. I glanced left and right and saw Uncle Lawrence following the tree line. He was heading for the river.

"Quick!" Zack said. "We can still catch him!"

I saw the tiny flash of light in the trees a split-second before I heard the *crack*. Zack went down without a sound.

TWELVE

"ZACK!" I screamed. Another muzzle flash flickered near the trees, followed by another *crack*. I dove back into the bushes and something buzzed over my head. Was Uncle Lawrence the shooter? No—wrong direction.

"Zack," I said, then clamped my lips together so I wouldn't give away my position. *Don't panic, girl,* I growled to myself. *Use your head.*

My head threw me an image of Zack lying dead on the grass and I bit the inside of my mouth to keep the fear and anxiety from pouring out in a long scream. More constructively, I grabbed the cell from my belt and punched in 911.

"I'm in the Arboretum," I told the dispatcher. "There's a man with a gun. He shot my companion. We need an ambulance and police."

My instincts were screaming at me to run out and help Zack. I told them to shut up—calling for help was the intelligent thing to do. Jesus, why had I left my gun in the Jeep?

"Where are you in the Arboretum?" the dispatcher asked, infuriatingly calm. "I need to tell rescue where to find you."

That stopped me cold. Where the hell was I?

"I don't know," I gasped, and forced myself to think, retrace my steps while Zack lay dead or bleeding a few feet away. "Shit. Uh… I came in at the hospital entrance, and from there came down into the valley."

"Ambulance and police are on the way, ma'am. Stay where you are, and stay on the line."

The hell with that. I clicked off, set the phone to vibrate, and crawled toward the tree line. In the growing darkness I made out Zack's frighteningly still form. I couldn't tell if he was breathing.

"Heyyyyy, girlie!"

The voice was cold and dead, and it echoed faintly across the valley. Ice slid up my spine and made the hair on my neck rise.

"I shoot your boyfriend, girlie," the voice called out. "Come out now. He still might live."

His accent sounded like...Slava's? My mind flicked back to what Ms. Hawk had said about the dead man in Uncle Lawrence's house. I couldn't remember his name, but he had come from Georgia, once part of Russia. I remembered the dog cages we had found in the warehouse, and a dreadful suspicion stole over me.

"Girrrrrlieee!" the man sang. "You come out! We find you soon!"

We? Was he bluffing or was there more than one of him out there? Tension twined my guts into a cold knot. Zack might be dying, but I couldn't help him without getting a bullet through the head.

Another flash from the muzzle of a pistol, and a bullet sliced through the leaves not far from me. He obviously didn't have a night scope. Otherwise he would have shot right at me. A small plus.

I knew what I had to do. No time to wait for the police. Zack could be dying, and every second counted.

Okay, calm. Breathe like *Kyosa* Parkinson taught you. This was nothing but a problem to be solved, a lock to be opened. But quickly. Zack might be bleeding to—no! Concentrate on the enemy. He had given away his position several times with the muzzle flash, the shots, and the shouting. He was a fool.

A fool with a weapon, I reminded myself.

The spot where the shots had come from was about thirty yards away, across the clearing. I was pretty sure the shooter was hiding beneath the drooping fronds of a willow tree. The main woods arced around to my right. I mentally traced a path, then oozed out of the bushes and dropped to my stomach. It was dark now, and a tiny sliver of moon gave weak silver light. Grass tickled my throat. Zack was a few steps away to my left. I shot him a glance. Was he breathing? I couldn't tell. My nerves screamed at me to help him, but the gunman would be expecting that, watching for it, and I would be dead in an instant.

Gritting my teeth, I got to my hands and knees, praying the darkness would be enough cover. Crashing through the bushes might keep me hidden, but the sound would give away my position. Grimly I crawled forward like a spider. My skin itched, waiting for the bullet to come.

"You help your boyfriend," the man called from his hiding place beneath the willow. "He dies soon if you do nothing."

My teeth ground together, but I kept crawling. Sweat broke out and trickled down my collar. Ten yards. Twenty. Rocks and roots dug into my hands, knees, and thighs. Something slashed my palm, and I bit my lip to keep from crying out. Thirty yards. I flicked a glance over my shoulder. Zack's form was just another shadow among many. Did he think I was abandoning him? Maybe he was already dead.

shut up, shut up, shut up, shut up.

I judged I was far enough away from the willow tree to make a run. With a quick breath and an equally quick prayer, I rose into a crouch and skittered across the clearing. The moon cast a wan shadow that kept pace with me. I tripped over something, rolled with the fall, regained my feet, kept running. Don't stop, don't think, just run. The opposite tree line was just ahead of me.

"You come out, girlie! I have nice bullet just for you. You cannot hide always."

Hatred of that voice boiled inside me, and I forced myself to keep calm. I reached the tree line, dropped to my stomach, and waited a dozen fast heartbeats. No response. I got back on my hands and knees and followed the tree line back to-

ward the willow. The ground was smoother on this side, for
which I was grateful.

"Maybe boyfriend still alive. Must be hard to keep hiding like coward."

Boy, was this guy *dumb*. Whoever hired him must have
really been desperate.

Like you? a traitorous voice whispered in my head. *Who's
the fool, the one hiding with the gun or the one sneaking
around without any weapon whatsoever?*

Maybe I should have just fled the Arboretum entirely. But
that would have left Zack behind, and the thought was absolutely unthinkable. The willow tree slumped just ahead of
me, a sleeping giantess with long hair that gleamed silver in
the moonlight. I went down to my stomach again and inched
forward a maddening millimeter at a time. Ten years later, my
outstretched hands touched the trailing fronds as they brushed
the ground. I stopped breathing and snaked forward. My arms
and legs were on fire at the unaccustomed exercise. I was used
to running, jumping, and fighting, not crawling like a worm.

I parted the fronds a finger's width and peered into the
space beyond. A shadowy male silhouette stood at the curtain of fronds only a few feet from me. He was peering out
across the clearing like a nosy neighbor, except this neighbor
carried a high-powered rifle. If he turned his head, he would
probably see me. I would have only one chance, and I would
have to move fast. Anticipation rose and tingled in my hands
and feet. Digging myself in like a racer on starting blocks, I
gathered myself and *lunged.*

Time slowed for me like it always does. The man turned as I
burst through the fronds and did a shoulder-smash straight into
him. His rifle spun away in a metallic arc. The man's body was
solid, but my momentum and his surprise bowled him over.

He went down with me on top. I rolled away, but he caught
the back of my shirt and yanked me backward. I brought up
my elbow and connected with something meaty. He "oofed"
and let go. I scrambled to my feet and spun to face him, shift-

ing my weight for a fast kick. But he braced himself and did that neat little maneuver that lets you shoot to your feet in one smooth motion. Shit. I'd been practicing that move for months and still hadn't mastered it, and this bozo flips upright like a gymnast.

We didn't speak. He swung a fist. I blocked with one arm and snapped a punch to his gut with the other. He grunted but managed to grab my wrist before I could yank it back. He twisted, yanked, and spun me around so I was facing away from him, my arm trapped behind me. His harsh grip left bruises around my wrist. I back-punched with my free arm and caught him on the bridge of the nose. His hand loosened and I broke free. I tried a spin kick, but he ducked beneath it, smooth as mercury.

"Your boyfriend die," he said. "We fight and he die."

That shook me for half a second, and he took swift advantage. His fist clipped my chin. Pain exploded through my head and I staggered back a step. The man landed a sideways kick in my midriff. The breath whuffed out of me and I landed flat on my back, halfway through the curtain of willow leaves. My right hand touched something cold and smooth, and the world rocked dizzily.

The man stepped through the fronds, stood over me, and drew a pistol. Dimly I wondered why he hadn't done that earlier. He flicked off the safety and took careful aim. My hand clenched around the rifle barrel I had touched.

"Now you die, too."

I swung. The long rifle caught him on the side of the head. His knees buckled. Anger seized me now. Before he could recover, I rolled to my feet and swung again. The rifle smacked his head with a sickening, satisfying *crack*. He dropped. Panting, I snatched up his pistol. Even in the dark I could tell it was a Glock. I pointed it at his head. Red anger blazed hot in my blood. This was the asshole who had shot Zack and tried to kill me. A quick death was more than he deserved. I held the pistol steady and squeezed the trigger.

At the last second, I jerked the gun sideways. The shot cracked through the night air and went wide. I sighed and lowered the pistol. I wasn't going to kill this guy. I wouldn't sink to his level.

I did give him an extra kick in the gut instead, though.

For a split-second I considered taking the rifle, then dismissed it as too difficult to carry. I flung it into the dark woods instead, holstered the pistol, and all but flew across the clearing to Zack.

He still lay where I had left him. My heart continued to pound and my aching head throbbed at every beat. *Please, please, please be alive.*

My CPR training took over. I knelt beside Zack, put my ear to his face and my fingers to his neck so I could simultaneously check pulse and breathing. His skin was cold. For a sickening moment I felt nothing. Then Zack exhaled warm breath over my cheek and I found a steady pulse. Relief weakened every muscle. I ran my hands quickly over his body, checking for wounds by touch and finding none, but the side of his head was sticky with blood. Where the hell was the rescue squad? I pressed the light on my watch to check the time and discovered not even five minutes had passed since my 911 call.

Zack didn't seem to be in danger at the moment, but with head injuries, who knew for sure? I pulled my flashlight from my belt and crashed through the bushes to Uncle Lawrence's tent, where I snatched up a pair of moldy-smelling blankets, returned to Zack, rolled him onto the first, and covered him with the second. Then I picked up two corners of the bottom blanket and pulled. Zack slid smoothly across the grass, heavy but manageable.

I was running on automatic pilot now. An exit to Geddes Road was at the top of the hill, and it was the closest way out. I hauled on the blanket, ignoring the protests from my back, amazed at my own strength and how fast I was able to move. Years of working out were paying off in ways I had never imagined. The blanket made a faint hissing noise as I drew it over grassy ground. I was almost at the gate when I heard sirens wailing in the distance, giving me a moment's relief— until I realized they were heading for the hospital entrance, where I'd come in. I was almost to Geddes Road, a completely different entrance. Shit! I yanked out my cell phone and dialed 911 again.

"I called earlier about the gunshots in the Arboretum," I said. "My friend needs medical attention, but we're not at the hospital entrance. We're almost to the Geddes Road entrance."

"I'll alert the ambulance and the police," said the operator, a different one. "Please stay on the—"

I clicked off and went back to hauling. Zack was a dead weight. I dragged him upward, refusing to stop and rest. At one point, I did pause to glance over my shoulder, thinking that there were people on the hill. Then the impression was gone, and I went back to work.

I was panting and sweaty, my muscles burning from the fast, continual workout. The sirens continued to wail, but were still far off by the time I got to the Geddes Road gate. The Arboretum is big, and the roads that make up its boundaries are twisty and difficult to navigate at night, which would slow the drivers down.

I left Zack on the ground and dashed through a gate in a low stone wall onto Geddes Road, a winding, tree-lined affair peppered with enormous houses that never run lower than seven figures. I peered left and right, hoping for a glimpse of whirling lights, then flung myself back into shadow.

A battered red truck with a camping top was parked across the road. Sitting in front of it was a brand new SUV. Two men dragged the limp figure of a third toward the truck. A dirty red baseball cap fell off the third man's head—Uncle Lawrence. He was either unconscious or dead.

A fourth man pointed a keychain at the SUV and chirped it open. He was blocky and square. His two partners hauled Uncle Lawrence to the back of his own truck, opened the camper cab, and none-too-gently shoved him into the back.

The sirens grew closer yet, and I saw red lights through the trees. The third man barked something in another language. Russian. My blood went cold, and my earlier suspicion exploded into full-blown certainty. Even before the man turned toward his men and the streetlight illuminated his face, I knew what I would see. A knife scar split the boss's right eyebrow like a lightning bolt and I recognized the square face of Stanlislaw Yerin, the *Pakhan* who had overseen the child-slavery ring in Russia.

Oh, hell, no.

Yerin jumped into the SUV and his two lackeys climbed into Uncle Lawrence's truck. Both vehicles started up, and I didn't hesitate. The sirens were almost on us, but explaining everything to the police would take too long and give Yerin too much of a head start. I sprinted across the street and reached the back of Uncle Lawrence's truck just as it started to pull away. I lunged for the lip of the tailgate and caught it. My feet dragged the ground for a moment before they gained purchase on the bumper. The door of the cab swung open, then banged shut on my hand, and I almost yelped at the pain. I was going to be a mess in the morning—assuming I ever saw the sun rise again.

I lifted the door just enough to haul myself underneath it and into the back of the truck. Then I lifted it again to peek out. Police cars and an ambulance were coming to a halt at the Arboretum entrance. They'd certainly find Zack, who I had left only a few feet inside the gate.

I *hoped* they'd find him. Jesus, I hoped.

The back of the truck smelled of exhaust fumes and old paper. All kinds of junk rattled around as we swerved and bumped down the road—newspapers, boxes, cans, bottles, even a dented trash can. I was knee-deep. A filthy window lay between the driver's cab and the truck bed, and I couldn't see anything through it. Conversely, this meant the driver and his hulking friend couldn't see *me*—a clear benefit.

My quarry lay beside me and, with an understandable sense

of *déjà vu,* I checked him for breathing, pulse, and injuries. Like Zack, he was unconscious but breathing, with a steady pulse. He smelled of stale body odor and leaf mold. So this was the elusive Uncle Lawrence. I had a thousand questions for him, but he was in no condition to answer. Why is it men always go to sleep just when you want to talk?

Okay, maybe that was unfair. But still.

I peered out the back door again, though all I could see was rushing road and dark trees. Adrenaline zinged through every nerve. If I got caught back here, I was dead. No ifs, ands, or buts. I fingered the Glock in my holster. The metal was comforting. I wondered if I should risk breaking it down by touch and counting the number of bullets. Best to leave it alone, I decided. I might drop a bullet in the dark, and I'd never find it again.

My cell vibrated like a frog squirming in my pocket, and I jumped. Thank God I had shut off the ring function. With a wary glance toward the front of the truck, I pulled it out, turned the volume way down, and answered. It was Ms. Hawk.

"Where are you?" she said. Her low, rich voice calmed the adrenaline fizzing in my blood. She was with me and everything would be all right.

"In the back of Uncle Lawrence's truck," I said in a voice just above a whisper. "Some guys shot at me and Zack in the Arboretum and—"

"Shot?" Ms. Hawk interrupted. "What happened?"

I explained as tersely as I could. The truck went around several turns, then sped up considerably. We were on the highway. "So I jumped into the truck just before they drove away," I finished. "Do you know if Zack is all right?"

"I'm nowhere near the Arboretum," Ms. Hawk said. "So I'm afraid I don't."

The hope that had been rising inside me abruptly dropped into my feet. "There's more," I said. "Stanislav Yerin is here."

Brief pause. "I'd guessed as much. Do you remember the other case I mentioned?"

The one she'd been working on while I searched the house alone with Zack on the Day of Many Doughnuts. "Yes."

"I was actually following another lead on the Peale case, cashing in some favors, and I learned what the Peale family has been smuggling."

"I know," I said. The sentences slid from my mouth like cold worms. "The kennels aren't for dogs, and that food wasn't for the Peales. They're both for the…the…" I couldn't say it.

"For the children," Ms. Hawk finished. "Yes."

I closed my eyes, feeling cold and sick. Until Ms. Hawk said the words aloud, I had been able to keep the knowledge at arm's length, pretend I didn't *really* know. It made dreadful, terrible sense. All this time I thought everything had been about the Peale family papers, but the treasure was a tiny footnote in a much larger story. Stanislav Yerin's branch of the Russian mafia needed American contacts, and the Chicago Peales had been looking to diversify their empire. A match made in hell. Yerin and his men snatched children off the streets and out of state-run orphanages and brought them by tramp steamer, most likely to Canada, which has a coastline much less crowded than anything America has to offer. The children would then be brought by truck to Windsor, right across the river from Detroit, a major point of entry for smuggling human slaves into the States. A quick boat ride across the Detroit River after dark, and *voila!* Instant slavery.

Dog cages, of course, would be so much easier than chains for long-term transport. Escaping chains is possible, but escaping a locked dog kennel? Hard for an adult, let alone a kid. Hell, you wouldn't even need to open the door for meal times. Easy enough to dump some canned stew through the bars and into a dog dish. I felt sick again.

Once the "cargo" was safe in Detroit, another truck could haul everything—every*one*—to Chicago, and from there— who knows? America is a big country, with lots of wealthy people who are happy to pay through the nose for their private kicks. I remembered the girl with the peanut-butter-cup eyes. She had escaped. How many girls like her hadn't?

Junk slipped and slid around the back of the truck as it continued down the highway and I wondered where the hell we were going. Uncle Lawrence didn't move. A shoebox fell onto his back and popped open. Rubber bands—thousands of them—cascaded over him like tiny snakes.

"The Russian mafia must have been watching me," I said. "They put the pictures in my mailbox and the jack-in-the-box in my car. So why didn't they just kill me?"

"They may have felt that another murder would call too much attention to the case," Ms. Hawk said. "Or perhaps they were hoping that if you didn't drop the case, you would lead them to Lawrence Peale."

"And I did. Dammit! But why didn't they kill him?" It was weird discussing this in the back of a drafty, smelly truck filled with junk and an unconscious old man. Not ten feet away sat two armed men who would happily fill my brain with bullets.

"They need Lawrence Peale alive," Ms. Hawk said. "Perhaps he knows something."

"The notebook," I breathed. "He had a complete schedule—time and place—of their arrivals. They must have learned about it and realized it could destroy their operation. That's why they were searching his house. They picked the lock and went in. They somehow avoided the cement-block deadfall, but that guy from Georgia triggered the magazine trap and suffocated. Problem was, they couldn't find the notebook—or anything else. So the Peales *and* the Russians need Uncle Lawrence to tell them where the notebook is, since they're working together on the child trafficking, but the Peales want him alive for something else—so he can tell them where the treasure is."

"That would be my assessment as well," Ms. Hawk said. "All we need to do is rescue the two of you."

"Is the GPS in my phone tracking where I am?" I asked Ms. Hawk.

"I'm just now checking on my laptop. Hold on…hold on…" I heard keys clicking in the background. The truck swerved abruptly and someone honked a horn. I almost dropped the phone before I recovered my balance.

"I have you," Ms. Hawk said. "You're moving eastbound on I-94."

"Heading for Detroit," I said. "The warehouse? Maybe you should call the police and have them meet us there."

"It would turn into a hostage situation," Ms. Hawk said. "Do you think you can escape?"

I glanced at Uncle Lawrence's prone form. "I probably could, but I don't know about—"

A tone beeped in my ear. Startled, I checked the display. A call was coming in from a number my phone didn't recognize. Could it be…? I told Ms. Hawk to hold on a second, then accepted the call.

"Terry!" came the welcome, reliable sound of Zack's voice. "Are you all right?"

Relief flooded me like warm water. "Me? What about you? I saw you get shot, but—"

"The EMTs said the bullet barely grazed me," Zack said. "I lost a little blood and I have a Godzilla-sized headache, but I'm perfectly fine otherwise. They wanted to take me to the hospital, but I took off."

I realized my throat was thick and a tear had leaked from my eye. I brushed it away impatiently. This was no time for that sort of thing. The car ride had smoothed out, and I cast a wary eye toward the cab of the truck. No sign I had been detected.

"Hold on," I said. "I've got Ms. Hawk. Let me get you on three-way."

A few button clicks, and the three of us could talk at once.

"I'm on my way to the Arboretum, Mr. Archer," Ms. Hawk said, after a terse explanation for Zack. "We can drive to the warehouse together. I think it would be best if we called the police."

"So do I," said Zack. "They get paid for this kind of thing. Besides, the *Free Press* will probably pay a pretty penny for the pictures."

"Just get my good side during the hostage negotiations," I said, feeling less tense by the moment. With Ms. Hawk on the way, everything would work out. It wouldn't dare not.

The three of us clicked off after that. I put my cell in my breast pocket, settled in next to Uncle Lawrence, and waited. And waited. I checked the time on my cell. It was taking way longer to get to the warehouse than it should have. This wasn't right.

The truck slowed, then made a quick turn that tossed me off balance again. I fell against Uncle Lawrence and thought I heard him groan softly. Another quick turn in the other direction threw me off again. A garbage bag full of empty milk cartons burst open and bobbled over me, dribbling sour milk everywhere. What was going on?

The truck halted. The doors up front opened and the truck rocked slightly as the thugs got out, though the engine was still running. Tension trilled through me. I was already half-buried in milk cartons, so I burrowed deeper into the truck's junk collection, trying to be quiet. For the first time, I was glad Uncle Lawrence was a trashaholic. I was just pulling my right foot farther into hiding when I heard the rear door of the camper top squeak upward. A waft of summer air caressed my ankle, and I froze. Was my shoe exposed? No way to tell.

The men spoke in harsh Russian sentences that I couldn't understand, and it sounded like they were only inches away from me. I wanted to yank my foot into hiding, but knew movement would only draw attention to it. I desperately wished I could see what was going on, but my vision was obscured by the very stuff that hid me.

One of the men said something that drew a harsh response from his companion. Someone hawked and spat, and I heard a tiny *splat* not far from my head. My heart beat like a hummingbird's, and I prayed with every ounce of strength that they wouldn't notice a size eight woman's tennis shoe sticking out of a pile of milk cartons. Just another piece of trash, nothing to investigate or get excited about.

Metal clanked and thudded. They were bringing down the tailgate. I heard junk spill out of the truck, and the stuff over my head shifted dangerously. One of the men said something that sounded like swearing. I held my breath. A sludgy trickle of old milk oozed down my cheek. It smelled awful, but I didn't move.

A third voice joined the first two—Stanislav Yerin's. He barked something that was obviously an order, and a moment later something slid out of the truck. The thugs were hauling Uncle Lawrence out. I took a slow breath tinged with the lovely smell of rotten milk, and hoped they would hurry up.

The tailgate went back up and the camper door came down with a double bang. Footsteps headed back to the cab of the truck. I stayed put, just in case.

The truck's engine abruptly raced, snarling like an angry chainsaw. Before I could react, everything lurched forward. I burst out of hiding, but less than a second later the nose of the truck dipped sharply downward. Junk poured over me as I fell back toward the cab. I almost screamed, but managed to hold it in. What was—

A terrible jolt, then a terrible splash. The dirty side windows showed water spraying in a thousand directions. Then the truck began to sink.

THIRTEEN

I CLAWED MY way forward as cold water poured in through the door above the tailgate. Junk swirled in dirty eddies, trying to shove me backward. The truck dropped toward the bottom in slow motion, and I felt the movement in my stomach. How deep was the water? Jesus, I had to get *out*. I batted aside a floating cardboard box and lunged at the tailgate. The back of the truck was pitch black, but my head was still in a narrow pocket of air, maybe six or eight inches' worth.

The truck was tilted at a forty-five-degree angle. My hand hit metal, but I couldn't see below the waterline. The water was cold, and my clothes dragged at me. Panic pounded at my chest. Where was the top of the tailgate? I fumbled around in the dark water, tilting my head back to keep my mouth and nose above water.

The truck's nose hit bottom with a jolting crash. I barely managed to gulp some air before I went under. A second later, the rear wheels hit, but with less force. Objects floated around me, and I heard my own heart pounding in my head. Already feeling desperate for air, I shoved myself toward what I hoped was the back of the truck. Utter blackness had enveloped me, and it didn't matter if my eyes were open or closed. I felt another box and shoved it aside, then another. My lungs ached. Then I felt metal and a latch. The back of the truck! I shoved against the rear door, trying to push it up. It resisted—the water held it back. Another burst of panic ripped through me. This truck would be my coffin. I was going to drown, alone in the dark. Ms. Hawk and Zack would never know what happened to me. I pushed again, and the door opened upward with aching slowness. My lungs begged me to exhale and take in a huge gulp of sweet air, but there was none to be had.

The door opened enough for me to slide through. I eeled out of the truck and kicked off the back bumper with all my fading strength. My belt, heavy with equipment, dragged at my hips and weighed me down, so I unclipped it and let it sink. The water was black as octopus ink, and I had no idea how deep I was. Water pressed painfully against my eardrums. I swam and swam. Was I going the right way? I couldn't tell. I had heard stories of drowning people who got confused and swam in the wrong direction. Lights flashed behind my eyelids and I felt dizzy. I needed air, needed to breathe. Another stroke. And one more. Come on, Terry, you can do just one—

I broke through the surface and breathed. It was the most delicious feeling. I sucked down breath after breath. An adrenaline rush took over, and I felt like I could swim the English Channel. Terry Faye—woman of steel!

Once my heart and lungs settled down, however, I took stock of my situation. The sky overhead was dark and cloudy, as was the water I was swimming in. A long wooden dock sat on low pylons just in front of me. Two men, their backs to me, were walking toward the shore. They dragged Uncle Lawrence between them. Now that they had gotten rid of the all-too-traceable truck, they were free to do whatever they wanted to Uncle Lawrence. City lights burned past them, illuminating unfamiliar buildings. We were nowhere near the Detroit warehouse.

A small motored yacht was moored to one side of the dock. Its running lights were off, but I heard a motor purring. Someone—Yerin?—shouted something in Russian at the two thugs, who stepped up the pace. They were going to take Uncle Lawrence somewhere, and if that boat took off, we'd never find him again.

Without a splash, I swam under the dock. Water lapped against the slimy pylons, and footsteps clonked on the wood over my head. I reached the boat and glided alongside it. Overhead, the thugs complained as they hauled Uncle Lawrence into the boat.

I managed to reach the stern. The boat had two levels, and I wasn't enough of a sailor to know what their names were. A glass-enclosed cabin sat up top. Below it, a deck ran all the way around the vessel. At the stern, a ladder went down to a little platform that lay just below the waterline in case a diver wanted to climb aboard. It was also perfect for a sneak like me. Thanking God the yacht's lights were off, I made for the platform.

Abruptly the sound of the motor intensified, and the boat started moving away from the dock. Biting back swearwords, I lunged and missed. The boat turned, picking up speed. I lunged again, and this time I caught the edge of the platform and managed to haul myself onto it. The platform itself was about three inches below the waterline, so it made for a wet seat, but I was already soaked through. I thought about trying to climb aboard the yacht, and then I thought about the Three Goons with Guns, and then I thought how nice and comfy my current seat was. Perspective—the woman of steel's best friend.

The yacht slipped into deeper water, and I suddenly realized I had no idea what body of water this was. It could be the Detroit River, Lake Erie, or even a small inland lake. I felt at my breast pocket, deciding to check in with Ms. Hawk on my—

—empty pocket. My cell phone, complete with global positioning system, currently lay buried in junk at the bottom of who-knows-what body of water. Automatically my hand flashed down to my belt. The pistol I had swiped from the thug in the Arboretum was gone, too, discarded with my belt. Great.

Abruptly I missed Zack. I wanted to know he was near. I wanted him to make a joke or drive up in his ancient VW bus and help me out of this. I wanted him to wrap me in a towel and rub me dry with his strong hands. Stranded out here on the back of a strange boat filled with men who would kill me without a second's hesitation made me feel frighteningly, achingly alone. Abandoned. I pressed my forehead against the back of the boat and prayed Zack and Ms. Hawk would somehow figure out where I was and ride to the rescue.

Right. I firmed my jaw. In real life, no one rides to the rescue. In the end, everyone is alone. In the end, everyone abandons you. My ex-husband, my mother, my father. And now Zack and Ms. Hawk. I knew it wasn't fair to blame them for my current situation, but there it was. Zack had gotten shot, the big idiot, and scared me half to death. If it hadn't been for that, we might *both* be on this boat, and I wouldn't be alone.

Or Zack might have drowned in the truck. Or been found and shot by the Russian thug guys. Maybe it was a good thing he wasn't here, in danger. But I *wanted* him here. It was all so mixed up. I was mixed up.

My teeth chattered. The spray kicked up by the boat was *cold.* And then it came to me—I had to be on Lake Erie. Even in August, the Great Lakes are never truly warm, and now that the sun had gone down, I was feeling the chill.

The trip went on and on. Water lay dark below me. The yacht didn't once turn on its running lights, and I had no idea how Yerin was navigating. By some kind of GPS system, probably. Several times we passed boats and even ships with their lights full on. My hand was cramping up from holding on to the ladder, and I felt cold as a naked penguin. I'd have to find a way to warm up soon or I'd be in danger of hypothermia.

The motor slowed and I tensed. I couldn't see around the yacht to our destination. I doubted I'd see much anyway— the darkness was almost absolute. As if in response to my thoughts, a spotlight speared through the night from the top of the yacht. It swept the surrounding water like a white finger. I held my breath and clamped my teeth together to stop the chattering. But the spotlight didn't move in my direction. Instead it picked out a dock to the yacht's port side. The motor shut off and the yacht glided forward, guided by the spotlight. It bumped against wood and rocked gently on the water.

Men shouted in Russian and footsteps thumped above me. I couldn't stay there. Bracing myself, I pried my stiff fingers from the ladder and slipped carefully into the cold water. I swam the few feet to the dock, slipped underneath it, and allowed myself a sigh of relief. I was safe. More or less.

While Yerin and his men *thumped* around on the boat and dock yelling at each other, I scooted into shallower water. This area was a little warmer, though I was still shivering. I supposed that was a good sign. Lack of shivering was a sign of impending hypothermia. After a few minutes, all three men thudded over my head, still talking. I also heard the sound of a body being dragged. Poor Uncle Lawrence.

The footsteps faded away. I counted to fifty, then crept out from under the dock and took a cautious look around. The yacht was moored not far away, its lights off. Beyond the dock, the island rose from the water like a hill floating on black ink. At the top of the hill sat a large, multi-story house, and several of the windows blazed with gold light. A path led up to it from the dock. It was too dark to see if the thugs were on the path, but I imagined Yerin and his thugs were hauling Uncle Lawrence along it. Once they got whatever it was they wanted, they would kill him.

A breeze zipped across the water and washed cold over me. I shivered violently. All I wanted was a mug of hot coffee and a chair by a roaring fire. Hell, I'd settle for a cup of instant and a stool by the heating duct.

The yacht looked deserted. Time was limited for Uncle Lawrence, but the boat had too many helpful possibilities for me to pass up. I dashed down the dock and jumped aboard. The deck rocked gently beneath my feet. I had to half feel my way toward the door to the main cabin, though the dim light that made its way down from the house helped.

The door was unlocked, thank God. I scuttled inside and felt around the door jamb with fingers stiff from cold. I'm not much of a boat person, but I *do* know a few things, including the fact that most people keep an emergency light on the wall—or whatever they called walls on boats— next to the door. And I was right. My numb fingers found a flashlight. I pulled my sopping shirt tail from my waistband, cupped it around the end of the light, and switched it on. The dim light was enough to see by but wasn't bright enough to alert the thugs that someone was sneaking around their yacht. I hoped.

The room seemed to be some sort of sun room, complete with a small kitchen area and wet bar. I guessed bedrooms were below and the bridge was above. High-class place, and all paid for with the lives of small children. Mama Bear growled softly inside me and I told her to be quiet— I needed to concentrate.

A steep, narrow staircase led downward, and I took it. Yep—a short hallway with three sliding doors that opened into three tiny bedrooms. A fourth door opened into a pint-sized bathroom complete with teensy linen closet. Score! I was never so glad to see terrycloth in my life. I grabbed a towel and entered the first bedroom. It had a closet and a dresser. A quick check revealed clothing. Score again! A bit of rummaging turned up a set of sweats that were only a little too big. Drying off and pulling on fresh, dry clothes had never felt so wonderful. I found no underwear and my shoes were still wet, but I was beyond caring. I did a quick search for useful tools or weapons and came up empty. My lucky streak over, I bundled my wet things into the towel I had used, crept back upstairs, and tossed everything overboard. No use leaving my stuff around for someone else to find.

I was getting nervous now. No one knew where I was or how to find me. I was completely isolated, completely alone. No Ms. Hawk, no Zack. Not even any cops. My breath caught in my throat, and I forced calm on myself. I'd be fine. I just needed to find a way to bring help.

I headed upstairs to the bridge, this time with a washcloth over the flashlight to keep it dim. The controls made no sense to me, dashing any hope I might have had of using the yacht to escape. I couldn't even figure out how to start it. My eye, however, fell on the radio. Yes! The Coast Guard would be here in a matter of minutes. I grabbed for the mike.

The stupid radio didn't work. It seemed to be on, but the mike was completely unresponsive, no matter how often I pressed the button. I fiddled with frequency dials and poked at switches. Nothing. A small green screen winked at me. It read: *Enter Security Code.* Beneath the screen was a keypad. Shit! How paranoid could Yerin get? I entered a few four-digit numbers at random, praying for a miracle. I didn't get one. The radio remained stubbornly silent. No way to summon help.

I looked up at the house, cold and distant on its hill. My heart pounded like it was trying to escape my rib cage. Me. Alone. Facing a houseful of armed thugs. My knees went weak. I couldn't do it on my own.

On my own.

Abruptly I realized that it had always been that way for me. I had *never* done anything on my own. I had never lived on my own. I had never investigated a case on my own. Hell, I had never even trained for a job on my own—Mrs. Hawk had walked me through everything. Even my fight training, someone else taught me every step. I had spent my life surrounded by people who told me what to do and how to do it. Now Uncle Lawrence needed me, and I had the ultimate chance to show I *could* do something on my own.

If I could pull it off without being killed. I swallowed hard. I could just wait, hide in the boat or on the island. Eventually someone would work out where I was.

And Uncle Lawrence would be dead.

I straightened. No. I could do this. I *would* do this. Terry Faye, woman of steel, would not flinch from what needed doing.

An oddly light-hearted feeling washed over me and a lot of my fear abated. I was a strong, capable woman, and I could handle this. By myself.

In the end, I left the yacht with only the flashlight and my own two hands. Sure, the latter two were semi-deadly weapons, but Wonder Woman to the contrary, they wouldn't stop bullets, not even with silver bracelets. I would have given up cheesecake for life in exchange for a Glock.

I paused. Well, no—if I gave up cheesecake for life, I'd at least have to get a pair of Uzis. Or a tank.

I made my way up the path in my squishy shoes. Now that I wasn't soaking wet, the air was pleasantly cool. Crickets chirped below and stars glowed above. It would have been a beautiful night if I had been anywhere else.

The path curved a bit as it went up the hill. It was lined with scrubby bushes, and I stayed close to them, trying to walk in a crouch like cops do in the movies, except that hurts after a few dozen yards. Stupid TV. I alternated between crouching for safety and running upright for speed. The gravel path crunched underfoot, and I prayed no one would hear. Going through the bushes would give me more cover but would make more noise, so I stuck with the path.

Eventually I reached an expanse of scruffy lawn. A white, two-story house built with peaks and gables and a wide front porch sat in the center of it, looking out across the water. The place was battered by weather and in need of paint. A couple of the upper windows had been boarded up. Several other windows glowed with light from inside, the panes throwing yellow squares into the yard. No outdoor light, for which I was grateful—the people inside wouldn't be able to see out.

I crept up to the house. My heart beat fast again, and adrenaline tingled in my arms and legs. The first-story windowsills were a little higher than the top of my head. Zack could probably have stood on tiptoe to peer inside, but I had to chin myself, using the tips of my shoes to gain a little purchase against the side of the house. Splinters dug into my fingers as I pulled myself just high enough to get a peek, hoping I would see Uncle Lawrence. No such luck. I was looking through a kitchen window at four guys sitting around a table, eating and smoking. I could make out their voices. One of the men was Yerin. He turned his head toward the window, and I dropped back down in fear. Had he seen me? I dashed around the corner, flattened myself against the wall, and listened. Crickets, the soft lap of water, a distant boat horn. No slamming doors, running footsteps, or shouting voices. I allowed myself a bit of relief, though my stomach was still tight with tension. The odds against me looked pretty grim.

A window on this side of the house also had its lights on. Moving carefully, I chinned myself again, hoping for an empty room with a phone sitting on a table placed conveniently under the window. Instead I saw a room with a bed, a couple ladder-back chairs, and Uncle Lawrence. He sat tied to one of the chairs, hands behind him, gray head drooping downward. The dirty red ball cap was gone. My heart twisted. I had never even spoken to the man, but I felt protective of him nonetheless. How could I get him out of here? I had no boat, no gun, and no way off this island.

Uncle Lawrence wasn't moving, though I could see him breathing. My forearms burned, and I dropped back down to the ground to think. I might be able to get in through the window and untie him, but then what? We might be able to hide somewhere until daylight, but that wouldn't get us back to shore. I needed more information.

I ran around to the rear of the house. The hill was higher back here, and the back door was level with the ground. Beside it were some garbage cans and a lawnmower that looked like it had been left out in the rain for longer than I'd been alive. A little roof jutted out over the back door to protect it from the weather, and above that was a glowing window. I eyed the window speculatively. Zack was—or had been—a second-story man, but he wasn't here.

Before I could lose my nerve, I backed up, took a running start, and *leaped*. I got a good handhold on the roof above the door. The shingles were rough and a little damp with dew. Blessing every moment I had spent in the gym, I swung myself sideways left, then right, until I had enough momentum to get one foot up onto the roof. My foot made a thump when it hit the wood, and I froze. My forearms were burning again and my fingers hurt, but still I didn't move. My eyes and ears strained to catch something in the darkness. Nothing but the normal night-time sounds I was used to hearing.

One of my hands was starting to slip. I hauled myself up onto the shingles, half rolling onto the roof. Carefully I duck-walked over to the window, taking each step as slowly and noiselessly as a deer sneaking past a hunter. Once I was close enough, I peered through the glass. What I saw turned my stomach. Bile roiled around my insides, and bitter acid burned the back of my throat.

A large bedroom lay beyond the window. On the bare wooden floor sat a dozen wire dog kennels, each one barely big enough for the child it contained. Mama Bear roared anger and I kept hold with the barest grip. I counted ten girls and two boys, all dressed in ragged, dirty clothes, all of them under thirteen. Some lay curled up on the floor of their cages, asleep, others sat and stared at nothing. Two of them were crying softly, and a third rocked herself, arms wrapped around her knees. Anger pulsed like a living thing. I wanted to smash the window, destroy the cages, take the children out of there, gun down the thugs who had done this to them. But I had no weapons, and there was only one of me.

The door to the room opened and a thug strode in. I flattened myself against the wall below the sill. The sound of him stamping about the room came faintly through the glass. I held my breath. The sounds ended. Had he left? No way to know for sure without looking. I counted to ten…twenty…thirty.

The window above me scraped open. My heart almost stopped. A shadow moved. Without moving any other part of my body, I rolled my eyes upward to look. The thug was peering out the window. I held my breath. Cloth rustled, and the thug pulled a small flashlight from his pocket. He shined it on the ground around the little roof. The smell of stale tobacco clung to his clothes. I could have reached up and flicked his chin. The flashlight beam skittered around the yard below like a beam cast from a miniature lighthouse. Then the thug muttered to himself in Russian and pulled back into the window. He slammed it shut. I exhaled, feeling weak and trembly.

I waited a few minutes, then peered into the room again. The children continued to huddle in their cages, but the thug was gone. I eased to the edge of the roof and dropped down to the grass near the garbage cans. I was feeling more and more out of my depth, with no idea what my next move should be.

The *clack* of a cocking pistol sounded right behind me just as a cold gun muzzle pressed the back of my neck.

FOURTEEN

"You move," hissed a voice with a Russian accent, "you die."

Hey, who wants to die? I didn't move.

"Hands up. Move to house."

I obeyed. An odd calm dropped over me, a feeling I recognized. It usually takes over during a terrifying situation like this one. My mind goes into computer mode, gathering data, analyzing, planning. Once the situation is over, I usually have a total freak-out.

The thug nudged me through the back door and up a short flight of stairs into the kitchen. Thick cigarette smoke hung like gray fog in the air around a simple table littered with the remains of a junk-food supper. A hard wooden floor creaked beneath my feet. Leaning against the stove, cigarette in hand, was Stanislav Yerin. He was still built like a wooden block, with skin the color of pale wood. His eyes widened at the sight of me, and the scar that split his eyebrow spread slightly. The thug said something in Russian, and Yerin answered. Then he turned to me. My hands were still raised.

"I am happy to see you, Miss Faye," Yerin said. His accent was more British than Russian. "You and your partner cost me quite a lot of business when you shut us down in Moscow."

Mama Bear rumbled inside me at the thought of all the children this man had sold into sexual slavery, and anger edged over my enforced calm. "Glad to hear it," I said.

He blew out a long stream of smoke. "You made a mistake when you came here. Sergei has very keen ears, and when he said he heard something, we started looking. This island is quite small, Miss Faye, so it is not hard to search. And speaking of searching…" He drew a pistol and spoke sharply to Sergei, who holstered his own pistol and patted me down. Yes, he copped a generous feel. Yerin watched without comment.

"Now that you know my tits aren't armed," I growled, "what happens next?"

Another stream of smoke jetted into the already-choking air. "I don't know. You made me very angry, Miss Faye, and it will take time to settle on something appropriate. Sergei here is ex-KGB and he knows many interesting ways to cause pain. I am sure the rest of my men would be pleased to assist him."

As if on cue, the back door opened and three more thugs boiled into the house. The casual way he said this ate away some of my crisis composure. A cold spike pierced my chest and I instinctively shot Sergei a glance over my shoulder. He was smiling, and his eyes brimmed with eagerness, as if he were a child looking at the tree on Christmas morning. His expression turned my stomach.

"In the process," Yerin continued, "you will also tell us how much you know about our current operation, despite the changes we made." He flicked his cigarette butt into a wastebasket. "You and Mr. Peale both."

He barked another order in Russian, and Sergei shoved me forward. I stumbled across the dirty floor and down a short hallway to the bare bedroom where I had seen Uncle Lawrence tied to a chair. He was still there, hands tied behind him, though now he was awake. He stared at me with silent, bleary eyes. Sergei shoved me into a second chair and tied me up with swift efficiency. The ropes cut into my wrists and ankles, but I didn't give Yerin the satisfaction of hearing me cry out in pain.

Sergei smelled like fried sausage and his breath had onions on it. He stroked my ear with a cool fingertip. I glared hard at him, though I was starting to shake inside. I was in the deepest shit since…since ever. Zack and Ms. Hawk had no idea where I was or even how to look for me. It was me, myself, and I, and right now the three of us were tied up tight with no weapons and no way to get off this fucking island.

Just as Sergei was finishing up, a man with salt-and-pepper hair rushed into the room. He was lean and his eyes were hard. "You found the little bitch?" he snapped.

Yerin was lighting another cigarette. "My men are efficient, Mr. Peale."

My mind fished around and came up with the name Jackie Gold, the detective in Chicago, had given me. "Quentin Peale?" I said.

In answer, he backhanded me across the face. Pain crashed through my head.

"Don't injure her, Mr. Peale," Yerin said. "It will make her interrogation harder if she is only half-conscious."

"Aliens."

Everyone turned, though in my case it only involved my aching head. Uncle Lawrence was the one who had spoken.

"What's that, old man?" Quentin demanded.

"Aliens," Uncle Lawrence repeated. "You're all aliens. I lost my hat, and you were able to read my thoughts. That's how you found me."

"Oh, God." Quentin spat on the floor. "Not this bullshit again."

"It's true!" Uncle Lawrence grew more agitated. "You can't fool me. I know you're in disguise! The government let you land on Earth so you could take my treasure, but you'll never find it! Never!"

Quentin drew back his hand again, then apparently thought the better of it. "Sure, old man. We're aliens." He leaned in until he was almost touching Uncle Lawrence's nose. "And if you don't tell me where the treasure is, we're going to *probe you*."

Uncle Lawrence whimpered, his face pale as pizza dough. I felt so sorry for him—and for myself. It was clear Uncle Lawrence had a few leaks in his submarine, and I had no idea how to get *myself* out of this, let alone a lunatic old man and a room full of little kids.

A wave of anger washed over me. Where the hell was Zack? Why had the creep left me alone to handle this? Intellectually I knew it wasn't his fault, that he'd be here in a pico-second if he could, but I wasn't thinking all that rationally right then. I pulled at the ropes, but they remained stiff and unyielding.

"So you just want the treasure," I said. "This has nothing to do with selling children?"

Quentin shot me a look filled with acid. "It has everything to do with the goods," he snarled. "Both paper and people." Then his expression changed. His eyes became hungry, predatory. He stepped closer to my chair, a wolf edging up to the flock. "You've been through my cousin's house. My boys took pictures." He leaned in. His breath oozed warmth across my face. "What did you find?"

He clamped my earlobe between two fingernails and squeezed. Hot pain lanced my ear. I cried out and struggled to get away, but the ropes didn't budge. Behind Quentin, Sergei and Yerin watched the show with mild interest. Quentin kept up the squeezing for several long seconds, then released me. The pain of release was almost as intense as the initial grab, and I cried out again.

"Jesus," I yelled. "What the fuck are you doing?"

This time he slapped me. "Watch your language! I won't put up with blasphemy from a woman."

Okay, this guy was beyond help. My computer-like calm had returned, and my mind was moving fast. Amazing how quick you can think when survival depends on it.

"I'm sorry," I said instantly, casting my eyes down. Meek, submissive little woman. No need to slap. You fuckhead.

Quentin grabbed a chair, reversed it, and sat facing me over the back. "Better," he said. "Now. Let's set some ground rules. You are going to die. That's a given. The only question is how slowly and in how much pain. You can make it less painful by talking. First—where are the papers?"

In a way, his little speech was helpful. He thought I had information he needed, and that meant I could stall. The longer I stalled, the more likely some kind of help might arrive or a chance to escape would present itself. The hard part—and here I had to swallow—would be convincing him not to kill me or cause me permanent damage. Maybe it was a good thing my hands were tied—no one could see them shaking.

"I don't know where the papers are," I said, forcing my voice to remain even. "But I might be able to figure it out if you tell me about them. Like you said, I've been through that house more than anyone, and I know where stuff is."

"This is idiotic," Yerin said abruptly. "We need to learn how much she knows about the trafficking routes, and who she might have told. That is far more important that a bunch of old papers."

"Shut up," Quentin snapped. "You'll get your turn." He fixed his attention back on me. "Nice try, Hawkgirl. You tell *me* what *you* know about the treasure."

"No!" Uncle Lawrence vibrated with agitation in his bonds and the chair legs banged against the floor. His eyes were wide with a mixture of fear and horror. "No! The papers are *mine!* You can't take them back to Mercury with you. They'll burn up!"

"One more word, old man, and Sergei will slice your tongue in half," Quentin hissed. Uncle Lawrence went still, though his expression was terror personified. Quentin looked at me again. "Well? Spill your guts, girl, unless you want me to cut them out of you."

"I don't know much," I said as slowly as I dared. "Uncle Lawr—I mean, Mr. Peale here has a huge collection of U.S. history books in his bedroom. Several of them have bindings that break open at sections dealing with the Constitution, so I'm guessing the papers have something to do with that."

"Good guess," Quentin said. "What else?"

"Mr. Peale's leaf collection is also pretty important to him," I said. "Though I'm not sure exactly why."

226

"After the invasion from Mercury destroys the forests," Uncle Lawrence blurted out, "we'll be able to use them to clone new trees. I saved leaves *and* seeds."

"Shut *up!*" Quentin's fist clipped Uncle Lawrence. Uncle Lawrence's head snapped back and he gave a harsh grunt.

"You didn't have to do that," I said hotly. "He's not hurting you."

"It's fun," Quentin said. "He's been hiding *my* family papers in that fucking house of his for decades. They belong to *me.*"

"How do you know?" I countered. "Do you have a will or something that says they're yours?"

"I have tradition on my side," Quentin said. "I'm a direct descendent of Luke Peale, who was a direct descendent of Roger Peale. And I'm the youngest son. Family tradition says the papers always went to the youngest son, and—"

"Not the oldest?" I interrupted.

"No. Roger Peale was the youngest in his family and he felt that the youngest always got the short end of any inheritance, so he stipulated that his papers would always go to the youngest son. After the Civil War, that was Luke Peale."

Uncle Lawrence burst in again. "Not true! Luke and Bradley Peale were twins, and no one recorded which was born first. Their father gave the papers to Bradley, but Luke got jealous and stole them when—"

"Yeah, yeah, yeah." Quentin waved a hand. "He stole them when the Union army invaded Charlottesville. Your side of the family has been saying that so often, you think it's true. Never mind that Bradley only *claimed* their father left him the papers. No will was ever filed."

"Because Luke found it first and burned it!" Uncle Lawrence said.

"Right, old man." Quentin leaned toward his chair again. "So you don't think I'm an alien after all, do you?"

"You're a clone made by aliens," Uncle Lawrence said. His chair vibrated again. "Made so you can pass for human. I read all about it in the coded messages the government put in the newspapers. But I gathered up thousands of newspapers and hid the coded ones among them. You'll never find them now."

"We are wasting time," Yerin said. "We have more important things to do."

"This is my country, Yerin," Quentin said. "You're not in charge here."

I was hoping Yerin would retort and keep the argument going, but he traded glances with Sergei and fell silent instead. I decided to step in.

"So the Chicago Peales stole the papers from the Detroit Peales, and the Detroit Peales stole them from the Chicago Peales," I said. "Until Victor's house burned down in the forties and everyone thought they'd been destroyed."

"Dad knew how to fool everyone," Uncle Lawrence said proudly. A bruise was darkening on his cheek where Quentin had punched him. "No one had any idea that Howard and I had buried the papers before Dad set the fire."

"He burned his own house down?" I said in surprise. This hadn't occurred to me.

"Yep, yep," Uncle Lawrence said, nodding vigorously. "Made everyone think the papers had been destroyed, and the insurance money gave him an extra bit of cash. It made it easier for him to get out of publishing and into the automobile industry while the new house was being built. Dad knew how to fool 'em, yes he did. Yep, yep."

"Those papers are my *birthright,* old man," Quentin snarled at him. "Where did you hide them?"

"Howard hid them," he said. "He said it was somewhere obvious, but I didn't want to know in case you aliens got me." His eyes grew misty. "But now Howard's dead. At least I can't tell you where they are. Go ahead and read my mind and you'll see."

Yerin looked like he wanted to say something but stopped himself. Quentin turned to me. "Okay, girl—what's your theory? Where are my papers?"

I had no freakin' clue. My mind was flying in a dozen different directions, though, and I was getting really tired of all the "girl" cracks. "What do you want me to say? 'Four hundred and sixth box from the right'? I couldn't begin to tell you."

"But you could show me, right? So all we have to do is take you to the house, right? So you can try to escape, right?"

I remained silent, disgruntled that he had seen my plan. Quentin slapped me again, but almost as an afterthought, and it barely stung. The ropes digging into my wrists hurt worse. Yerin, meanwhile, gestured at Sergei, who stepped forward and grabbed the front of Uncle Lawrence's shirt. His eyes widened in fear.

"I want to know who else you told about the trafficking route," Yerin said in a voice as cold as a shark's underbelly. "You obviously told this girl. Who else did you talk to?"

"I didn't talk to anyone," Uncle Lawrence protested. "You paid me. We had a deal."

That got my attention, or it would have if I had let it wander. "You paid him?" I blurted.

"It was an enormous sum of money," Yerin said.

"Ten thousand dollars?" I said.

That got *Yerin's* attention. His eyes glittered as he turned to me. Sergei released Uncle Lawrence's shirt.

"How much do you know?" Yerin demanded.

Stall, stall, stall. "I know that Mr. Peale paid off his property taxes with a sudden large deposit to his savings account. I saw his financial records in the house." I paused to lick my lips, which were dry as sandpaper. "Could I have a drink? I'm parched here."

"Talk first," Yerin said. "Go on."

"Mr. Peale was spying on you for months. He even set up a little nest on top of the warehouse and wrote down every time you brought a *parcel*—" I spat that last word "—into Detroit and when it left for Chicago. Once he had enough evidence, he blackmailed you. Ten thousand dollars for his silence. But you didn't believe he'd keep his mouth shut, which is why you sent guys to pick the lock on his house and search for the evidence. You weren't looking for the treasure at all. But one of your guys—I forget his name. The one from Georgia."

"Ilya," Yerin said. "He was clumsy."

"That's for sure. He tripped one of Mr. Peale's deadfalls and suffocated under a pile of magazines. Mr. Peale didn't call the police, either because he was afraid of them or because he was worried about being linked with you, or both, so the body just stayed there. He was unable to throw that out, either, I guess." Ew. "Then *I* showed up and started searching."

"You mean *we,*" Yerin said, tapping his foot with impatience. "We know all about Hawk Enterprises and your photographer lover."

"He's not my lover," I shot back. "He only wishes."

An accompanying thought landed like an airplane: I wished it, too.

The sudden knowledge—okay, admission—dropped hard on me, and I felt unexpected tears come to my eyes. I was probably going to die, and I'd never hear Zack's voice again. We'd never hold hands or kiss or talk on the front porch while the moon rose. Stupid thing to be thinking about under the circumstances, but I couldn't help it. The tears threatened to spill over, and I blinked them back hard. These guys would only think I was crying because I was scared of them. Not that I *wasn't* scared of them—I just didn't need them thinking I would cry over it.

"Anyway," I said, suppressing the quaver in my voice, "with all these people going in and out of his house—including me—Mr. Peale became more and more nervous. Finally he fled and hid in the Arboretum." I cleared my throat. Still dry. "There's one thing I don't understand, though."

"And what's that?" Yerin replied, on cue.

"How Mr. Peale here found out about you in the first place."

"I saw him," Uncle Lawrence said. "I was looking for equipment. Sometimes the CIA hides stuff in Dumpsters. No one would think to look for it there, except me. I know the truth. Once, I was down at the docks in Detroit—the FBI building is there, and they're just a shell organization for the CIA—and I saw the Quentin clone. He's my sixth cousin. Or he was, before the aliens kidnapped him and put a clone in his place. I thought the warehouse was a secret clone farm, so I started watching it. No one pays attention to an old man going through Dumpsters. That's how I learned everything."

"What is this nonsense?" Yerin said. He paced back to the door. "I suppose it does not matter whether the old man talked or not. Too many people know about the warehouse in Detroit. The route has been compromised. We must change it before we bring in any more parcels."

"Why don't you just call them children?" I couldn't help asking. "That's what they are."

"Kill her, Sergei," Yerin said in the same sort of voice most people ask for fries with their hamburger. "We don't need her anymore."

An ugly pistol appeared in Sergei's hand, and I found myself wondering how he had managed to smuggle one into America. Stupid last thought to have. Sergei's finger tightened on the trigger.

"Wait!" Quentin snapped, and Sergei paused. "I still want to know where my family papers are. This girl is my only chance."

"It is too dangerous to let her live," Yerin snapped back. "Especially for a handful of stupid papers."

"Those papers are my *birthright*," Quentin thundered for the second time since this conversation had begun. "I won't let an old man and a simple girl keep them from me."

Man, this guy had some serious control issues. Me, I was floating in a small cloud of relief that I was still breathing.

"Do with them as you wish, then," Yerin said. "But they will not leave this house."

He turned on his heel and strode for the door with Sergei in tow. Quentin went after him.

"Where are you going?" he demanded.

"To oversee my men," Sergei said over his shoulder. "We need to remove every trace of our presence on this island. I am thinking we should set fire to the house just before we leave. It will be easiest." He left.

"What?" Quentin raced after him. "You aren't going to burn anything. I paid a fortune for this—"

The door slammed shut, cutting off his final words. Once their footsteps had receded down the hallway, I gave my ropes an experimental tug. No slack, no way to wiggle free. I swore under my breath. Maybe I could find a way to break my chair. No, too noisy. I wanted to scream in fear and frustration.

"I don't suppose you've managed to work your hands free and were just biding your time until they left," Uncle Lawrence said. His eyes were remarkably clear for a man who'd been babbling about aliens and the CIA mere moments ago.

I glared at him. "Faker."

"Of course." The wild look stole back over his face. "The CIA has bugged my house and they report everything to the Mercurians, yep, yep. You bet." His expression returned to normal. "You can get away with a lot when people underestimate you."

"All right, then," I said. "My equipment belt and the weapons in it are at the bottom of Lake Erie along with your truck. No one knows where we are or how to find us. We're both tied up tight by a bunch of thugs who are going to sell a dozen terrified little kids into prostitution. They're also going to burn this house down, probably with us in it. Have I underestimated anything?"

"Me," said Uncle Lawrence. "I have a knife."

I blinked at him. "You do? Why didn't they find it?"

"It's zipped into a secret pocket at the back of my belt," he said. "Just in case my hands were tied behind me. I can't reach it, though—the chair slats are in the way. Can you scoot around and get it?"

It took some scooting, but eventually our chairs were back-to-back. Every scrape and thump made my heart jump, but the door never opened. I reached backward with my bound hands and groped around until I was able to reach between the ladder-back slats and grab Uncle Lawrence's belt. That done, I inserted a finger and found the tab of a small zipper. The tab was small and kept slipping through my fingers. Uncle Lawrence's back was warm, and I could feel the knobs of his spine. His clothes were gritty with dirt. It felt strange to be in such close contact with him.

"Hurry," he said. "My cousin might come back. And my left arm is killing me."

"Not that I'm ungrateful or anything," I said as I worked at the zipper, "but I thought the paranoia was just an act."

"It's not paranoia if they're really out to get you." He was panting, as if he couldn't breathe right. "I found this belt in a trash can ten years ago and stored it away just in case I might need it. Once all this nonsense started up, I figured the time had come to use it."

I worked the little compartment open and my fingers found a sliver of metal. A sharp pain told me I had sliced a finger on it, and I hissed a little.

"How come you pushed those pans down on me?" I asked. "And why did you keep running away from us? We were trying to help."

He shrugged, and the motion made me lose my grip on the stiletto. I swore, and he apologized. "I didn't know who you were," he said. "People kept breaking into my house, and all of them shouted that they didn't want to hurt me, that they just wanted to help. And you were with a woman who spoke with a Russian accent."

"Slava," I said. "She's actually from Ukraine."

"Goodness, the difference was so obvious," Uncle Lawrence said. "How was I supposed to know?"

I managed to get the stiletto out of the pocket and reverse it so I held it by the handle instead of by the blade. "You should have known because you yourself pointed Belinda toward Hawk Enterprises."

"Ah. Figured that out, did you?"

"Belinda said she'd found a Hawk Enterprises business card among the promotional pamphlets at her motel." I pressed the blade against a bit of rope that felt promising and started sawing. Hard to do when you can barely move your wrists. "Hawk Enterprises doesn't advertise, and even if we did, we wouldn't place ads among pizza pamphlets and zoo flyers. You put that card in there, hoping Belinda would come to us and we'd come looking. What's up with that?"

Uncle Lawrence sighed. "I'm sorry. It's my fault you're here, isn't it?" He paused, still panting for breath. "I'm not... I'm not a good person, Terry. You don't mind if I call you Terry, do you?"

"As long as I can call you Uncle Lawrence," I said. My wrists were getting sore, but the rope was parting, strand by strand.

"Sure." Another pause, and I sawed through another strand. "Part of what I said is the truth. I did happen to see my cousin Quentin down by the docks, and I did start spying on him. I knew about his Chicago dealings, and I was curious what he was doing in Detroit. I found out about the...the children, and I started keeping a log of all their activities. Beyond that, I didn't know what to do. I figured the police wouldn't believe me if I called them. I was still trying to figure out what to do when...when Howard died." His voice grew thick, but he kept going. "I was so sad, I could barely get out of bed in the morning. I couldn't even bear the thought of making funeral arrangements. It was too much, too overwhelming."

I felt a twinge of sympathy for the old guy. "He was your brother and your best friend," I said.

"I never married, never had children," he said. "It was just me and Howard. I couldn't eat or sleep or go out to hunt new stuff. I also stopped writing to Belinda. After a couple months, though, I started spying on the warehouse again, mostly for something to do. One day I was hiding in a trash bin and overheard some of the men talking about how two women from a group named Hawk Enterprises had messed up their operation in Moscow. Yerin had to flee the country, in fact, and that's why he's here now. I did some detective work of my own and learned you were based in Ann Arbor—a lucky break for me!"

"Right." The rope was about halfway cut. My wrists were on fire and my arms ached, but I gritted my teeth and kept at it.

"I scrounged around your Dumpsters and eventually found a card. I even called you once, but you told me you only worked for women. Do you remember?"

"No," I said truthfully. "We get about a dozen calls a month from men, actually. I'm supposed to be polite, then hang up."

"You were that," Uncle Lawrence said. "Then Belinda showed up, and I realized that you wouldn't work for me but you might work for her."

"Why didn't you just go talk to her yourself?" I asked. I could barely feel my wrists now and was sawing on simple faith.

"Because I didn't want to put her in danger. If Yerin or Quentin saw me talk to her, they might decide she knew something about their operation and hurt her. So I bribed a motel worker to put the Hawk Enterprises card under her door with some flyers, hoping she'd call you. She did. So you see—it's my fault you're here."

The rope parted and my left hand jerked sideways. I was so surprised, I dropped the stiletto. It clattered on the floor. I had been sawing through my own ropes. I quickly worked my hands free. Pins and needles lanced through them and I took a few seconds to shake some life back into them.

"Where does the blackmailing fit in?" I asked, untying my ankles.

A long pause. I untied the last rope and turned to face Uncle Lawrence. The back of his neck was bright red.

"I told you I wasn't a good person," he said in a small, gasping voice. "See, I was desperate. The last of Dad's money was gone, and I was going to lose the house and all my possessions forever. I didn't know what to do. So I called Quentin.

I know I should have gone to the police with my notebook, but I told myself they wouldn't believe an unwashed, ragged old man like me. It was a lie, of course. I was just too scared to face them, too ashamed of…of my house. Dozens of children were sold into slavery while I watched and did nothing."

I didn't say anything. He was right. How many children had paid for his inaction? On the other hand, I couldn't hate him. In many ways, he had spent his life trapped in a terrible prison. I picked up the stiletto and started work on his ropes.

"No!" Uncle Lawrence gasped. "I'm old, and I'll slow you down. Get the kids out of here first—they're more important. Every second counts."

I didn't want to leave him, but I also didn't want to argue. Uncle Lawrence was right—I had to save the kids and he would only slow me down. I darted over to the window. With one last look at the old man, I opened it, climbed out, and dropped to the ground below.

FIFTEEN

THE FRESH NIGHT air tasted sweet after the nicotine poison I'd been breathing inside. I dropped to the ground and scuttled into the shadows well away from the house. What time was it? I'd completely lost track, and my timetable had been bumped up. Originally I had been thinking of searching the island for a rowboat or canoe and running for help. That, however, would take several hours, well past the time Yerin planned to torch the house and flee. I had to get Uncle Lawrence and the children off the island tonight. Now.

Crickets chirped. I looked at the yellow lights of the house, then down to the dock. The white yacht, which I had no idea how to pilot, still lay at anchor. But maybe I wouldn't *need* to pilot it. If I could get the kids onto the boat and cut it loose, the current might push it away from the island. Eventually someone would notice us.

The plan was lacking in detail, including how I was going to get a dozen scared kids who probably didn't speak English past the thugs and down to the dock, but hey—you have to start somewhere.

No sense waiting. I probably had less than half an hour before Yerin discovered I was missing. I ran around to the back of the house, hoisted myself up to the little roof over the back door, and peered through the window. The kids were still in their kennels. Standing near one of them was Sergei. His fly was open and he was reaching for the latch on the cage of a girl who couldn't have been more than ten. She cringed away as best she could. Mama Bear roared inside me, but I kept my head. I reached up and gently scrabbled at the window. Sergei spun around, and I thanked God nothing had popped out of his zipper. He couldn't see outside because the lights inside were on, so I scrabbled at the window again, then flattened myself against the wall beside it. Blood zinged through me and my heart pounded with fear and anticipation.

The window opened, and Sergei leaned out. His eyes met mine, and he barely had time to gasp in surprise before I grabbed his shirt with both hands, braced myself against the roof, and *yanked.* Sergei came through the window with a yelp. I deliberately went over backward. His momentum combined with mine to let me throw him past my head and off the roof. He hit the ground with a bone-jarring *thud.* I scrambled to my feet and looked over the edge. He wasn't moving.

I poked my head into the bedroom. All twelve children stared at me with silent, round eyes. "It's okay," I said in a loud whisper. "I'll be right back."

I jumped off the roof. Sergei was alive but out cold. I searched him and came up with his pistol. Yes! I kicked Sergei once in the head, partly to make sure hc would stay out and partly to satisfy Mama Bear. She grunted in contentment. I stuck the pistol in the waistband of my stolen sweats, chinned myself back up to the roof, and climbed into the bedroom. The children, clearly confused and uncertain, didn't make a sound. I put a finger to my lips anyway and pointed to myself.

"Police," I said, hoping the Russian word was similar to the English one, even if the description was inaccurate.

One of the children—an older blond girl who had to curl up to fit inside her cage—said, "Police? You help?"

A translator. Thank God. I nodded and opened the latch on her kennel. "Stay quiet. We go fast. Out the window."

The girl scrambled out of her cage, then winced as cramped muscles protested. I opened another cage, and the girl said something in Russian. I caught something that sounded like *policia* and assumed she was explaining who I was. The other children were all obviously afraid, but they were more than willing to escape their cages. A little boy abruptly grabbed me in a hug, and I almost burst into tears. I hugged back, then gently disentangled myself long enough to wedge a chair under the doorknob.

"What's your name?" I asked the blond girl.

"Sveta," she said. She kept her voice low, as I did.

"I'm Terry," I said. "We're going out the window and we have to be quiet. Tell them, okay?"

She did. The kids were bewildered. One of the girls started to cry. I scooped her up and headed for the window, every footstep a potential alarm to those below. I scooted out onto the roof and helped the crying girl through. She was so thin and weighed barely anything. Sveta urged the next child out, and the next.

"Get them all out," I told her. "I'll help everyone down."

I jumped to the ground, landing beside the unconscious Sergei, and stretched my hands up to the first girl. She looked down at me uncertainly. "Jump!" I said, crooking my fingers. "I'll catch you."

I thought she would hesitate, but she surprised me by jumping right away. I caught her, set her down, and reached up for the next child, who followed her example. I was setting the fifth child down when the first girl gasped. I spun around and found myself looking straight into the barrel of a pistol. I didn't recognize the thug behind it, but how much did that matter?

"Hi!" I said, amazed at my own bravado. "Just taking the little ones for a quick walk through the park. Ice cream might be involved later. Wanna come?"

"I kill you now," he growled. Then he yelped in pain. I didn't bother to figure out why. I swept the gun aside with my forearm, then gave him a good slug in the gut. He doubled over. I grabbed his head and slammed his face into my knee. Something cracked, and he dropped to the ground next to Sergei. I grabbed his pistol, pulled the clip for the extra ammo, and flung the gun itself into the bushes. Only then did the first girl let go of the thug's leg. She had bitten him. Mama Bear grunted approval.

In short order, I had twelve kids with me. Gesturing at them to keep quiet, I herded them down the path toward the yacht. Sveta tried to get them to hurry, but all that time spent in kennels had taken their toll. The best they could manage was a fast walk. My skin prickled. Yerin and Quentin had to know I had escaped, and by now they had probably broken into the bedroom. They weren't stupid, and had to know I'd make a run for the yacht.

I picked up the two smallest kids. Sveta took the hands of two more, and we scurried as best we could down the rough path toward the dock. I gave the house another glance over my shoulder as we went. Uncle Lawrence was still in there. I wanted to run back and get him out, but Mama Bear snarled that such a thing would only endanger the children. And he had told me to go without him.

"Hurry!" I told Sveta. The kids clinging to my neck were growing heavy. "We have to hurry!"

A girl stumbled. Sveta helped her to her feet, and we kept going. Night closed in around us, and my ears strained for sounds of pursuit. So far I only heard normal night sounds and the occasional distant barge horn. I was getting tired. It had been a long day and night, and fatigue pulled at my muscles. And I was starving.

We got down to the dock, and I breathed a sigh. One hurdle overcome. Shouts echoed down the hill. Someone had found Sergei and his friend. I got the kids down to the yacht as it rocked gently in the dark water, sloshing like a barfly who's had too much to drink. Sveta and I boosted them to the deck. Everyone was panting with exertion, and the night had turned hot and sweaty.

More shouts, and they were growing closer. Hadn't taken the bosses long to figure out where we'd gone. The yacht was moored to the dock by two thick ropes. I unwound both with shaking hands, then grabbed a long pole from the deck and used it to push the yacht away from the dock. The problem was that the current worked against me, pushing the yacht back against the wood. The kids huddled together on the deck, watching me with big eyes. I changed tactics and used the pole to shove the yacht forward instead. It felt like my bones were bending, but the prow slid past the front of the dock. I heard footsteps thudding down the path, and sweat slid down my back.

"Get down!" I told the kids. Sveta obeyed, and the other children followed her lead. The yacht was halfway clear of the dock, then three-quarters. Abruptly the prow swung around, caught in the current. The side scraped against a pylon, and then we were in open water. Feet pounded on wood, and I made out shadows coming toward us. I shoved down with the pole like Charon on the Styx, but the water was already too deep. Gunfire boomed, and I dropped to my knees by the gunwale. I snatched the thug's pistol from my waistband and fired blindly back. The gun kicked in my hands, and all twelve kids screamed. Five shots, and the clip was empty. The thug didn't keep his piece fully loaded. Someone shouted an order in Russian, and the shooting stopped. By now, we were ten or twelve feet away from the dock, though, and I felt almost safe. I was reaching for the second stolen clip when a dark shadow leaped over the gunwhale and smashed into me.

I crashed to the deck, the extra clip flying from my grasp. Wind burst from my lungs and hot fire lanced my shoulder. A second shadow thudded to the deck, and I heard a dim splash as someone else tried to swim for it. Reflexively I kicked away from the guy who had landed on me and rolled to my feet, empty pistol up. My opponent did the same. Facing me in the dim starlight was Stanislav Yerin. Quentin Peale staggered to his feet beside him. Behind them, a bunch of shadowy men clustered at the end of the dock. Swearing drifted up from the water as the third man realized he couldn't swim fast enough to reach us.

Yerin and I trained our pistols on each other.

"Stand off, Stan," I said. My heart felt like it would burst free of my ribs. I was facing down a mafia boss with nothing but an empty gun.

"Shoot her!" Quentin barked. He didn't seem to have a gun of his own.

"I. Hate. You," Yerin spat at me. I could almost taste the anger in his words. "You have ruined my life, foiled me every step of the way."

"Dirty job, but I'm glad to do it. Drop the gun, Stan."

"Drop yours."

"You're a fucking idiot!" Quentin screamed. "Kill the bitch!"

Yerin spun and fired three shots. The children screamed. Quentin Peale gurgled and fell over the side. His corpse hit the water with a splash. Yerin aimed his gun at me again.

"I will take no more orders from American trash," he snarled. "Now drop your gun!"

I thought fast. The longer this went on, the more likely Yerin would try a shot. I took a chance.

"You don't want to shoot me," I said in a soft, steady voice. "You want a piece of me. I can see it. Standing right in front of you is the little woman who helped destroy your Moscow operation and made you a fugitive. Who ruined you forever. Tell you what—let's lower our guns to the deck. Then we'll kick them out of the way, and you can take me."

He hesitated. Behind him, the kids had pushed themselves against the gunwale.

"Scared an American woman will beat a Russian man?" I taunted. "No wonder we won the Cold War."

Yerin's face hardened. "We lower them slowly," he said.

Together we lowered our pistols, dropped them to the deck, and kicked them aside. The boat continued to drift as Yerin and I went into fighting stances. I licked my lips. If I won, the kids went free. If I lost, Yerin would kill me and sell the kids into slavery.

Yerin lunged, faster than I expected. He snapped the heel of his hand into my chest and knocked me off balance. He followed with a foot sweep and I landed flat on my back. The back of my head cracked against the deck. *Kyosa* Parkinson would have been disappointed. I had underestimated Yerin, a beginner's mistake.

Yerin leaped, intending to land full-force on my throat. I rolled away, and his feet crashed on the wood beside my head. I grabbed his ankle and yanked upward. This time *he* fell. We both scrambled to our feet. Yerin's eyes blazed with a hatred that turned me cold inside. This time I didn't wait for him to move. I swept an axe kick at him, but he dodged aside and flicked a punch at my midriff. I blocked it, but barely. Then the fight began in earnest. We traded blow and block, counterblow and kick. I clipped the side of his head, and he slammed my mouth hard enough to split my lip. My blood sang and I felt the power of muscle moving beneath skin. My world narrowed to my opponent.

I connected with his shoulder, and Yerin staggered backward. Then he dropped and came up with the pole I had used to push the boat away. He whirled it twice, then jabbed it at me, quick and sharp. I ducked and weaved, then dove past him. I landed on my hands and used a tuck-and-roll to come back upright. The children cowered against the gunwale less than a foot in front of me. Yerin spun and brought the pole down. I flung myself aside. The pole cracked against the deck and broke in two. I snatched up the free half, brandishing it like a truncheon. We paused, panting, then rushed at each other again.

Our makeshift weapons clacked and clattered against each other. He swung at my ribs. I parried and punched at his throat. My rage at this man, this monster, channeled itself into every swing, every strike. His lips curled in a fury he had no right to feel. After a while, I realized I had him on the ropes. Yerin gave ground until he was close to the gunwale. I landed a blow on his wrist, and his half of the pole went spinning into the water. Without pausing, I drew my makeshift truncheon back, intending to crack him upside the head with it and drop him like a dead rat. But Yerin dropped for me. He hit the deck on his knees.

For a split-second I thought he was going to beg for mercy. I should have known better. In his right hand he held the pistol he had kicked away—the reason he had allowed me to back him here in the first place.

"Drop it," he snarled, aiming the pistol up at me. Blood dripped from his nose and he swiped at it with his spare hand. "Then back away."

"I beat you," I snarled. "Fair and square. Take it like a man."

He fired. The kids cried out, and pain scored the top of my shoulder. He had winged me on purpose. "Drop it and back away!" he yelled.

I obeyed, the muzzle flash still on my retina. The deck rocked gently beneath my feet, and I heard a strange rumbling sound. Now that I had stopped moving, the battle rage subsided and I felt shaky. My shoulder burned. Yerin got to his feet, never letting the gun waver. I cast about for an idea, something to say or do, but nothing presented itself.

"You will die now," Yerin said, and fired.

The strange thing was that no muzzle flash blinded me this time. I also felt no new pain. Was this what it was like to die? A painless slide into darkness? Yerin was staring at me, his eyes blank in the starlight. Then he fell forward and hit the deck with a wet *thud*. I stared down at him, uncomprehending.

Then white light flooded the entire area and blasted my eyes six feet into my skull. The rumbling noise I had heard resolved itself into the sound of an engine. Another boat was drawing closer. Someone had shot Yerin, and I might be next. I automatically dropped, seeking cover. The light lessened, and I blinked furiously to clear my vision. The children didn't make a sound. I groped forward on my stomach until I found Yerin's body—and his pistol. I grabbed it and checked the action by touch. My heart was racing again as I carefully brought my head up high enough to peer over the gunwale railing.

"Terry! Thank God!"

"Terry! Are you all right?"

Zack and Ms. Hawk. The two sweetest voices in the world. I pulled myself upright, suddenly shaky again. Now that the searchlights weren't trained directly on me, I could see their boat, one rather smaller than the yacht. Zack stood at the helm, the wheel in his hand, and Ms. Hawk stood beside him. She carried a pistol. Both of them wore night-vision goggles from the equipment stash in Ms. Hawk's trunk. I gave a weak little wave.

"I'm all right," I said. "Except I'm bleeding. And I've got lots of bruises. And—"

Another searchlight stabbed at us. This one was attached to a Coast Guard boat that was already throttling back so it could drift to us. Voices shouted over bullhorns, but I ignored them and my bleeding shoulder. Instead I staggered over to the children, still huddled at the stern like a litter of puppies. Most of them were crying, including Sveta.

"It's going to be all right." I knelt to embrace as many as I could with my good arm. "Everything's fine."

They continued to cry. As Ms. Hawk and Zack jumped aboard the yacht, I realized my tears were mingling with their own.

I GOT THE full story later. Zack and Ms. Hawk had gotten "concerned," as Ms. Hawk put it, when my GPS signal abruptly winked out. Realizing that the Detroit warehouse wasn't part of tonight's equation, Ms. Hawk had driven like the wind to the place where my GPS signal had last shown itself. They found no sign of me at the dock, of course, and Ms. Hawk had decided the only option was to check the coordinates from Uncle Lawrence's notebook. Zack said he would locate a speedboat while Ms. Hawk got on her laptop to figure out where to go. All this took time, and Ms. Hawk said she had been forced to keep Zack calm so he could hot-wire the boat he found.

They radioed the Coast Guard along the way, but it took

lots of talking to get them to listen. As a result, Zack and Ms. Hawk reached the island before anyone else. They shut their running lights off to keep their presence quiet and arrived just in time to see the yacht drifting away. Their night-vision goggles let them see that Yerin and I were fighting. Zack desperately brought the boat close enough for Ms. Hawk to get in the shot that saved me.

The Coast Guard cutter brought the children aboard, took the yacht in tow, and headed back to the island, where it joined two others. Zack had to physically restrain me from running off to find Uncle Lawrence. He didn't have to try very hard—I was bandaged, wrapped in a blanket, and feeling weak as a spring flower. The children refused to let me out of their sight.

The Coast Guard arrested Yerin and Quentin's entire goon squad and easily broke into the house. They found Uncle Lawrence tied to his chair. He was dead. A heart attack.

I suddenly remembered how Uncle Lawrence had gasped for breath and felt pain in his left arm—symptoms of an imminent myocardial infarction. Sorrow filled me up and spilled over. I sat down and cried in harsh, wrenching sobs. Zack put warm arms around me. Even though I had spent less than an hour with him, Lawrence Peale felt like someone I had known all my life. Eventually, however, the tears had ended, though Zack's embrace had not.

"AND THAT BRINGS us here," I said. "To the last loose end."

"I assume you mean the treasure," Belinda said, "and not the fact that Mr. Archer—I mean, Zack—and I are related?"

Zack laughed. All five of us—Ms. Hawk, Belinda, Zack, Slava, and I—were standing at the top of the stairs that led down to the basement entrance. Two days had passed since the island, and my shoulder was almost healed. Clouds had moved in, blunting the worst of the sun and muting the green leaves overhead, as if they were sad. Zack had his big yellow backpack with him, and Belinda carried a mask provided to her by Ms. Hawk. Slava had asked to come, and Ms. Hawk had reluctantly agreed that she had been at least a little help on the case and deserved to see how it ended.

"I'm definitely talking about the treasure," I said. "Let's go in."

"Watch your step, Ms. Harris," said Ms. Hawk.

When we got to the bottom of the stairs, Belinda put the mask on. It was the sort of mask that painters and other people who work with toxic fumes use to cover their mouths and noses. Two cannister filters jutted out from either side. It made Belinda look like an alien, but it would allow her to enter her uncles' house without choking to death. We led her carefully upstairs to Uncle Lawrence's bedroom. She looked around with a sort of sorrowful interest. Slava put hands on hips.

"My mother always tell me," she said, "'Your room will be messy if you do not clean.'"

"Actually, Slava," I said, "it was your mother who helped me figure out where the treasure is."

"Explain this," Slava said, surprised.

"Uncle Lawrence told his cousin Quentin that Howard had hidden the papers someplace obvious," I said. "Lawrence may have been lying, but I got to thinking—this room is the most obvious place in the house. All the important papers are here, and the treasure is made of paper. All these books deal with the Constitution, and I think the treasure does, too."

"You think it's hidden among these books?" Belinda said.

"In one particular book," I said, taking down the lone, enormous volume of the *World Book Encyclopedia.* "This is what Slava helped me figure out. She told me to look for something out of place, for something not logical. So. Why would someone who was so anal about organization separate this book from the others in the set?"

"Volume C," Zack breathed.

"For Constitution," Slava added. "Let's look!"

Everyone gathered around as I opened the thick, heavy book. Someone had cut away the interior pages, creating a hollow space. Inside lay a second, smaller book bound in brown leather and sealed inside a plastic bag. The diary of Roger Peale, just like Zack had said on our little picnic. A second plastic bag contained a pile of yellowed papers. I carefully lifted both out of the book, set the book down, and started to open the second bag. Zack grabbed my wrist.

"Don't," he said.

I raised an eyebrow at him. "Why not?"

"They're old and fragile and they're stained with mud."

"Ah ha! You *do* know what they are. You lied to me in the Arboretum when you said you didn't."

"I never said I didn't know," Zack said impishly. "*You* said it. I was going to tell you, but you decided to eat espresso beans instead of kiss me."

"Why, you little—"

"Perhaps you could finish that portion of your conversation later," Ms. Hawk interrupted. "And Mr. Archer could explain about the mud stains."

"I know I'd like to hear it," Belinda said.

"My pleasure." Zack sat on Uncle Lawrence's bed. "I told Terry that Roger Peale was a printer's apprentice who had a passion for history and recognized that important events were taking place around him. My dad said Roger wrote about most of them in his diary, including the event that involves the papers."

"And that event would be?" I prompted.

Zack crossed an ankle over his knee. "Some background first. The Bill of Rights was drawn up in 1789, two years after the Constitution was ratified. George Washington ordered fourteen copies of the rights printed up so the colonies could discuss them. Washington signed each copy, kept one for himself, and sent the others by horseback to the colonies."

"That was in one of the books," I said. "The one with the underlining."

Zack nodded. "What the history books don't know is that when Washington's secretary left the building, he fumbled the papers and dropped them in a puddle. He couldn't send them

off all muddy, so he ran down to the shop that had printed
them up in the first place."

"The shop where Roger Peale was an apprentice," Ms.
Hawk said.

"Yep. They hadn't broken down the template yet, which
meant they could print up another set on the spot. The secretary took the new copies back to Washington. He signed them
again, and this time they reached the colonies, no problem.
The original copies, with Washington's original signatures,
were tossed on the shop's kindling pile."

"But Roger saved them," Belinda breathed.

"He did. They've been passed down to the youngest Peale
son ever since. But then a set of twins were born not long before the Civil War, and both brothers claimed the papers were
theirs. That started the feud between the Chicago and the Detroit Peales. You know the rest."

"Oh, my," Ms. Hawk said. "The original thirteen states
keep their signed copies of the Bill of Rights on display, as I
recall. They're priceless."

"And they're nothing but seconds," Zack said. "Terry is
holding the originals. Roger's diary will help authenticate
them. Their existence will send a few shockwaves through
the government and historical circles."

The plastic bag suddenly felt very heavy. I held it up to the
light and made out the words "Congress shall make no law
respecting an establishment of religion" in slightly smudged
type.

"But who do they belong to?" Belinda asked. "The government might try to claim them."

"Won't stick," Zack said. "A government official threw
them away, so they're found property. They belong to the
Peale family. Quentin isn't in any position to put in a claim,
and the uncles were in possession when they died, so the papers will go to their estate."

"But they left everything to each other," Ms. Hawk mused.
"This could get complicated."

"Not so much." Zack unzipped his backpack and pulled out two more pieces of paper. "I've been keeping back some information, Terry. I'm sorry."

My stomach clenched. "What do you mean?"

"The wills I found in that shoebox weren't the latest ones." He held up the papers. "I found these on top and hid them. They're the uncles' newest wills."

Belinda gasped. I dashed across the room and snatched them from him. My temper cranked up the rheostat. "Why did you keep quiet about this?"

Zack didn't resist me. "You didn't know I was a Peale yet. The wills would have revealed who I was."

"Why didn't you tell me this down in the Arboretum?" I demanded, trying to read and talk at the same time.

"I didn't have a chance. Everything happened so fast."

"Zack," Belinda said quietly behind her mask, "did my uncles name you the beneficiary?"

"*A* beneficiary," Zack said. "I guess Uncle Lawrence was pretty impressed with the way Dad thumbed his nose at the entire family and decided I was worth leaving something to. Plus he did like me." He cleared his throat. "They left you the house and property, Belinda, but they left me the Peale family papers. I'm a youngest son."

"An only son," Slava corrected. "Unless you have siblings you fail to mention."

"Nope. Just me."

"I see," Belinda said. The mask prevented me from reading her expression.

"Jesus, Zack," I blurted out. "Those papers are worth millions and millions."

"Yeah." He gently took the plastic bags from my unresisting fingers. "Kinda weird, thinking about it. Um… I hope you aren't upset, Belinda."

Ms. Hawk and I both turned to look at her. I found I was holding my breath.

"Upset?" Belinda said. "Honey, I'm *relieved*. Whoever

owns those papers is going to end up in the middle of a media circus, you understand. I'll sell this place and head back home to watch everything from a safe distance."

"What about the money?" I asked. "We're talking a fortune here."

Belinda laughed. "Oh, lord—my husband has more money than I could spend in three lifetimes. I'm just glad everything got settled." Her tone grew misty. "Though it's strange. In a way, I lost Uncle Lawrence twice."

"I wish he hadn't died," I said, my throat thick.

Slava shrugged. "He helped you escape so you could rescue the children," she said. "Is not bad way to go. Almost heroic. And might help make up for evil he did."

"Evil?" Belinda looked shocked.

"Slava!" I said.

"Perhaps 'evil' is too strong a word," Slava agreed with another shrug. "But mafia sell many children into slavery because Lawrence fails to come forward sooner. Perhaps FBI will find them, perhaps not. But Lawrence is partly at fault. My mother always say, 'Some people good, some people evil, but most are little bit of both.'"

The thought silenced all of us. After a long moment, Ms. Hawk patted Belinda's hand. "Well, we've no need to stand around in here. Let's go outside for some fresh air."

We did. The air outside was fresh as summer air can be. I looked up at the tired old house, perfectly happy that I'd never have to go inside again. Maybe it was my imagination, but the place actually looked a little brighter, a little happier now that it didn't have to hold so many secrets.

Ms. Hawk, Slava, and Belinda headed for Ms. Hawk's car while Zack and I headed for my Jeep. Zack carried the wills and the papers in his backpack. It was strange to think that he was carrying millions in it.

"Have you decided what to do with the papers?" I asked as we climbed into my Jeep. "I'm guessing eBay."

He laughed, and his green eyes sparkled. "Not." Then his face grew serious. "Actually, I *have* decided."

"Well?" I slammed the door. The inside of the Jeep was hot. "Don't keep me in suspense, Sunshine."

"I'm going to donate them. To an historical museum."

I stared at him, amazed right down to my boots. "No shit."

"What happened to words like 'patootie'?"

"Fuck 'em. You're really going to do it?"

"Yeah." He gave a smaller laugh. "It's…it's kind of a gesture, you know? After everything I've stolen. Maybe it can make up for some of that."

Sunlight broken by the overhead leaves dappled his golden hair. Jesus, he was growing more beautiful by the second. Beautiful, reliable Zack. "You'll more than make up for it, unless you stole the Hope Diamond."

"Besides," he added, "the photos that go along with the story will make *Time* and *Newsweek* and all the major news services. Plenty of money there."

"I *knew* it!" I howled.

He gave that irresistible impish grin. "No one's perfect. What did Slava's mother say about good and evil people again?"

I sighed and reached for the keys. Zack abruptly grabbed my wrist. Startled, I looked into his eyes. They looked teary. "I didn't get a chance to tell you," he said. "I'm glad you're okay. When your GPS signal disappeared, I almost died. I never want to go through that again."

"I'm fine," I said, swallowing the lump in my throat. "Really. It's all right."

"And you keep saving my life," he said. "Three times now, I think. What other woman would do that?"

I kissed him. His eyes widened, then slipped shut. I became aware that his arms were around me and my back was twisted uncomfortably, but I didn't care. His tongue found mine and I pressed against him, feeling our bodies mold together despite the cramped conditions of the Jeep. We parted, then met again, our lips warm together, his scent washing over me. He ran his hands through my hair. My hands wandered over his face, his cheeks just a little scratchy. I couldn't get enough of him. A longing I had felt since I had first laid eyes on him swelled and burst, leaving me satisfied but wanting more.

My cell rang. Reluctantly I pulled away and answered. It was Ms. Hawk. She was almost back to the office with Belinda.

"I will tidy up the loose ends with her," Ms. Hawk said. "Why don't you and Mr. Archer take the afternoon to celebrate?"

Zack, who had overheard, gave me a knowing grin.

"Thanks, Ms. Hawk," I said. "I think we will."

* * * * *

REQUEST YOUR FREE BOOKS!

2 FREE NOVELS
PLUS 2 FREE GIFTS!

Your Partner in Crime